Cross Check

Ridder U Hockey

Lynn Stevens

Lynn Stevens

Copyright © 2022 by Lynn Stevens

All rights reserved.

No portion of this book may be reproduced in any form without written permission from the publisher or author, except as permitted by U.S. copyright law.

Contents

1. Chapter 1 — 1
2. Chapter 2 — 9
3. Chapter 3 — 18
4. Chapter 4 — 26
5. Chapter 5 — 38
6. Chapter 6 — 44
7. Chapter 7 — 52
8. Chapter 8 — 60
9. Chapter 9 — 68
10. Chapter 10 — 75
11. Chapter 11 — 81
12. Chapter 12 — 87
13. Chapter 13 — 92
14. Chapter 14 — 100
15. Chapter 15 — 107

16. Chapter 16 — 116
17. Chapter 17 — 123
18. Chapter 18 — 132
19. Chapter 19 — 138
20. Chapter 20 — 145
21. Chapter 21 — 151
22. Chapter 22 — 158
23. Chapter 23 — 164
24. Chapter 24 — 169
25. Chapter 25 — 175
26. Chapter 26 — 182
27. Chapter 27 — 188
28. Chapter 28 — 196
29. Chapter 29 — 201
30. Chapter 30 — 209
31. Chapter 31 — 216
32. Chapter 32 — 222
33. Chapter 33 — 231
34. Chapter 34 — 238
35. Epilogue — 243

Get Hooked on Ridder U Hockey — 248
Also by Lynn Stevens — 249
About Lynn — 250

Chapter 1

Elora

The arena rose above me. My first hockey game. I came to Minnesota for new experiences, right? That's what I told my parents when I left Galveston almost two months ago. October in Texas, not the same as October in Minnesota. I missed the sand, the sun, and the sea air.

"You ready for this?" Melody asked over her shoulder. Her long blonde hair flowed down her back in thick waves. With her bright green eyes and perfect proportions, she belonged more on my parents' yacht than in the freezing landscape of the upper Midwest. We'd hit it off immediately, and she'd taken me under her wing the last two months as I adapted to land life.

"Not really." A light breeze hit my bare skin, and I shivered.

Melody laughed, and it sounded just like her name. "This will be fun. Trust me. You haven't been out much since you got here."

The line moved forward. It wasn't entirely true. I had gone to the freshman mixer and a couple of parties, and I'd never done anything like that before either. This whole college experience has been harder than I anticipated, but I finally felt somewhat adjusted. Melody and I had a great heart-to-heart, and she invited me to go to the game with her. I accepted because she was right. I needed to get out of my comfort zone. Well, more than the over 1200 miles I was already out of it.

We walked toward the metal detectors. A security guard waved me to her table to check my bag. I opened it, used to this when my dad took me to Houston to see the Astros. He loved baseball, and we'd go once or twice a year after we'd docked in our slip in Galveston. She raised her eyebrows. Melody looked into my oversized purse.

"Seriously? You brought a book to a hockey game?" Melody shook her head, and my face flushed.

"I know nothing about hockey. I didn't want to get bored." I always took a book to the Astros games. It gave me something to do in between innings.

"Trust me, you won't get bored." Melody flipped her hair, drawing the attention of a few guys around us.

I couldn't do the hair flip to tease her, even though I wanted to. My dark brown hair had been artistically pulled up into a bun. Okay, not artistically, but still. I shivered under my parka. It wasn't even cold yet, according to my roomie. She grew up in Minnesota and loved the cold. I'd never even seen snow, and I was really looking forward to my first time.

People parted for Melody as she strode through the crowd. She wasn't being a bitch and demanding people move for her. She just knew who she was and where she was going. I admired that.

We went through the gate, and the temperature dropped even more. Despite the amount of body heat being produced in the three-thousand seat arena, it was downright frigid. I glanced around, tugging my parka closer to my body. Most of the people were in hoodies or jerseys with the school's team, Ridder University Beavers. Worst school name-mascot combination ever.

Melody didn't stop until we were in the first row behind panes of glass that had to be at least six feet tall. A big machine rolled down the middle of the ice, leaving a wet sheen behind it. Water. I wondered why, but I was distracted by the players in black and red jerseys, shooting out of the bench area. Their skates kicked up tiny shavings of the ice. Interesting.

I looked at Melody, but her gaze was on the bench a couple of sections down from us. Our seats were in a corner. I wasn't sure if that was good or not. There was a net in front of us, so maybe it was good.

"I'm glad you came." Melody grinned, and we sat down. She took off her zip up hoodie and draped it over the back of her seat. Her Ridder U t-shirt was long-sleeved with the blue and gold school colors. I'd freeze to death in that. "You need to experience Minnesota."

"I know." I tried to sit straight, but it was so cold, and my body wanted to curl in on itself. "It's tough, you know. After spending my life on the water, being inside is ... different?"

"I can't believe you grew up the way you did." She nudged me with her elbow. "I'm jealous. Never going to school, traveling the Caribbean. That's what dreams are made of."

"Yeah, so I've been told." The other truth was college itself hadn't been what I expected. Sitting inside stuffy classrooms, hunched over desks, and being expected to listen and not say a word? My mom taught me to ask questions, be inquisitive, challenge everything. That didn't go over well with some of my professors. Others loved the discourse. College was weird.

"You're eighteen, out on your own for the first time. Live a little." She hugged my shoulder.

"Nineteen," I said absently as I stared out the glass. "Today's my birthday."

"Oh shit, why didn't you tell me?" She pulled out her phone and snapped a picture of us, then thumbed rapidly over her screen before putting her phone back in her pocket. "There. I sent it out so anybody who sees you will wish you a happy birthday."

"Sent it out where?" I narrowed my eyes at her.

"On the school's social media site, duh. Don't tell me you still haven't gotten on that." Her wide hazel eyes admonished me with one look.

I shrugged and thought about my parents. They had a charter this week and were in open water. It was the first time we hadn't spoken or celebrated my birthday together. They had called me before they set out two days ago. It wasn't like they were ignoring me or that they forgot. Knowing that didn't stop the sting of loneliness.

"Look," she said, snapping me out of my reverie. "There's Damon."

My gaze followed her finger to the giant TV hanging from the ceiling. Damon Anderson's photo glared from the pixels along with his name and number, 27. It flashed away to Wyatt Birch. My breath caught in my throat. He didn't glare like Damon did. His head tilted slightly down, and a knowing smirk touched his lips. He had messy light brown hair with dark eyes that glistened mischievously.

The image flicked off to another player, but I was frozen. Literally and figuratively. I couldn't feel my toes. Melody wasn't paying attention to me anymore. I wondered if he was friendly. Most people I'd met so far were. Melody laughed at something the guy on the other side of her said.

I pulled my book from my bag and picked up where I left off in *The Gathering Storm* by Winston Churchill. History was a weakness of mine. I loved reading about it, but I also loved biographies and memoirs. Learning how people lived, coped, survived trauma, that fascinated me. Human nature, our reactions and inactions, why they did what they did. I always wanted to know more.

The parka held my body heat in a little too well. I unzipped it and shrugged it off. My shirt barely kept my arms covered. It wasn't my normal style. Then again, my normal style was a bikini with a tank top over it. I knew nothing about dressing for colder weather. Melody had put me in a white button-down shirt that strained over my chest with three-quarter sleeves. After the game, we were heading to a party with the players. Her goal was for me to meet more people.

I'd lost myself in Churchill's writing. The man had been brilliant on so many levels.

A loud slap on the glass made me jump. The heavy book fell from my hands. I glanced up to see a guy from the other team laughing before he skated away. My face burned. I reached down, wiping the cover with my hand.

Hockey was nothing like baseball.

Wyatt

Damon wasn't focused again. The game hadn't even started, and he was already thinking about hooking up with his new girl. More than once during our warm up, he'd glanced toward her.

I followed his gaze again just in time to see Mesher smack the glass right in front of her seats. A girl with a mess of dark brown hair jumped out of her chair. Her tits bounced, straining against the buttons of the tight white shirt. Impressive. But totally puck bunny.

Damon saw it too, and I had to hold him back before he started a fight and got ejected without playing a single shift.

"Melody's not his target." I put my arm down once I knew he wasn't going to take Mesher out just yet. Then I smacked him on the back of the helmet. He didn't take his gaze off the corner seats. "Get her out of your head until the game's over. We need to start this season with a home win, got it?"

"Yeah, yeah, yeah." He glared at me, then skated away. Mesher had a target on his back, and Damon wanted to be the arrow. We had a game to win. He wouldn't jeopardize that, but he would take Mesher down if he crossed the line again.

It was tight in the first two periods. Coach chewed us out during each intermission, but we were up by two goals after the second. Damon had one, I had the assist. We made a line along with Linden. Two years together, working on and off the ice to improve our flow, our shifts, and our overall game showed.

At the start of the third period, Mesher decided he wanted to impress someone.

We battled for the puck in the corner. Our sticks slapped and cracked against each other. He dropped his shoulder, then lifted his stick to hook my knee. Asshole move, and it cost him a chance at the puck. I cleared it behind the net.

Mesher glanced up at the girl he'd been flirting with and blew her a kiss. Disgusting. I slammed my hand into the back of his black helmet, pushing his face guard into the glass so he could kiss that with his teeth. Mesher threw an elbow and turned fast, punching me in the side of the helmet.

Game fucking on.

I dropped my gloves. Go time. He reached for my jersey as he skated around me. I waited, faking him out, until he dropped a hand an inch too far. Then I reached in, grabbed his jersey and slammed my fist into his stomach until his blades slipped and he tasted ice. I didn't hesitate as I skated to the penalty box.

This year, I wasn't taking any shit. No more Mr. Nice Hockey player. I was going old school. My first two years at Rider, I had gotten into two fights total. Game one my junior year, one fight down. I wasn't going to start them, but I sure as fuck was going to finish them.

We won by three goals. Mesher finished the game with blood caked on his lip. He wore it like a badge of honor. What a prick.

"You ready?" Damon asked as he threw his duffle over his shoulder once we'd all showered and changed.

I shrugged and finished shoving my sweaty pads into my bag. "I guess."

"Time to get back on the horse, cowboy." Damon laughed at his stupid reference. He thought he was making fun of me since my family hailed from Deadwood, North Dakota. Like I hadn't heard that shit my entire life. "Find a puck bunny, get over Veronica, and move the fuck on. It's been six months. She's over you."

I snorted at that. She was more than over me. She was married with a newborn. Worse, she married my former roommate. When I thought back on the months leading up to our breakup, I should have seen it. She was at our apartment before I got home from class all the time. I'd wake up and she wasn't there, coming back into my bed a few minutes later, looking flushed. Then she told me she was knocked up. I thought it was mine until I walked in on her with her legs high and my best friends slamming his dick into her.

Talk about taking a puck in the nuts. We'd been together almost two years, and she'd spent the last three months getting down and dirty with my best friend. I spent the past summer in a drunken stupor back home, and the last three months working my ass off to get back into shape.

"I'm not screwing some puck bunny who probably has had every guy's dick already." I did that already and look how that turned out. Veronica had been a sophomore, experienced, and ready to take on a freshman when she hit on me. I was ready and willing. Dumbest moment of my life, and I wasn't interested in repeating it.

"Fine, don't find a puck bunny. Find a date, make out with a chick. Do something. Just get over Veronica." Damon pushed open the door of the locker room and walked out.

He was right. I needed to move on. It was well past time. I followed him to the parking lot and climbed into his SUV. He blared his music, which was fine on one hand and horrible on the other. I loved music. What he listened to was not music. It was all computerized bullshit. Music should be actual instruments with actual people playing them. Not that the people who did the techno crap weren't talented, they were. It just wasn't music, in my opinion.

Damon parked on the street and practically rushed into the house, looking for his new squeeze. Melody was not his usual type. Confident, hot, and actually nice, and, bonus, she wasn't a puck bunny, but she was a hockey fan. Just a normal girl he met in one of his classes.

He found her fast, standing to the side of the fireplace. Standing next to her was the girl Mesher flirted with, and her gaze was glued on me.

Chapter 2

Elora

I looked away from that guy, Wyatt. His eyes were the blue of a stormy sea, and his glare told me enough. Just don't talk to him. I'd seen it before from other cultures on the islands. Most people were friendly, but there was always a handful who hated tourists and made it known. The way Wyatt looked at me reminded me too much of those people.

Damon hurried over to us, and Melody threw her arms around his neck. The kiss was anything but PG-13. I stared at the ceiling while they greeted each other and fought a smile. It wasn't hard to see why she was attracted to him. Damon had dark brown hair that tumbled over his forehead. His sharp chin curved in a balanced arc under thin lips that became fuller as he smiled.

"Hey," Damon said to Melody once they stopped sucking face. Did people still say that? My brother, Apollo, used that term, and it seemed appropriate.

"Hey," Melody replied, just as lovesick as him. It was sweet, really. She grinned and stepped out of his arms. "Damon, this is my roommate, Elora Castellanos."

He held out his hand, meeting my stare with his chocolate gaze. "Nice to meet you. My..." He glanced around and shrugged. "One of my roommates was just here. He probably went for a beer. Can I get you guys anything?"

I shook my head just as someone shouted, "Happy Birthday, Elora."

A bunch of other people chimed in. My cheeks flushed, and I was certain I looked like an elf. At just over five feet, I was the shortest person in the room. The last time this many people had wished me a happy birthday had been my thirteenth party on a beach in Curacao. They had been tourists and locals who just stopped. That was the best gift I'd gotten that year. The Macbook was the second best.

"It's your birthday?" Damon grinned wide, revealing perfect white teeth.

"Oh, yeah, I found that out on the way to the arena." Melody laughed and threw her arm over my shoulder. "So I spread the word. She's been hearing about it all night."

Damon thought this was hysterical, and apparently, decided to sing "Happy Birthday" at the top of his lungs, which a lot of people joined in on. My face had to be the color of a pomegranate by the time they finished. A few people even high fived me. That was awkward but appreciated none the less. Damon kissed Melody and disappeared toward the kitchen.

"Sorry, he's ... something else," she said with a sigh. When I didn't respond, she glanced down, her eyebrows furrowed. "You okay?"

"Yeah, I'm just going to step outside for a bit. I'll come find you, okay?" I'd never been claustrophobic before, but I'd never been in a room with this many people. Even the clubs I snuck into in the Caribbean were outside. I felt so trapped, and the crush of people only seemed to grow as more shifted by and dropped birthday wishes.

"You sure? If you want to leave, we can go. I'll walk you back." Her eyebrows wrinkled, and she pressed her lips into a thin line.

"I'm sure." I smiled, and that seemed to reassure her. I fought my way through the crowd toward the sliding glass doors in the kitchen. The air hit me hard, and I gulped in an icy breath. Just being outside eased the tension. Normally, I liked being around people, but it was just too much at the moment.

I tugged my coat closer around my middle. The backyard wasn't any better than the house, but at least I could breathe fresh air. Two fire pits flickered in the center of groups of chairs, each occupied couples. As much as I wanted to warm my hands by the fire, I didn't want to interrupt.

I ducked in and out of students, sneaking around them and trying not to bump anyone and spill their drinks. A few minutes alone, that was all I needed to get myself together. Finally, I found a piece of quiet at the side of the house. The music was muted, and the conversations dulled. The house even stopped the breeze, giving me a tiny relief from the cold. I leaned back against the gray siding and exhaled.

"Not a party person?" a voice asked from the darkness.

I jumped and stepped back toward the yard. "Who's there?"

"Don't worry, I don't bite unless asked." A tall guy walked into the faint light from the nearby window. His brown hair was styled back from his forehead like a small wave. It was lighter than Damon's, but not by much with the product that kept his tresses in place. He kept his head down, and I stepped back even more. "You came in with Melody. I'm Damon's roommate. Well, one of them. T.J."

"Oh." Now I felt foolish. Still, there was something dark about him, and I wasn't really into the dark. "I'm Elora."

"The birthday girl?" He lifted his head, and a smile revealed a crooked tooth. His eyebrows lifted, and I noticed his eyes. One hazel, one pale blue. Heterochromia, if I remembered right. I remembered reading about it after watching *Dr. Quinn Medicine Woman* with my mom. Fascinating. I wanted to ask questions, but that was too personal. "Happy birthday. How are you celebrating tonight?"

"This." I motioned around the party, stepping more into the yard. The wind whipped a loose strand of hair into my mouth. T.J. didn't seem like a bad guy, and my shoulders relaxed. "I ... uh ... I should get back. It was nice to meet you."

"See ya around, birthday girl." He nodded, his gaze drifting down my chest.

I turned around and headed back toward the house, a yawn catching my breath.

Wyatt

This party sucked. I just wasn't in the mood for the congratulations and drunken fun. It all felt like bullshit now. The puck bunnies were out in full force, and I did everything in my power to stay away from there. Damon was right. I needed to move on from Veronica. Just not with anybody who wanted to be with hockey me. I was more than just a hockey player. Most of the bunnies wanted to talk hockey, give out blowjobs (not that I was opposed to that), and put me on a pedestal. That was pretty much how it started with Veronica.

I nodded to a few of my teammates and snaked my way toward the back door. Just in time to see the girl Mesher screwed with hurry away from the side of the house. T.J. sauntered out after her with a mile-wide grin. That was all I needed to know about that chick.

There wasn't anything outside except the same shit as inside. I went to find Damon. It didn't take long. He was still with Melody by the fireplace, just where I'd left them. They were in deep conversation, and I was glad not to watch another make out session. That was a point in her favor. I didn't know much about Melody, except she was a freshman and not the type he usually scored with. She also didn't care that he played hockey, even though she knew plenty about the sport.

At Ridder U, hockey was second to none. Not even football beat us. Of course, the football team hadn't had a winning season in ten plus years. Basketball was slightly better, but not by much. It wasn't a good thing or a bad thing, just a thing. Some of the guys used it to their advantage to score the bunnies. I wasn't among them. Don't get me wrong, I wasn't a saint. I just didn't bag every bunny who wanted me.

Maybe I *had* been off the market too long.

"Hey," I said, to get Damon's attention.

He lifted his head and met my gaze. A knowing smile curled his lips. Damon was one hundred percent a smart ass. I loved him like a brother, and that kept us from kicking each other asses. He waggled his brows and nodded toward the person hovering near Melody. I glanced that way and there she was again.

Jesus. I couldn't get away from this girl. Her brown eyes widened, and they were pretty. I'd admit that much. Okay, she was sexy in a bundled up, frozen kind of way. Who wore a parka in sixty-degree weather?

I opened my mouth to introduce myself. Mama didn't raise me without manners.

Her gaze shot away from mine, toward her friend. "I think I'm going to go. I'm exhausted."

"I'll go —"

"No." She held up her hand and cut a glance at Damon. "Don't leave for me. I can walk. It's not that far."

"Wyatt will walk you back, Elora," Damon volunteered, slamming a hand on my shoulder and squeezing. "Our apartment's not far from Aldridge Hall."

"That's our dorm," Elora said. She shook her head. "Sorry, you knew that. Just... I'm a little flustered."

"Yeah, I'll bet," I deadpanned. Her gaze shot to mine and she tilted her head to the side. A lock of dark brown hair with a hint of gold fell across her cheek. I was leaving anyway, and I was on foot since Damon drove. Like I said, Mama didn't raise me without manners. "Come on. I'm heading out. I'll walk you back."

She nodded to Melody and Damon, then stepped up beside me. I wondered again about the parka. It wasn't any of my business, but curiosity met the cat. Once we stepped out onto the porch, she literally shivered.

"What are you going to do when it gets cold?" I asked, taking the steps down to the sidewalk. "This isn't even close."

She sighed, pulling the coat closer. "I don't know. I keep telling myself I was insane to move up here, but this isn't just college. It's a lifestyle change."

I snorted at that. "Explain that to me."

"Being in a classroom, going to parties, being away from my family, the ocean." She shrugged, and a wistful expression came over her face. "Maybe I should've stayed closer to home."

"Where's home?" Not that I cared, but making polite conversation went along with manners.

Her phone rang, and I almost laughed as she struggled to get her phone out of her pocket. "Excuse me." Her world seemed to brighten when she saw the names on the screen. She swiped to answer, and a middle-aged, very tan couple's faces appeared. "Hi, Mom. Hi, Dad."

"Happy Birthday, Elora. We're sorry it took so long to call." Her mom waved at the camera.

"We just docked in St. Thomas. Finally got service." Her dad peeked over her mom's shoulder. She shared the wide brown eyes with her mom, but her dark hair matched her father's even in volume. "How'd you spend the big day?"

"Melody took me to a hockey game." Elora glanced at me out of the corner of her eye. "It was interesting."

"That's great." Dad leaned farther in, and her mom pushed him back. "What're you doing now? It looks dark."

I must have leaned too far over, because the next thing I heard was, "Who's that?"

Elora's eyes widened, and she glanced at me, then pulled me into the frame. "This is Wyatt Birch. He's walking me home."

"Hi, Wyatt." Her mom waved again, and something crossed her expression. Probably motherly concern. I'd seen something similar when my sister Jane brought home her future husband. That was not necessary in this situation though. "We'll let you go. I'll call this weekend, okay?"

"Of course," Elora said. She waved again and ended the call. Her shoulders fell. "Sorry."

"Why are you sorry?" I asked, moving away from her. The wind whipped that strand of hair toward me. She smelled really good, like sunscreen and grapefruit.

She shrugged, and I didn't push her. "So where are you from?" she sputtered, then added, "If you don't mind my asking."

"North Dakota. Near Deadwood." I thought about my mom making fresh bread in our kitchen. That always made me smile. Maybe I'd call her later and ask her to send a loaf. "You?"

"We're based in Galveston, Texas, but I lived on a yacht all over the Caribbean." She smiled wistfully again.

"Wait, your parents are in St. Thomas? Right now?" That was interesting. I'd never really been out of the Midwest. She had traveled all over the Caribbean and she's only nineteen. "How did that work with school?"

She laughed, a sincere, hearty sound. "Mom homeschooled me. Before my parents decided to buy a yacht, they were both teachers. My grandfather left Dad a lot of money when he died. Now they run charters out of Galveston for weeks at a time."

"That's amazing," I said, truly awed. Life on a boat could be interesting. Living for the next destination. I couldn't even imagine it, and I kind of wanted to. "So, you're not a puck bunny?"

"What's a puck bunny?" Her eyebrows furrowed, and she stopped in the middle of the sidewalk. "And why do I think I should be both flattered and insulted at the same time?"

I bit my lip. She had a point. There wasn't a way to talk myself out of this. "A puck bunny is a girl who chases hockey players."

A light bulb went off behind her eyes, quickly followed by a flash of anger.

"Sorry," I said with a shrug. "It comes with the territory. What about T.J., though?"

"What do you mean?" She stared at me with haughtiness. Her arms crossed. For added impatience, she tapped her foot. It was kind of cute.

I felt like such an asshole. "I saw you come around the building and T.J. followed you. He likes to take girls there to, well, you know... I just assumed..." My words trailed off and guilt sank into the pit of my stomach. "I shouldn't have assumed. Sorry."

She stared at me for a moment, but she stopped tapping her foot. "Okay. I guess I shouldn't be mad. You had your reasons for whatever you thought, even if they were so very wrong." She paused again and blew out a breath with a shiver. "I went around the side of the house to escape all the people. He was already there. He introduced himself, and I decided it was time to go. That was it."

I nodded. That made sense, actually. T.J. liked to scare people. He was good at it. One of the reasons he was a great goalie on the ice. T.J. liked playing the bad boy, but he was pretty decent, if he let you know him.

"No wonder you're cold," I said, trying to ease the tension by not-so-deftly changing the subject. "Did you have to buy a new wardrobe?"

She grinned, and I knew I was forgiven. "Melody helped. She thought it was crazy I hadn't thought of socks." She shrugged with a wider smile, rocking on her heels. "I've never owned socks."

I laughed, and we started back toward the campus. Although this time, I slowed my pace.

Chapter 3

Elora

Melody didn't come back to our room that night. Truth be told, I knew she was with Damon, but I still worried. It wasn't until almost one in the next afternoon that she rolled in with a huge smile on her face. I curled up in our loveseat with my comforter and watched a hockey movie called *Miracle* to kill time after a light lunch.

"Good night?" I asked, closing my laptop before cuing up a movie called *Goon*.

"The best." She twirled on her heel then collapsed onto the grass green comforter on her bed. A giggle erupted, and she rolled to face me. Her cheeks were flushed a light pink, and her eyes danced. "Damon's amazing."

I set my laptop beside me, then leaned forward. "Do tell."

Her eyebrows lifted, along with a smirk on her lips. "A lady never kisses and tells."

"You did more than kissing if you're getting home this late." I pressed my lips together in an O. That only set her off into more giggles. "That good, huh?"

Melody shifted her legs under her, sitting on her heels. "Have you ever had someone treat you like you're the most precious thing on the planet? Like just being able to touch you is a gift? And kiss you like he's worshiping you?"

"I can't say I have. I mean, I've had great sex, but nothing like you're describing." I tucked my legs under me and waited for more. The truth was, I'd had one boyfriend when we were stuck in Nevis a year ago. The yacht had an oil leak, and it took longer than expected to get the part. For two months, Nigel had taught me how to be a woman and how to tell a lover what I needed. By the time we left port, I knew what made me tick in that arena. Unfortunately, a year is a long time to wait for a repeat of great sex.

"Really? I thought you might still be a virgin," she said.

I laughed hard at that. "No, not even close, but we can talk about that another time. Tell me about Damon. I'm assuming you're going to see him again."

"Duh." She threw a pillow at me. I slapped it away before it hit me in the chest. Melody giggled again. Her happiness was infectious, and I giggled along with her. "He's got another game tonight, but it's over in St. Paul, and I don't have a car. Sometimes being a freshman sucks."

"That no car rule is silly." I shrugged, but the school's rules existed for a reason. "Do you love him? I mean, it's been since the end of August. Is that long enough to fall in love or was it just sex?"

Melody's eyebrows furrowed. "I think I do. I mean, I love being with him. I think about him all the time. My heart beats faster when I'm around him. Is that love? I don't know. I've never experienced it before."

"Me either." Melancholy dripped in my words. The euphoria of being with Nigel felt like love at the time, but I didn't pine for him after we left. I mean, I did at first of course. After a few weeks, he was just a very fond memory.

"Well, we're going to find out." She yawned and stretched her arms above her head. "I'm so tired."

I stood and opened the fridge. "Here." I tossed her a water bottle. "I'm sure you're dehydrated too."

Melody missed the bottle, but it wasn't a good throw. It bounced off the wall and back onto her bed. "Thanks." She nestled against her pillows and chugged a third of the water. "I'm going to crash."

"I'm going out. Text me when you wake up. We can get dinner at the student union or maybe go off campus to that Thai place you like." I slid my feet into my boots and shoved my laptop into my bag. "Mel?"

A soft snore answered me. I put on my light coat of Melody's to stave off the cold. I had a paper due Monday, anyway. It was done, but maybe it could be better. There was a study floor at the student union that might be better suited for my needs. It was an open area with fireplaces centered around various chairs and couches. Most people socialized, but I liked sitting by the fire and reading. Maybe I'd do that instead. I was ahead in most of my classes. A night reading by a fireplace sounded perfect.

I just needed something to read. I'd finished the Churchill book already, so the library it was.

After twenty minutes of searching for the perfect biography or memoir, I checked out two: *A New Conscience and Ancient Evil* by Jane Addams and *Gretzky: an Autobiography* by Wayne Gretzky. Jane Addams was a prolific suffragette. I'd read a biography about her before, but nothing written by her. I walked toward the student union with my head down, and I didn't get far before someone called my name. Turning around, I couldn't help but smile at who it was.

"Hi, Lawrence," I said when he stopped beside me. His hoodie was dark blue, white, and orange, with Chicago across the white stripe. He paired it with his usual jeans and gray New Balance sneakers. "How'd your open mic night go?"

Lawrence smiled widened. His perfectly white teeth gleamed in the afternoon sun. Lawrence was the definition of tall, dark, and handsome. His grandparents were from Jamaica on his mom's side, and his dad's side was Puerto Rican, but Lawrence was one hundred percent American. We had Intro to Philosophy together and hit it off easily.

"Well?" I prodded when he wouldn't stop smiling at me.

"It was... better than perfect? Is that even possible?" He rocked on his heels, humming with excitement. His warm brown eyes reminded me of the wet sand at the edge of the sea. Lawrence laughed, and it rolled deep from his chest. "I can't believe I actually got up there with my guitar. You should've been there."

"Next time, I'll try." He'd invited me, and I felt a little guilty about ditching him for the hockey game. I pointed toward the student union. "I'm just going to study."

"I'll walk with you." He offered his arm, and I slid my hand into the crook of his elbow. Lawrence had manners. It was nice, and I appreciated the old-fashioned gesture. "I sang an original song. It was so much fun. I've never experienced anything like that before."

"I get it." I squeezed his arm, and he flexed his muscles a bit. Odd. Lawrence was shy about his music, mainly because his parents didn't think it was a viable career option. Any success needed to be celebrated. "Guess what I did? I went to a hockey game. It was so exciting."

"That why you have that Gretzky biography?" He nodded to the books clenched in my other arm.

I glanced down at it. The hockey player on the front smiled like he knew Lawrence was right. "I guess so. It just sounded interesting, and I know nothing about it at all. Why not read a biography?"

"It's not your normal read." He shrugged, and my hand lifted with his arm. "So, what're you doing tonight? There's an open mic poetry slam at Wildflowers Café. I was thinking about trying some of my lyrics as poems. I mean, should I? Last night was..."

"Better than perfect?" I smiled, repeating his words. We stopped outside the student union, and I let go of his arm. "You should totally do it."

"Will you come?" His cheeks turn a slight pink under his smooth almond skin.

"Yeah, I'll bring Melody. We'll be your cheering section." I grinned, but something in his eyes shifted. It was gone before I really even noticed it, so I figured it must have been my imagination.

"Great. I'll see you, I guess. It starts at eight." He stepped back and offered a half smile.

I waited for him to turn away before I stepped into the warmth of the building. Somehow, I felt like I screwed something up. What, I had no idea. I climbed the stairs to the second floor and found my favorite quiet corner with a fireplace. Lawrence's expression bugged me. I couldn't focus on anything in either book, so I turned back to my laptop. After putting on my headphones, I cued up *Goon* and got lost in the hockey movie.

Wyatt

Damon was unbearable before the game. Getting laid hadn't eased his tension. It only upped it more. He itched to get back to Melody. We'd all seen that look of puppy love and desperation before. Most of us had experienced it.

"Jesus, man, you're pussy whipped already," T.J. said as he strapped on his goalie pads. Tall and gangly, T.J. moved fast in front of the net. He was one of the reasons we won more often than lost.

He was focused on the puck, and in the back of his head, being better than his pro father.

"Yeah, kiss my ass. You're just pissed you couldn't get your dick sucked last night." Damon threw his jockstrap at T.J. who dodged it easily. It smacked Elton in the back. He didn't even turn around.

"I almost had a chick. She was fine." T.J. stopped what he was doing to emphasize the girl's hourglass figure. "Her dark hair piled on top of her head, wide brown eyes, and her tits were spectacular from what I could tell under that parka."

I froze at the description of Elora. He hadn't had a chance with her. Not after what she said about him. I believed her more than T.J. He wasn't interested in anything long term, and I got the impression that Elora wasn't a one-night type of girl. I ignored his posturing.

"You could bounce a quarter off her perfect ass." He mimicked smacking it. "I could've ridden that all night."

My fingers balled into fists. Okay, maybe ignoring it wasn't going to work. T.J. talked shit about women all the time, most of it of the bull variety, but he also loved a challenge. She shot him down. That was enough for him to try again.

"But you didn't." Damon laughed as he pulled his jersey over his shoulder pads. "Elora ran from you. She's not your type. She's too classy."

"Yeah, that's what made her perfect." T.J. laughed and dropped back onto the bench behind him. He stretched his legs out, almost tripping Linden as he walked by on his skates. "Too bad she's skittish. I'll wear her down, though. They all come around to my cock."

My nails dug into my palms. No way he'd get to Elora. I glared at him, but he didn't notice. And why the fuck did I care? I walked her home last night. That was it. We chatted about her family, her life growing up, but only briefly. There wasn't any reason for me to go all caveman over her.

"You okay, man?" Damon said quietly beside me.

I buried the anger building in my chest with a fake smile and nodded once, keeping my mouth shut.

"Thanks for walking Elora home last night." Damon grinned like he was replaying his night with Melody. The goofy, lovesick grin wouldn't go away. "I owe you big time for that. Mel would've ditched me for sure if you hadn't come through."

I shook my head, not in the mood to talk about last night again. "Are you going to get your head out of your ass in time for the game?"

His smile widened, and I wanted to punch out his two front teeth. "Not my ass I'm thinking about."

This was going to be a very long night.

Three hours later, with an overtime win under our belts, Coach took me aside in the locker room. I'd gotten two minor fighting penalties in the third. The first was more jersey grabbing and circling each other. The second almost cost us the game, but he'd tried taking out Linden by cross checking him into the boards. Linden went down hard, and I fucking lost it.

My jaw throbbed from a nasty right hook, and my eye started swelling after a left jab. Fucker had pulled my helmet off and ripped the chin strap. I doubted I looked pretty, but I guarantee he looked worse.

"What the fuck is going on with you?" Coach snapped once I closed the door to the visiting office. "Two games, three minor fighting penalties? That's not the finesse player I know."

"Just upping my game." I stood in front of him, holding his gaze. "And Milford slammed Linden headfirst into the boards. Can't let anybody fuck with my line."

"Yeah, he deserved a wake-up call, but that's not your job." Coach leaned forward on the desk and stared hard. He was pissed, and I didn't really get it. Linden could beat the shit out of someone who even looked at T.J. wrong, but I'm getting my ass chewed for a legit fight. "You get assists, you score goals. Focus your damn effort there and stop taking stupid penalties when I need you on the ice."

"Yes, sir." I stepped toward the door, knowing I'd been dismissed. It was hard not to argue with him, and I wanted to. He'd bench me if I did.

"I mean it, Wyatt," he shouted before the door slammed shut behind me.

Yeah, yeah, yeah. And fuck that. I was done playing by everyone else's rules. Time to make my own.

Chapter 4

Elora

Monday was warmer than it had been, so I ditched my parka and wore a thick hoodie with Ridder U's logo across the chest. Crazy as it sounded, I never owned a hoodie before. I had long sleeved hooded t-shirts, but nothing thick and soft like this. I loved the rich blue color too. It reminded me of the deepest waters of the Caribbean. Extra bonus I hadn't planned on was that it was way too big and hung down to the middle of my thighs. Melody laughed when I brought it back to the room after I bought it. Then she said all girls wear their hoodies too big.

My morning classes had gone by fast. There was so much information to take in. Child Psychopathology was my favorite, but I still felt like I was missing something. Like the real meaning of my education. It was my junior year, and my coursework focused on my major. What if my major was wrong?

I sat on the edge of the round fountain in front of the student union, contemplating my courses and basking in the warmth of the sun. It reminded me of home. A light breeze lifted my loose hair around my chin. I raised my head to the sky, relishing the heat that burned off the chill of an October morning in Minnesota.

"Hey," a deep voice said.

I opened my eyes and smiled at Lawrence. "Hey."

"Can I join you?" He motioned to the open space beside me.

"Of course." I watched him pull an acoustic guitar around from his back so he could sit, and I moved a few inches over. He'd practically sat on my lap. Maybe he just misjudged the distance. "Did you write something new?"

He bobbed his head left to right. It was almost shy, which normally, Lawrence was not. "Yeah, kinda. It was something I was going to do at the open mic night."

"Oh, yes," I said, my voice pitching high. Guilt welled in my chest and lumped in my throat. I'd totally forgotten about it, and that wasn't something I was proud of either. "I am so sorry. Melody and I started watching the hockey game and lost track of time."

It was a small lie. The truth was harsher, and I really didn't want to hurt his feelings. Melody flat out refused to go to the poetry reading, and she begged me to stay with her. We did watch the game, though, so that was true.

"Yeah, it's cool." He ran his hand over the chestnut-colored guitar. "You wanna hear it now? I kinda turned it into a song."

"Sure." I scooted farther down along the fountain's edge and turned toward him, resting my leg on the rough concrete.

Lawrence smiled and shifted his guitar onto his knee. "It's still a little rough."

He started to strum, and after a few chords, the lyrics began. It wasn't rough. It was terrible. I faked my smile as he sang about some girl who wouldn't give him the time of day. It was sugary sweet and kind of silly. Not that I told him that. Music should make you feel, move you. Not make you want to stuff your fingers in your ears. He was trying to take something beautiful and create something more beautiful, only it just didn't work.

"That was nice," I said as politely as I could. My phone buzzed off my lap, vibrating off my leg. I caught it before it hit the ground. The words Spam Risk popped up, but it gave me an excuse to make a quick escape. He'd ask me more questions, and I couldn't tell him the truth. It wouldn't be good. The last thing I wanted to do was make him feel bad because his music was... well, bad. I faked a wide-eyed expression and grabbed my bag. "Oh, I'm sorry. I really have to take this." I waved the phone at him, careful not to let him see the screen, and swiped it to answer. "Hello?"

"Your vehicle's warranty is about to expire," a robocall began.

I glanced over my shoulder at Lawrence as I hurried away. "Hi, Mom."

He looked like I kicked his puppy. I'd make it up to him. Lawrence wasn't a bad guy. I just didn't want to break his heart. This was awkward. I wasn't used to it, either. One of my goals in coming to a school so far from my ever-moving home was to expand my knowledge of humanity. I'd met a lot of different people on our travels, but I'd never gotten to really know someone. I wanted this experience to be different. Lawrence's heartbroken face was not one I knew how to react to.

As soon as I stepped into the student union, I ended the spam call and hurried upstairs toward my favorite chair. The fireplace wasn't cold beside it, but my usual seat was thankfully empty. I sank into the overstuffed seat. Later, I'd ask Melody how I should've handled the situation. Maybe Deidre and Claire down the hall could give me some insight. At this moment, I just wanted to lose myself in something that made sense. I pulled out my book and started reading. It was three chapters later when a hand on my shoulder made me jump.

Melody laughed and plopped on a chair across from me. "You jump every time."

"I'm not used to people touching me at random. You live on a boat and see how many times that happens." I smiled despite my words and closed my book over my finger. "How'd you find me?"

"I saw that guitar player who has a huge crush on you outside." She shrugged, crossing her legs and leaning forward. Her expression turned grim. "He said you got a call from your mom and came inside. Is everything okay?"

I grimaced. "Would you think I'm terrible if I said I answered a robocall to get away from him?" I hated how that sounded. Really, I should've apologized. "I'm horrible."

Melody stared at me for a beat, then she burst out laughing. People turned toward us, their mouths agape and their expressions curious. No doubt they'd be on the school's social media page talking about the crazy chick in the student union. If we were lucky, they'd even post a picture. I wasn't a fan of the Beaver Blaster. Besides the terrible name that the administration didn't quite understand why it was inappropriate.

"Shush, people are staring." I slapped her leg down.

"Oh, who gives a shit." Melody roared for another minute, then wiped the tears from her eyes. "Damn, I needed that."

I shook my head, but a smile formed on my face. Ugh, I was a doubly horrible person. I opened my mouth to defend myself against the indefensible, but I was interrupted before I could say a word.

"Hey, babe," Damon said as he walked past me to sit in the chair by Melody. "What's so funny?"

Melody shot a glance at me, still smiling. "Elora answered a robocall and pretended it was her mom to get away from a guy who's got it bad for her."

"Melody!" My horror showed on my face, and I could feel my skin burning hot. It was going to blister from embarrassment. How could she just blurt that out?

Someone sat in the chair next to mine, and I turned to see a wide-eyed Wyatt. He pressed his lips together before grinning. "Didn't think you had that in you."

I dropped my face into my hands. The last person I wanted to think I was this horrific person was Wyatt. Or Damon. Or Melody. God, this was a mess.

"What's wrong?" Melody asked, the mirth gone from her voice. She tugged on my hands, but I wasn't about to move them.

"I'm horrible," I said into my hands. "I'm a terrible person. He just wanted my opinion on his song, but I couldn't tell him it sucked, so I ran. I'm a terrible, horrible person."

"No, you're not." His voice was soft, gentle, and I turned toward him, peeking out between my fingers. Wyatt's grin was as sweet as his voice. His blue eyes were as clear as the water at St. Kitts. "Sounds like you were trying to spare his feelings. That's not a bad thing."

My hands fell away, and I sniffled. "You don't think that was mean? To fake taking a phone call? I could have told him the song was good, right? I mean, is that worse or better?"

Wyatt raised his eyebrows. "Was the song good?"

"God, no." His smile widened, and I bit my lip to keep from laughing. Wyatt's gaze shot to my mouth for a minute. Or not. I could've imagined it. Yeah, I totally imagined it.

"Then you saved him the real pain." He licked his lips, and *that* I didn't imagine. Melody giggled with a snort. He glanced at Damon and Melody. "What?"

"Didn't say a word, bro," Damon said as he reached for Melody's hand. "Did you eat?"

"Yeah, you?" She leaned closer to him, and suddenly their conversation was hushed, intimate.

My fading blush deepened again. I could feel the lava flowing around under my skin. Wyatt shook his head and pulled out his phone. Needing a distraction, I picked up my book and started to open it to the page I thankfully remembered I was on. Using my fingers as a bookmark wasn't the best idea when I talked with my hands.

Wyatt's hand filled my vision as he pressed the cover back down. "Gretzky?"

"Well, yeah." I arched my eyebrows and pressed my lips together. Wyatt held my gaze. It made me want to lean closer. "Biographies are kinda my thing, and since the game, I've been trying to learn more about hockey. I mean, it's a fascinating game, and I don't know a thing about it."

"You want to learn about hockey?" He slid his hand away and put it in his lap. "From a book?"

"I watched some movies, too." I sounded like a little girl who had just been busted stealing a cookie. Probably looked like one too. Wyatt must've thought I was a little weird.

"What movies?" he asked. There wasn't any judgment in his tone, and his blue eyes shone with curiosity. At least, I hoped that's what that was.

"*Miracle, Goon, Slapshot, The Mighty Ducks.*" I paused to think if there was anything else and remembered one more. "Oh, and *Cutting Edge.*"

"*Cutting Edge* is not a hockey movie." He shook his head, his lip curling in fake disgust. How did I know it was fake? I wasn't positive it was feigned, but it didn't seem real.

"Well, there's a hockey player in it so I watched it." I fake swooned with my hand on my chest and a hefty sigh. "So romantic. And now I know what a toe pick is."

Wyatt laughed softly. "At least you learned something. Which one was your favorite?"

"*Slapshot.* Maybe *Goon.* I'm not sure. They were both pretty good. *Slapshot* was intense, and *Goon* just got to me, you know? I loved the way that Doug overcame everything to find some happiness. What about you?" I turned farther in my chair, pulling my leg up and tucking it under myself.

"*Goon.* It's actually got a good story." He met my gaze head on, and my breath caught in my chest. The intensity surprised me, and I liked it too. It takes courage to meet someone in the eye and hold it. Most people glance away after a few seconds. At least in my experience. Wyatt wasn't most people. "So you really want to learn about hockey?"

"Yeah. I didn't understand anything the other night, and it moved too fast. Melody tried to explain it to me when we watched the second game, but I just... It's a lot." I leaned forward. My own need to know everything was enough to close the distance. He smelled like musk after a fresh rainfall. "Can I ask you a question?"

He nodded.

"Why did you fight that guy in that first game? The one I was at? And what about the second game? You got into a fight then too. I mean, is that really common in hockey? Or is that just something you see in the movies?" My heart raced at the thought of so much brutality. It was crazy and weird. I waited for his response, but after a minute, I didn't think I would get one.

Wyatt

Why did I get into those fights? That was a great question. Mesher had pissed me off before the game even started just by the way he eyed Melody and Elora. Of course, I hadn't known Elora then, but I knew Damon was seeing Melody and that wasn't cool. Not after the shit I went through. And the second game? I just needed to get it out of my system and protect my team.

"I'm sorry," Elora said softly. She bit her lip again, and damn it, that wasn't what I needed to see. Elora was beautiful, with her wide brown eyes and her small nose, perfect chin, dark brown hair that was kissed by the sun and copper-streaked. Those thoughts were not helping me. They were too distracting, and I needed to not think of her in any other way than a friend of my friend's girl. "It's none of my business."

I rubbed the back of my neck. God, this was awkward. "It's just a hockey thing. No big deal." Her face had a nice pink hue under her tanned skin. I wanted to reach out, touch it, but that was kind of creepy and totally not appropriate. "So, Elora's kinda of an unusual name."

Her face brightened. "Right? Dad insisted on it being my name." She leaned in with a grin. "Especially after Mom named my brother Apollo. My great-grandmother on my dad's side was Elora. I barely remember her, but she was sweet."

"What do you remember?" I asked, suddenly interested in something that made her so happy.

She glanced at the ceiling, pressing her perfectly manicured nail to her lips. "She let me sit on her lap and snuggle her even though she was in a wheelchair." Her hand dropped, and she smiled at me. Her wide eyes shone with delight. "She'd sing 'Twinkle Twinkle Little Star.' I'd fall asleep every time."

The thought of Elora sitting in *my* lap leapt in my mind. I shook it off. "That sounds nice. I never knew my great-grandmothers."

"Oh, Grandma Elora was amazing. She lived this crazy life." Her hand became animated, like she needed them to tell the story. They flew around the air, emphasizing her words. "After she graduated high school, she took off and backpacked around the world for two years. I don't know how she survived. When she came home, she started college and protested everything she could. She called herself a Freedom Fighter. She became a teacher after college, but she never really settled down."

"She sounds pretty cool." I wondered what a life like that would be for me. The mere thought of me backpacking anywhere wasn't going to happen. A life like that wasn't for someone like me. I had obligations. My dad wanted me to take over the chain of hardware stores he owned. It wasn't that I didn't want to because I did. It appealed to me. I enjoyed the old guys who would come into the store, loyal to locally owned businesses, and just talk. And I was damn good with tools. I knew more than most people my age. So it wasn't the job. It was more about the timing. I wanted everything Elora just described before I settled into the life waiting for me.

"It broke my heart when she died, but she lived to be almost a hundred." Elora smiled, lost in her memories. It warmed my cold heart. "It's kind of why I decided to come to school here instead of staying close to the south. Well, one of the reasons." She grinned at me. "Did I tell you how I picked Minnesota?"

I shook my head, and I was dying to know. And so fucking glad she had.

"Apollo and I rolled out a map of the US on a beach in St. Kitts." Her eyes widened, like this was some crazy secret. "He turned me toward the water and had me throw seashells over my head until it landed somewhere. It hit Minnesota first. I applied to every school in the state that offered my degree." She lifted her hands in a playful shrug. "Voilà, here I am."

"What if you hadn't gotten into any of the schools here?" I asked, secretly thanking God she was here.

"Well, he made me land on three states, so I had options. Washington State was second, and New Mexico was third." Her nosed wrinkled. "I'm glad I didn't end up in New Mexico. I mean, I want to go there, but I was kinda looking forward to seeing snow."

"I thought you regretted moving here the other night." Her eyebrows furrowed, and I wanted to rub my thumb over the deep crease between her eyebrows. "When I walked you home, remember?"

"Oh." She pressed her lips together and leaned closer again. "I guess I was a little homesick. It was my birthday, and I really missed my parents. Mom called me again the next day, though. I felt better after talking to her." Her grin returned, and she pulled her phone out of her back pocket "I should show you what my brother sent me."

Before I could stop her, she turned it toward me. A guy slightly older than Elora grinned into the screen. It was pretty clear he was holding his phone up like a selfie, and it was equally clear that this was Apollo. They had the same wide eyes and sharp chin. Behind him was a stage with an entire cast of people in neon colors. Music started and everyone sang 'Happy Birthday' to her. Her brother blew her a kiss, and that was it.

"He's crazy like Grandma Elora." Her voice took on a wistful, lonely air.

"Where was he?" I asked. If I was honest, her family sounded amazing. My sister was cool, and my little brothers were annoying. Mom and Dad were typical South Dakotans obsessed with the Wild West.

"He works for a cruise line. I'm still shocked he got the theater cast to do that. Then again, he could charm the pants off a shark." She turned the screen back around and smiled at the image before putting her phone back in her pocket.

"It's nice he thought about you. My younger brothers can't remember the passwords to their phones, much less anyone's birthdays." Virgil and Warren were still kids, though. Virgil just turned fourteen, and Warren was twelve. Mom and Dad thought they weren't able to have kids after me, and whoops.

"How many brothers do you have?" she asked. Her open expression made me believe she was sincere. I wasn't used to that. Her eyes closed and she leaned back. "Sorry. I just meant if you don't mind telling me. I forget that some people aren't as free flowing with information as I am."

I smiled at her. "Two, Virgil and Warren, and an older sister, Jane."

"That's so cool," she said, and that sincerity reverberated in her voice. "Are you named after anyone? I mean, I'm named after my great-grandmother, and Apollo is named after the Greek God." She pressed her lips together. "Sorry. I like asking questions."

I chuckled and glanced down at her hands. For once, they were in her lap and not fluttering around. "Yeah, my parents are Western enthusiasts. Mom and Dad named me and my brothers after the Earp family, but Jane got the worst of it. Her full name is Calamity Jane Birch."

Her eyes lit back up again, and before I could say anything else, Damon stood and said my name.

"What?" I asked, letting my irritation show. I'd been enjoying this conversation. It had been a long time since I'd talked to someone who was so open.

He held up his phone. "Emergency meeting. We got to go. We'll probably be the last ones there."

I pulled my phone from my pocket, and sure enough, there was a text to haul ass to the rink. And it was sent thirty minutes ago. I was already on thin ice with Coach. This would only make it worse. Just fucking great.

"Are you in trouble?" Elora whispered before I stood.

I glanced at her, and I couldn't help but smile. "Nah."

Even if I was, it was totally worth the extra workout.

Chapter 5

Wyatt

The entire team stood in the locker room around Coach. None of us dared to sit down, except him, of course. He sat reclined in his office chair, a tattered black leather seat on wheels, but his relaxed appearance was just a rouse. His glare was enough to make most people shit their pants. A few of the freshman looked like they already had.

Coach made eye contact with every single one of us. "Anybody missing?"

I glanced around, and there was one huge omission. Steinberg, our captain. His best friends and roommates dropped their heads. They already knew what was up.

"Where's Steiny?" Halston, another junior, asked. He was on the line with me and Damon most of the time. His six-five frame was built for defense, and he loved roughing guys up.

"And Linden?" Waldmann asked. Another center, Waldmann could score beyond the blue line with his slapshot. Dude was badass accurate.

Murmurs erupted as I looked toward Linden's roommates. They seemed as clueless as everyone else.

"Jones and Reeves, you're in for the next game." He pointed at two freshman, who were chomping at the bit to play. "Steinberg's done for the season. Why is none of your business. Linden's not here because he had to head home for a family emergency. He'll be back in a few weeks. I know most of you are done with classes for the day. Those who aren't, get the hell out of here and get back right after you class. The rest of you suit up. We've got a lot of shit to adjust for." He turned to me and grimaced. "Wyatt, my office now."

Damon stared at me, but I didn't even acknowledge it. He wasn't the only one either. I felt all of their eyes on me as I walked behind Coach, as he pushed his chair back toward his office.

"The rest of you get dressed." Coach shouted over his shoulder and strode to the closet-like space known as his office. It was actually bigger than it felt. Coach stuffed it with gear and sticks. One shelf above his desk had nothing but skates. I closed the door behind me without being told. "Sit."

I wasn't about to argue with him, so I sat in the only cleaned off chair. The other two had stacks of DVDs on them. My throat tightened, but I kept calm. If he was kicking me off the team, this was a hell of a time to do it. "What's up?"

"You think about what I said the other night? About getting your shit together?" He leaned back in his chair, plopping his large feet on the desk.

"Yeah," I mumbled.

"You gonna straighten your shit up?" He cocked an eyebrow that had spattering of gray matching his salt and pepper hair, still mostly on the pepper side.

"Yeah," I said a little louder. Jesus, didn't he get the point?

"You sure?"

"Yes, damn. What do I have to do to make you believe me?" I snapped. My body surged up and toward him. I caught myself, but not before coach noticed my sudden anger. A lump the size of a puck sat in my throat. I forced myself to relax, but that anger still filled my chest, burning a hole inside me.

He dropped his feet and sat up, resting his arms on the desk. "Kid, everyone knows what happened last May. You had a right to be pissed. You been letting this shit simmer for four months."

I sat back, dropping my gaze to the tops of my Nikes. My hands shook in my lap. I pressed my lips together, trying to stay calm. He didn't have to bring up last May. He didn't have to say a fucking word.

He rapped his knuckles on the wood, and I glanced up at him. "I get it. Look, you need to let the anger go, Wyatt." He tossed a card across the table. "You have two choices. The easy one: talk to him. The hard one: get benched."

"That's bullshit," I snapped, ready to leap off the chair again. "You can't bench me. Not with Steiny gone."

"It's bullshit that you keep risking your game. That's not fair to the rest of the guys. You don't fight unless you have no choice, but you've been starting them. I don't think you can control it." He pointed to that card, ignoring the Steiny comment. "One appointment. That's all I ask. For now. You call him right now, in front of me, and make the appointment. Then I don't tell Norris he's playing Friday."

"I don't need to talk to some shrink," I said, but I picked up the card. Coach didn't back down on shit like this. I wasn't going to get out of it, even if I tried.

"One session won't kill you." He leaned back in his chair and put his hands behind his head.

I glared at him, but I pulled my phone out and made the call. What choice did I have?

Elora

"So, what's going on with Wyatt?" Melody asked later that night. She sat on her bed with a textbook and her laptop in front of her.

We'd just finished dinner with Claire and Deidre, who lived down the hall. We spent the entire time talking about classes and guys. Well, I mostly listened. Of course, Melody told them how I escaped Lawrence earlier.

"Well?" she prodded, tossing a pencil in my general direction.

"Nothing." I shrugged, but I felt that slow burn in my cheeks again. It wasn't a lie. Nothing was going on. I thought I wanted something to go on, though. He was gorgeous with his blonde hair, and those eyes were so easy to get lost inside. I put my philosophy book on the table. "He noticed my book, and we talked about hockey movies. That's all."

"Didn't seem that simple." She slid off the bed when the microwave beeped and took her popcorn. It smelled delicious, and I stole a handful after she poured it into a bowl. "Hey."

"Sharing is caring," I said, tossing one piece in my mouth.

"So share what's going on between you and Wyatt." She grinned and added enough salt to fill the sea.

I wrinkled my nose at the too much salt. "I'm serious. There's nothing going on. We talked. It was nice, actually."

"Nice?" She smirked and went back to her bed, pushing the book out of the way to make room for the popcorn.

"Well, yeah. He seemed interested in what I had to say. It wasn't about ... I don't know. It just was different. I liked it. I like him, I think." I shook my head and covered my face. It was a confusing mess, and I was pretty sure this wasn't normal. Didn't people know if they found someone attractive and liked them as a person? It shouldn't be too hard. I took a deep breath and looked up at Melody. "I mean, other than that first night when he thought I was a puck bunny, he's been kind to me. He asked about my family, and we talked about his."

"Oh my God, Wyatt thought you were a puck bunny." Melody laughed and spilled her popcorn over her comforter. She quickly brushed it back into the bowl before the grease could stain it, but the salt stayed behind. That ended up on the floor. "What gave him that idea?"

"I think because I was with you and you're dating Damon." I wasn't really thrilled that she laughed at me again. "It's not funny." I paused and pondered; something my mother said I'd always done. "Is it really so crazy that he thought that about me?"

"Yes, totally. You're not the one-night stand kind of girl. Seriously, most of the girls who are puck bunnies just want to screw a hockey player." She pointed a perfectly manicured nail at me. "Tell me I'm wrong."

I sighed and sat back against the arm of the loveseat. "You're not wrong. I just didn't think it was that funny."

Her mouth dropped into a frown. "I wasn't laughing at you, honey. Please don't think that."

"I know, I guess." I pulled my knees to my chest. Melody frowned deeply. Great, I'd hurt her feelings. "Sorry, I'm being a little bitchy. I'm not used to people making assumptions about me like that or that it might be funny."

Melody set her bowl on the bed and moved to the loveseat. She lifted my feet to sit beside me. "Sometimes I forget that you didn't have a normal childhood. Not that I don't envy yours, because that would have been amazing, but it's not the usual."

"It was pretty amazing, but it was pretty lonely too." I picked at the fringe on my jeans, avoiding her gaze. "I've never had a friend until you. Unless you count my brother."

Melody tackled me, pulling me into a hug. I couldn't stop the giggling from bubbling in my chest, and I didn't want to. "I'm so glad we're friends. And I'm sorry I laughed."

"It's okay." I hugged her back then pushed her off me. Melody laughed, and I thought again how appropriate her name was.

"So you like Wyatt? As in you'd like to date him?" She waggled her eyebrows. "Or kiss him?"

This time I laughed. My stomach ached from all the food and the laughter. It was a nice feeling. We'd had that when I was a kid, but this was different. "Yeah, I think I would like that a lot."

"Well, we need to make sure you keep running into each other, then." She scrambled back to her bed and grabbed her phone. "I'll tell Damon—"

"No, don't. I ... If it's meant to be, then it will happen naturally, okay?" I reached for my philosophy book to finish rereading the chapter. It had become my favorite class over the last week. I started to wonder if maybe this was really what I was looking for and not psychology. "If it doesn't, then it doesn't. I'm just going to keep being me."

"Well, if Wyatt's got any ounce of sense, he'll see how awesome you are." Melody emphasized that statement by tossing a popcorn in her mouth. She dropped her phone, and I wondered if she'd texted Damon anyway.

I just smiled. If all else failed, at least I really had a friend.

Chapter 6

Elora

I wasn't sure if I was getting used to the cold weather or if I was just being stupid, but I didn't wear a coat all week, just a light jacket. Whenever I got back to the dorm, I took the hottest shower I could stand to warm up. Baby steps. Psyching myself into believing I wasn't cold helped. It wasn't until I got under the steaming hot spray that I realized how cold I really was. Of course, I'd get out of the shower and be twice as cold as before. I curled up under my comforter until the chills left me.

"Hey, girl," Melody said as she opened the door with two bags in her hand. "You here?"

I pulled the cover off my face. "Just warming up."

Melody laughed and plopped on the end of my bed. "Stop trying to be brave. If you're cold, you're cold. Wear a coat."

"I'm just trying to adjust." I sat up and the warm air chilled my skin. "You said it gets colder?"

"Sorry, but yeah. Much colder." She held up a bag. "I got you something for the game tonight. Well, kind of."

"Kind of?" I reached for the bag and opened it. Inside was a white hockey jersey with blue and gold stripes around the upper arms and around the waist area. I freed it from the back and laid it on my lap. It was huge.

"Damon's loaning you his road jersey." She grinned and bounced on the bed. Then she pulled out a dark blue jersey out of the bag with white and gold stripes around the waist and arms. "He bought me a home one and had his name put on it." She turned it around so I could see Anderson over the number 27 in white with gold piping. "Cool, huh?"

"This is his?" I lifted it to my nose and Melody laughed. It was a legit concern. Those guys sweat like crazy during the games. I wasn't about to wear something that smelled like a men's locker room. "Doesn't smell, at least."

"Duh. They have them cleaned." She pushed off my bed and went to hers. "You are going with me tonight, right? I just assumed. I didn't even think to ask you."

"I didn't even know you had tickets," I pointed out as the jersey fell from my hands.

"Sorry." She rubbed her hands over her face. "As long as Damon and I are dating, I'll have tickets. I just.... It makes me a little nervous. He's a great guy, and I love being with him. That should be enough, right?"

"It's not?" My chest tightened. I thought she loved him or was falling in love with him. If I was honest with myself, Melody's relationship with Damon seemed like the gold standard. They just seemed to fit.

"I don't know. I ..." She let herself trail off and stared at the wall where a poster of her high school production of *Les Misérables* hung. "I'm only eighteen. I thought I'd come to college, date around until I found the right guy. First guy who asked me out, and boom, we're in a committed relationship."

"This is more about what you expected versus what you're experiencing. It's not really about Damon at all." I wanted to grab a pen and notebook to write that little gem down. It was basic psychology. I thought. Maybe it was basic philosophy. "Do you want to date other guys or do you think you want to date other guys?"

Melody didn't glare at me. She pressed her lips together as she thought about what I asked. When she finally looked at me, confusion etched that line between her eyebrows. "I don't know. Damon's perfect in every way. Why would I want to see what's on the other side of the fence?"

"Because you had preconceived expectations?" I scooted across my mattress to the edge of the bed. "Look at me. I had no expectations. And I also had no clue. My only ideas of what college would be like were from movies. You, at least, had an idea of what you planned." I smiled and lifted my shoulders for a long moment. "Life doesn't always let us stay on the path we set out for ourselves."

Melody grinned and huffed a small laugh. "You're saying to let it happen naturally?"

"Totally." I nodded in agreement with myself. "And, if I can be honest, maybe don't spend every waking minute with him." I pressed my lips together hard and pointed at the poster. "You love musical theater. Get involved with that. Damon's kinda been your college world."

Her eyelids snapped shut, and she fell back on her bed. "God, you're right. I go to class, hang out with Damon. Rinse, repeat. I mean, other than hanging out with you, Claire, and Deidre." She lifted her phone above her head and started thumbing like crazy. "There's a theater group meeting in ten minutes across campus. I'm going to go. You want to come with me?"

"No, I'm going to put on my jacket and head over to my favorite spot in the student union. I've got two chapters to read for my child psych class."

I pushed the comforter off my bare legs and stood. "What time do you want to meet for the game?"

"Six." She rolled off her bed and rushed to the door. "I'll text you."

I got dressed in a pair of jeans, my favorite Key West long-sleeved t-shirt, and pulled on my black Columbia jacket. It was warm and fashionable without being overly bulky like my big parka. After packing my laptop and a copy of *Beauties: Hockey's Greatest Untold Stories* by James Duthie, I hurried out of the dorm. I read my textbook as I made my way across campus. Walking and reading was an acquired skill. I made it just outside the student union when I saw Lawrence sitting on the fountain. Guilt welled in my chest.

"Hi, Lawrence." I stopped beside him, but not too close. Melody thought he had a thing for me, and I didn't want to encourage it too much. I just wanted to be his friend. I glanced at the page number before closing my book. "Can I join you?"

His face lit up with a huge smile. "Always."

"I wanted to apologize about the other day," I began, but he cut me off with a wave of his hand.

"Don't worry about it. Everything okay with your mom?" He was either sincere in his concern or he knew how to fake it. I had no reason to think he wasn't sincere.

"She's fine. Thanks for asking." I pointed to the guitar on his lap, ready to change the subject. "Working on a new song?"

He shrugged and strummed a few notes. "Still working on the same one. The music's good, but I think the lyrics need work."

"It never hurts to improve things," I said gently. That big ball of guilt sat in my stomach.

"Hey, Elora," a deep voice said to my left. My knees quivered at the sound of it. I turned, and Wyatt's small smile electrified me. "Mind if I join you?"

"Well—" Lawrence began, but I was not losing this opportunity.

"Of course." I turned so I was facing more toward Wyatt, then I realized how rude I was and adjusted myself to not shut out Lawrence. "This is Lawrence. Lawrence, this is Wyatt Birch."

They gave each other the bro head nod. I hadn't entirely deciphered it, but I thought it meant 'hi, I don't like you' in this situation. In others, it just meant 'hi.' Guys are hard to read.

"Going to the game tonight?" Wyatt asked.

"Yeah, Damon gave Melody tickets. I'm looking forward to it." I smiled and forced my body to not turn toward him. "I still wish I knew more about the game."

Wyatt smiled and opened his mouth, but Lawrence was quick to interrupt. "I can teach you what I know, if you want."

"That's so sweet," I said. Deep down, I wanted to tell him to shut up. I glanced at Wyatt's furrowed eyebrows. He looked downright angry. "But Wyatt's already offered."

The sweet smile returned. "Yeah, I have. Oh..." He reached into his pocket and pulled out a small rolled up plastic bag. "I was at the store getting a new showerhead and saw these. I thought you might use them."

My face burned, and my heart raced around my chest. My breath was a little shorter, too. I liked this feeling. I liked that he thought of me. It didn't matter what was in the bag either. He'd bought it for me. That had to mean something, right? I unrolled it and pulled out hand warmers.

"You just bend them, and they heat up. Hunters use them all the time. I thought they might keep you warm at the games." His cheeks took on a soft sunset pink, and I wanted to touch his jaw. I wanted to lean closer to him, feel his arms around me. Yeah, okay, I really liked him.

Instead, I put my hand over his and squeezed gently. His skin was warm and smoother than I expected. "Thank you. That was very thoughtful."

He held my gaze, and I didn't need hand warmers or a coat to feel the heat building between us. He turned his hand over, his thumb circling my palm. The shaking in my knees spread to other parts of my body. His soft touch echoed along my nerves, setting them on fire. My breath hitched as he tilted his head. I moved forward just a little. Hoping.

Then his phone buzzed. He closed his eyes and let go of my hand. The moment was gone, but there was definitely a moment. He looked at his phone, then back at me.

"Sorry. I have an appointment." He started to stand and leaned toward me. "I'll see you tonight, okay? After the game?"

"Yeah, tonight." I smiled, my heart going to cloud nine.

He grinned and glanced at my mouth. I waited for it again, but it didn't happen. He bit his upper lip and straightened. Giving me one more long look before he walked away. I watched him until he disappeared around the building.

When I remembered Lawrence was there, I turned to talk to him, but he had disappeared. I didn't even notice he left.

Wyatt

I aired it out. All the dirty laundry. Everything that happened between me and Veronica and my traitorous teammate. I couldn't even say that fucker's name. Nothing went untouched.

"They even had the balls to invite me to their shotgun wedding," I said, bitterness lacing each word. "Who does shit like that? Who knocks up his best friend's girl, then expects a wedding gift?"

The shrink stared at me with so much calm it only pissed me off more.

"I have every right to be pissed." I crossed my arms and glared at him. The guy could've been a spy. He blended in with the décor.

"Everyone has a right to their anger, Wyatt. It's how we manage it." He glances at the file in front of me. "How did you explain this betrayal to your family, your friends?"

Was this guy kidding me? "I didn't tell them shit."

"Leaving your feelings bottled inside you can only make things worse. Tell me, are you angry all the time?"

Pretty much. I didn't say that, though. I wasn't stupid. "No. Just on the ice lately."

"Do you think that's because your friend was a fellow hockey player?" His calm tone made me want to beat the fuck out of something. "That perhaps you're manifesting your feelings on the ice as your subconscious imagines punching him instead?"

I shrugged, because I thought of beating the shit out of him every damn day since I walked in on him balls deep in my girl. The first two months, I replayed my entire relationship with Veronica in my head. How had I missed it? What did I do wrong? It was a vicious cycle only broken by my need to pummel that asshole. Then I thought of different ways to make it really hurt.

"Wyatt, I think you would benefit from more sessions. Nothing long term, but you need to talk about your feelings and why you're having a hard time with your anger." The shrink leaned forward, resting his elbows on his knees. His precious legal pad of notes tilted vertically.

"You'll tell Coach I was here? That I did this, right?" I stood and stretched my arms above my head.

"Yes, of course, but I think —"

"Great. That was the deal. One session and I'm still on the ice." I walked toward the door and left without saying another word.

I'd done what Coach demanded. The shitty thing was all those emotions resurfaced. I'd kept a few things back from him. Things I'd never tell anybody. Like how it really went down. I'd left to get her ice cream at the small grocery three blocks from my place. She'd asked for it, and I never let her down.

A block from the apartment, I'd realized I'd forgotten my wallet. I turned around, walking quickly back to my place. When I walked in, Veronica was naked and bent over the kitchen counter with a knee propped on a stool. The asshole was hammering her from behind. With her leg propped up, it gave me a full view of his cock entering her pussy.

What made it even worse was that he came inside her before I even screamed.

I did beat the living fuck out of him then. The only thing that kept me from killing him was Veronica begging me to stop, telling me she was pregnant. We'd never had sex without a condom. Clearly, as the evidence showed down her thighs, asshole didn't use one.

I walked out and went to Damon's. For the next four nights, I slept on his couch in the same clothes. They all knew what happened. It spread like wildfire through the school. The only saving grace to my humiliation was the term ending in a week. Damon, being the good guy he was, went over and cleared out my personal shit.

Nobody ever asked me about it, and I wasn't going to offer up any information.

When classes started back this fall, the entire thing was swept under the rug. I went on as if it didn't happen. But every day it burrowed deeper. The only time I let it out was on the ice. That was where it needed to stay.

Chapter 7

Elora

Melody couldn't stop talking about the theater meeting she went to earlier. It was nice to see her excited about something. I'd went to the school's open swim hours and did a few laps after my run-in with Wyatt. I got there as often as I could, usually four or five times a week, plus weekends. Lately, it was the only place I felt warm. Winter was going to make me suffer.

We settled into our seats in the same corner of the arena for the game. Damon's jersey was heavier than I thought, but it still wasn't enough to keep me warm. I added a hoodie under it so I could take my coat off during the game. Nobody else wore their coats, or even sweatshirts right now. Ugh, it was so clear I was an outsider.

I pulled off my coat and took the hand warmers from my pocket. My fingers were ice cold. I couldn't feel the plastic as I tore a pack open.

"Where'd you get those?" Melody asked as I broke one.

"Wyatt." My fingers warmed instantly, and I sighed with contentment.

"Wyatt?" Melody poked me in the side. "Do tell."

"I was outside the student union, talking with Lawrence—"

"The bad singer?" Her eyebrows slammed together. "Why? I thought you didn't like him"

"I don't dislike him, but that's not the point." I waved her off with my warm hand. "Anyway, Wyatt came up to us and sat down. He asked if I was coming to the game, then he gave me these." My smile could've cut the Plexiglas in front of us. "He said he was buying a new showerhead and saw them, and he thought of me. Isn't that sweet?"

"Sickenly so." Melody grinned, offering me her popcorn. I shook my head. Too much grease, and my stomach rolled with nerves. "He likes you."

"Maybe, but ..." I thought about how much I wanted to kiss him and how it didn't happen. He'd leaned in. I'd tilted my head. The only thing that hadn't happened was contact. "I don't know. He's probably just being nice to me because of you and Damon."

"Nah, from what I've gathered, he's probably just being cautious. Damon said he had a girlfriend for two years until something bad happened and they broke up at the end of the spring semester. He didn't say what happened, though." Melody wiggled in her seat, then propped her feet on the boards. Her hand dug into the kernels. "Believe me, I pried, but Damon either didn't know or it was that bad of a breakup."

I let that rock around my brain while Melody chatted to the guy to her right. The team came out to cheers. I zeroed in on Wyatt, knowing it was him before I even saw the number on his sleeve or on his back. It was the smooth way he moved on the ice, like he was born there. My heart slammed hard against my ribs. He didn't look our way, not that I expected him to, but Damon did. He was so head over heels for Melody. It was sweet and very romantic.

Yeah, I was a little envious.

The guys warmed up, and I studied their movements. There was something artistic in how the blade of the stick cradled the puck. The passes had to be accepted or the puck would just bounce away. Several times, Wyatt passed to a teammate without looking. I wondered how he did it.

Melody stopped talking and started sipping a beer. I stared at her when she took a second sip. She smiled and shrugged. Guess she wanted to keep that little secret to herself.

The puck dropped at center ice. I lost myself in the game, the movement, and learning the rules. Melody supplied information as it came up, like what icing meant. I'd read about it, but seeing it happen made much more sense. Penalties were a little confusing. The referee, I learned that fast after I called him an umpire, would call what looked like a trip a hook or not even call a penalty at all. It was very confusing. After two periods, the game was scoreless.

I sipped on my water, nervous like most of the other fans around us. This was entirely new for me. Whenever Dad took me to a baseball game, it was fun and exciting, but I never got nervous when the game was on the line. This one wasn't even close to being over, and the butterflies in my stomach fluttered furiously.

The clock ticked down, with each team trading the puck back and forth. Then Wyatt had the puck, and he was alone at center ice. He skated toward the goal, the other team's defenseman fast on his skates behind him. I held my breath as Wyatt shifted his body left, then right. He closed in on the goalie and flipped his wrist.

The crowd erupted as the puck flew over the goalie's shoulder, but I gasped. The defenseman's stick lifted high, and Wyatt's head snapped back. He fell onto the ice, his gloved hand covering his neck. Someone in a suit rushed onto the ice. I pressed my hands and face against the glass, trying to get a better look to make sure he was okay. He was on the other side of the rink across from us. Blood splatter the ice near him. The crowd was silent.

Then Wyatt stood, and everyone cheered. Blood dripped from his glove. Tears filled my eyes, and I swear I stopped breathing. He skated off the ice on his own. That was a good sign. My gaze never left the bench as I waited for him to come back out, but he didn't.

It wasn't until the players started shaking hands, or more like gloved fist bumps, that I realized the game was over. We'd won on Wyatt's goal.

"Hey, let's go wait outside where the guys will come out. Damon will let us know if Wyatt's really hurt. Or maybe Wyatt will come out himself and you can see he's okay."

I nodded fast. "Yes, please. I just... That didn't look good. Do you think he'll be okay?"

Melody smiled gently and put her hand on my shoulder. "I'm sure he's fine. It probably looked worse than what it was."

"Okay." I wanted to believe her but all that blood.

We made our way slowly out the doors toward the players' entrance and then waited along with a bunch of other women for about thirty minutes. I couldn't even feel the cold. The team slowly started to trickle out, and some of the crowd thinned. Still no sign of Damon or Wyatt.

Melody kept glancing at her phone, then she smiled. "Damon's coming out now. He didn't say anything about Wyatt. Come on."

She grabbed my hand, pushing through some of the women who had to be freezing in their tight tops. Maybe these were the puck bunnies Wyatt told me about. Damon stepped through the door, smiling the minute he saw Melody. I didn't see what happened next because Wyatt was right behind him.

Our eyes met, and I started toward him, but two women moved in front of me. Wyatt smiled at both of them, even hugging one. He didn't look back at me. I felt like a fool. Of course, he might have had a bad break-up last spring, but that didn't mean he hadn't moved on. Stupid me. I thought there was something between us. Maybe there was, but it wasn't serious enough for him to explore. Unless he was one of *those* guys, the type that just wanted to get laid. He'd been so adamant against puck bunnies, so that couldn't be it. It was probably just me.

I turned around and left to catch the last shuttle back to campus.

Wyatt

Halston's girlfriend hugged me once I stepped outside. India was sweet, and she always worried about the team if we got hurt.

I looked for Elora, but the puck bunnies were in the mood to play. Two different hands landed on my arms, and I shook them off. Damon and Melody appeared out of the corner of my vision. Neither one of them appeared happy. They both looked across the parking lot with frowns. I followed their gazes and saw Elora's back heading toward the shuttle. She was in one of Damon's jerseys.

"Excuse me," I said as I forced my way through the crowd toward her. "Elora."

She didn't hear me, or if she did, she ignored me. I didn't want to run, to appear desperate, but damn, I wanted to talk to her, not those puck bunnies. I held back and regretted it as she climbed onto the shuttle.

"Damn it." I turned back toward the players who were still picking out their bunnies for the night. Damon stared at me with raised eyebrows. I was his ride. "Let's go."

I ignored them as I hurried to my car. The shuttle let people off at the parking lot behind the student union. I plotted the route in my head, flipping my keys in my hand.

"Drop us off at the frat house, okay?" Damon said behind me.

I ignored him.

"Wyatt?" Damon pressed.

I climbed in my truck and started the engine. Melody slid next to me on the bench seat, and Damon sandwiched her in. I peeled out; my only thought was getting to the student union to catch up to Elora there.

It didn't make sense to me. I just knew I wanted to talk to her.

"You okay?" Melody asked.

Again, I ignored her.

"He's focused. When that happens, just roll with it." Damon was fucking right. All I could think about was seeing Elora and making sure she was okay. She'd walked away with her head down. That wasn't her. She always held her head high. "He'll never answer you."

"On what, though?" she asked. Damon didn't respond, or if he did, it was his usual shoulder shrug.

I hit the light two blocks from campus. Damn it. Damon must have said something to Melody, because they hurried out of the truck. We were only a block from the frat house. I gunned it the minute the light turned green. Less than a minute later, I pulled into the parking lot.

The shuttle was still unloading, and I could see her walking toward the quad. I parked illegally, but I didn't care. Ticket me, campus police. I just needed to talk to her. Jesus, what the fuck was wrong with me. Whatever it was, the only way I'd figure it out was if I chased after her.

"Elora," I said when she walked by the fountain in the front of the student union. She jumped at the sound of her name. "Wait up."

Slowly, she turned to face me, an unreadable expression on her face. I stopped a few feet away from her. She didn't move, and I wasn't sure I could. There was something in her expression that bothered me. Disappointment? Anger? Hurt?

"Are you okay?" I asked quietly.

She nodded, then stepped closer. Her eyebrows curled toward each other. She lifted her hand, her fingers hovering over the bandage on my neck. "Are you?"

"Yeah, just a scratch." I wanted to lean into her touch.

"I was worried. That was a lot of blood." Her hand fell back to her side.

"Why didn't you say hi after the game?" My body was frozen in place. I couldn't even put my hands in my pockets.

"You looked busy," she said, shrugging, but she glanced away from me. "I didn't want to bother you."

I nodded, not sure what to say. Those girls didn't mean anything to me, and I would've preferred it if they left me alone. I finally found the ability to move and pointed at her jersey. "Where'd you get that?"

She looked down, a small smile appearing on her lips. "It's Damon's. I kinda like it, though. It felt like I fit in at the game."

A little finger of anger wrapped around my heart. I didn't like that. I didn't like her wearing Damon's jersey. Saying it to her, though, that would kill that little bit of happiness she just showed me. I wasn't about to ruin it for her.

"Do you have a swimsuit here?" I asked out of nowhere. Even my brain wondered where that came from. Then the perfect idea formed.

"Yeah, I swim every morning." Her eyebrows curled in again, but this time not as severe. "Why?"

"It's a surprise." I nodded toward her dorm. "I'll meet you over there in ten minutes."

She didn't say yes or no, but then again, I hadn't actually asked her anything.

"If you want, I mean. If not, I get it." I stepped back, the sting of silent rejection piercing me.

"You don't have to."

Elora smiled softly. "Okay. Ten minutes."

I grinned back at her. Damn if I didn't feel like I just won the Stanley Cup. I ran to my truck, pulling out my cell phone as I went. The minute I fired up the engine, I made the call to arrange everything. Elora was going to love this. I knew it like I knew my own name.

This might've been the best damn idea I ever had.

Chapter 8

Elora

I had no idea what Wyatt was up to, and I liked that. I also liked that he found me after the game. My body reacted to him. My heart raced, my breath hitched, my skin quivered. I'd never experienced anything like it. And I wanted more.

My dorm was virtually empty. Only a few people wandered around. Claire waved from down the hall before disappearing into her room. She was nice, and I liked hanging out with her almost as much as Melody. Claire's major was physics, and I wasn't ashamed to admit it was over my head. Still, I was curious, and I read a book about Stephen Hawking at the beginning of the semester. Claire explained the things I couldn't quite wrap my head around. Having friends, that was a nice new feeling.

I hurried into my room and grabbed my favorite pale green bikini. It didn't take long to change and redress with a pair of leggings and my favorite Ridder U hoodie. I looked casual, but my hair wasn't right. After checking my watch, I had two minutes left. That wasn't enough to do anything sexy. Did I want to do sexy? Yeah, I really did. I pulled my hair up into a messy bun, pulling a few strands down to frame my face. Nothing he hadn't seen, but it would have to do.

A giggle escaped my throat. I felt like a naughty teenager sneaky out of her parents' house to meet a boy. At least the teenager part was right.

When I walked out the front door of the dorm a few minutes later with a beach towel on my arm, I didn't see Wyatt.

I saw Lawrence.

"Hey, Elora." He strode up to me with a huge grin that widened at the sight of my beach towel. "Going swimming? I could join you."

"Actually—"

"It wouldn't take me long to change." His gaze took a tour of my body, and I didn't appreciate it. Lawrence was a nice guy and all, but I didn't like him that way. I'd thought I made that clear without being mean. "Swimming sounds great tonight. It's a little chilly here."

"Yeah, it does," a sexy voice said behind me.

I turned and smiled, but it fell at the expression on Wyatt's face. "But that's not what we're doing?" I walked over to him, standing as close as I dare. "Or is it? Is that the surprise?"

Wyatt's face relaxed and that small, sexy smirk emerged as he stared down at me. "If I told you, that would defeat the purpose." He glanced up at Lawrence and shook his head. His eyes narrowed, and that friendliness disappeared from his tone. "Thanks for keeping Elora company. I was running a little late."

Lawrence grunted a "no problem" and offered me a sad smile. "See ya later."

"Goodnight," I said softly. It killed me to hurt his feelings. He just wasn't what I wanted. I looked up at Wyatt, who glared at Lawrence's retreating form. "Ready?"

"I don't like that guy," he said. When Lawrence disappeared into the dark, he glanced down at me. "You changed."

"Yeah, someone spilled beer on my jeans at the game. I'm surprised you didn't smell it." Plus, if we're swimming, these are more comfortable.

"Good." He tugged at the blue string of my oversized hoodie. "I like this hoodie."

"Me too."

There wasn't a lot of room between us, and I wanted to close it. His lips looked very kissable. I sucked my lips, pressing them hard together. There was no way I was making the first move. He liked me; I was almost sure of it. Then there was that story Melody told me, about the long-term thing that didn't work out.

His fingers touched the back of my hand, and just that little bit of contact sent my body on high alert. Then it was gone.

"Let's go," he said, his breath a little rough.

I couldn't talk, so I just nodded. Wyatt took my towel, tossing it over his shoulder. Then his fingers brushed against mine again. I shivered.

"You cold?" he asked as he put his arm around me. I snuggled against him, melting. "Better?"

"Much," I said. He smelled like a spring in Trinidad. "Thank you."

"You're welcome." His arm stayed over my shoulders until we got to his truck. I missed the warmth of him instantly. But not just the warmth, the comfort and security it provided. I felt safe with Wyatt.

The truck wasn't anything new and fancy. Just a simple pickup with two doors and a short bed. He pulled the door open and held my hand as I got in. I smiled at the chivalry. He got into the driver's seat and looked at me, then his gaze dropped to the space beside him. I thought about scooting closer, but that seemed presumptuous. That was the last thing I wanted. His arm around me could've simply meant he didn't like that I was cold. Jesus, this self-doubt thing was horrible.

"How's the cut?" I asked, as he put the key in the ignition and started the engine.

He shrugged. "I've had worse." He put the care in gear but kept his foot on the break. "Does it bother you?"

"Why would it bother me?" I turned as much as my seatbelt would let me. "I mean, it bothers me you got hurt. I was worried that it was serious. It still seems serious. Are you sure you're okay? I don't want to make it worse by doing whatever it is we're doing. I don't like that you're injured."

Wyatt smiled and pulled out of his parking spot. "Thanks. I'm not sure anyone has been that concerned except for my mom. Maybe my older sister. She's not a hockey fan."

"What's she like?" Having a sister sounded like fun. Melody was kind of like the sister I never had. I think. I don't know what being a sister even means.

"Jane's pretty cool now. When we were kids, she was always playing mother hen." He didn't look at me as he drove, but I couldn't take my eyes off him. All the tension he'd held was gone. His face had softened, and I wanted to reach out to feel the smooth skin along his cheek. "She's got her own kid now. He's two."

"You're an uncle? That's awesome. My brother's never having kids. Or so he told me." I shook my head as I laughed. Apollo as a dad, that would've been interesting to see. "His boyfriend, Carlos, has other ideas, though, so we'll see."

"Did your bother grow up on the yacht, too?" A red light filled the cab, flashing off Wyatt's relaxed features. The cut on his jaw had a small patch of gauze over it. The chances of a scar were likely.

I tore my gaze from his profile. "Yes, but he was already in school when the money came in. I was only a few years old. Mom and Dad debated about following their dream before taking him out." Apollo remembered school, and he remembered the heartbreak of leaving his friends behind. I always asked him what school was like. At first, he was almost wistful about it, but as we both got older, his bitterness disappeared. He loved the ocean. "It was hard on him at first, but he's part fish."

Wyatt chuckled. "Are you part fish?"

"Sort of." I grinned before biting my lower lip. "I swim five miles at the pool almost every morning. My first week here, my philosophy professor told me the pool had open swim times. I think he noticed I was miserable. It's not the same as salt water, but it helps. I tried running, but that's not me."

"Are you miserable now?" he asked softly.

I reached across the bench seat, touching his arm softly. "Not at all."

Wyatt

I felt her through my long-sleeved tee. It was like the sun searing through my clothes to warm my skin. I shifted, and her hand fell away. A small sigh escaped her lips, like resignation.

"Good," I said, gripping the wheel tight. "I'm glad you're happy."

She stared at me. I could see the intensity of her face out of the corner of my eye. Whatever she saw in me, I wasn't sure, but she bit her lip and shook her head almost imperceptibly. "So, where are we going?"

"It's a surprise," I said again. *I hope you love it.* If I was honest with myself, and that damn therapist told me I needed to be, I was terrified. Elora was sweet, sexy, and I just liked being in her orbit. The jealousy that twisted around my chest like barbed wire was a problem. Seeing her with that guitar nerd who clearly wanted to get in her pants skyrocketed my heart rate and made me want to pummel his face. I needed to get that under control.

Elora didn't say anything else, nor did she touch me again. I hadn't tried to knock her hand away. That was the last thing I wanted. I'd shifted in my seat to get closer to her, and her hand fell away. There's that internal honesty again. I pulled into an alley and parked in the back lot in front of a nondescript gray door.

"Can I make this a complete surprise?" I asked, turning toward her. Handing her a small brown bag, I bit my tongue as she opened it.

She pulled out the sleep mask, holding it up by one finger. Doubt covered her features, and for the first time, she looked apprehensive. "You want me to wear this?"

"Just until we get to the surprise." I didn't like how my heart ricocheted around my ribcage. "I swear on my family that nothing will happen to you, but if you're not comfortable, I get it. I just thought it would be fun, and ..." I slammed my hand into my hair, turning to look out the driver's window. "I'm sorry. I feel like I'm fucking this all up. We can go."

"Wyatt," she said softly.

I turned toward her, expecting complete rage or disappointment or fear. None of the things I wanted for her. She had the sleep mask over her eyes.

"It smells like you," she said, and I swore she took a deep breath. "I trust you."

It took everything in my power not to kiss her then and there, but it wouldn't be right. When I did finally kiss her, I wanted to do it with her eyes wide open. Jesus, was I really thinking about kissing her already?

"You're going to have to help me out of the truck." Her nervous giggle went straight to my heart.

I jumped out of the cab, locking my door before I closed it. Keeping my cool was hard, but she couldn't see me, so I jogged around to her door. I opened it and took her soft hand. It was warm in mine, and she gave a little squeeze. This was going to be harder than I thought. She slid down, bumping into me.

"You ready?" I asked as I tried to keep a little distance between us.

Elora nodded, biting her lower lip. Jesus, I wanted to do that to her. I tightened my grip on her hand and walked to the gray door. Swallowing hard, I knew this was going to be great, but that inkling of fear wouldn't go away. Fear, doubt, I never had that problem until Veronica fucked me over.

I turned to the door and knocked three times. Hugh Helmsey opened the door. He was a beast of a man at six-two. I'd met Hugh my freshman year when I needed to get away from campus. His gym looked like a good place to hang out. He let me in and gave me a tour. Once he found out I played for Ridder, even though I was a measly freshman, he made a deal with me. He'd let me work out whenever I wanted on the condition I helped him coach his youth hockey team. It was a no brainer. We'd been great friends since.

"This door will lock automatically when you leave," Hugh said in a deep voice. Elora scooted closer to me. Hugh raised his eyebrows and pointed at the sleep mask. I shrugged my shoulder, and he chuckled. "I'm going out the front, so you'll have the place to yourself. See you tomorrow, Wyatt."

"Thanks, Hugh," I said, letting the real gratification in my voice. We stepped inside, and I led her to the elevator. Hugh, true to his word, walked out the front door and locked it. He waved and gave me a thumbs up. "He's gone. You can relax."

Elora nodded, but the tension didn't leave her body.

"I'll tell you all about him in a minute. Right now, it will ruin the surprise." I twisted my hand, so our fingers intertwined. Her small palm fit perfectly against my larger one. "Ready?"

"As I'll ever be," she said with a laugh, as the elevator dinged on the next floor. "Wow me with your surprise."

Chapter 9

Elora

"Okay, but this is just a tease until you get your suit on." His soft voice washed over me, but the nerves were still there. He led me out of the elevator and through a door.

I held up my finger. In one swift move, my sweatshirt was on the floor. Wyatt's sharp intake of breath hit me in the heart. I kicked off my shoes, then tugged my leggings down. "See? No need for a tease. Hit me with the whole surprise."

"I think you hit me with the surprise," he said with a laugh. It wavered a bit, and I tried to hold back a smile. He was nervous. I liked that, too. I didn't think anything could unnerve Wyatt Birch.

With the sleep mask on, I had no idea where I was or what I was surrounded by. I was one hundred percent sure we were alone based on what that Hugh guy said. There was a hint of sweat in the air, but it wasn't overpowering. More like it had been cleaned. I wasn't at all cold, even in my bikini, but I wasn't feeling the steam of a pool area either. And definitely no chlorine. Wyatt's finger skimmed down my lower arm until he linked his hand with mine. Goosebumps covered my arm. I shivered from the sheer joy of his touch.

"You cold?" he asked softly, his lips somewhere near my ear.

It took a lot not to lean into him. I knew what I wanted, but I still had no idea what was on Wyatt's mind. "A little."

"Trust me," he said. He pulled me gently forward, then let go.

I stepped into steamy warmth, and I stopped to inhale the humidity. My body instantly reacted, relaxing with the heat. All I needed was a nice sea breeze and I'd feel like home. I closed my eyes, even though I still had the mask on, and just stood for a moment.

Wyatt's fingers lifted the sleep mask. He was so close. His blue eyes bright with something I didn't know, but I wanted to think it was because of me. I put my hands on his now bare chest and stared up into his eyes. His skin was hot, smooth, softer than I anticipated.

"Thank you." I lifted on my toes and kissed his cheek. He didn't react. Well, he did. When I glanced down, his fists were clenched tight. I dropped my hands and stepped back, putting distance between us. A lump caught in my throat, and I tried to keep my voice normal. "This is wonderful."

"I thought you'd like to feel warm again," he said, tossing the mask out the door. He fiddled with some nobs, then stepped out of the steam room. A large bucket of water with a giant wooden spoon was in his hand when he came back inside. He set it near the hot coal, then poured water over them. The steam was delicious. "I usually come once a month to get away from everyone. Hugh lets me in after hours, and I just sit and think. It's kinda like a spa day."

I laughed and sat on the higher bench. Wyatt tossed me a towel. "I can see that. This... is great. I can feel my bones again."

"Are you really that cold all the time?" he asked as he settled on the bench beside me. I tried not to notice how close he was. He could've sat anywhere else in the small steam room, but he didn't. The teak bench was slick beneath me. He draped his own towel over his lap, covering the red trunks he'd quickly changed into.

"I think I'm getting used to it a little, but yeah. I'm freezing until I'm in the shower or under my weighted blanket." I shifted my legs until I was sitting in Lotus position. "I guess if you stayed on the yacht for a month, you'd probably be hot."

Wyatt turned his head toward me. "Probably. Our summers can get warm, though. For about a week or two."

"It's not *really* hot, though. There's always a breeze." I raised my eyebrows and smirked. "Plus, there's plenty of swimming."

Wyatt laughed. His head fell back, and I noticed how long his neck was. He'd shaved too. There wasn't any of the stubble I'd seen earlier.

"Do you swim?" I wanted to move closer, but after the whole clenched fist thing, I didn't think he wanted me too close. But he sat close to me, so maybe he did. I was getting mixed signals.

"Yes and no. I learned how to survive the water in our pond back home." His shoulders relaxed, and he leaned back against the wall. "Jane wasn't exactly the patient type when it came to teaching me. I hope my nephew learns though."

"What about your parents? They didn't teach you?" I didn't hide my surprise.

"Nah, they were too busy. Dad has the store and the farm. Mom had the house to run plus her job and the historical society." He grinned just talking about his parents. "They were there for everything important, but sometimes we'd just take off into the pasture for fun and trouble."

"Sounds freeing." I couldn't imagine it. My parents were around us all the time unless we docked. Even then, we didn't have a lot of freedom until we were sixteen. "Sounds amazing, actually."

"You grew up in exotic places. That sounds amazing." Wyatt's eyebrows furrowed. "Wasn't it?"

"Yes and no." I smiled sadly and glanced away from him. "I loved it, don't get me wrong, but sometimes I wish it had been more normal. This is the first time I've ever had to sit in an actual classroom. It's totally different from sitting on the boat and learning through my computer. And I never had any real freedom. Plus, I'd have to leave friends behind all the time. Melody's the first real friend I've ever had, other than my brother. It could get lonely."

Wyatt's hand covered mine and squeezed. "I'm sorry. Loneliness sucks. Especially when you're lonely with someone."

I wanted to know more, but I didn't want to break this thing between us. It was like we were baring our souls. And I wanted him to know everything about me. Good or bad. "We docked for three months once. It was like having a real home. I met someone, and we... became close. It killed me to leave him, but I didn't have a choice." I shrugged as he squeezed my hand again. "I like that I have choices here, decisions I can make on my own. Although it took me a while before I could sleep comfortably. My bed doesn't rock."

Wyatt smiled and let go. I missed his hand, his warmth.

"Do you miss your family?" I asked, in order to keep the conversation going.

He nodded as he stared at the ceiling. "My parents are great. My little brothers annoy the shit out of me, but yeah, I miss them." He moved to the bucket and added more water. "Do you miss the guy?"

I sighed and laid down. "Honestly, yes. He treated me like I was precious. It was nice to feel like the center of someone's world, even if it was really just a fantasy. He taught me to live in the moment because life is fleeting."

"Lift your head," Wyatt said gently. I did, and thick muscle became my pillow. His thigh was hard, but it was soft too. "Did you... love him?"

I opened my eyes and stared up at Wyatt's tight jaw. It hurt to see him so tense. I reached up, running a finger along his stubbled jaw. "No. I loved the *idea* of him. Of being in love. The normal for a seventeen-year-old. But I was never in love with him."

Wyatt leaned into my touch. "Does it make me a Neanderthal to admit I'm glad?"

"Not at all." I continued my gentle caress as I sat up. "Wyatt."

He turned his gaze toward me, and there was pain in it. I wanted to kiss him. I wanted to let him know I was all in. I wanted this to happen, but that pain held me back.

"You're a really great guy," I said softly, still caressing his cheek. "Thank you for this. For being a good friend. If that's all you want, I understand."

He swallowed hard, but he didn't say another word.

The tension was too much. My hand fell away, and I laid back down with my head on his thigh. Then I regaled him with stories of cliff diving in Jamaica, cooking authentic jerk chicken, and swimming in the lagoons of various islands. Wyatt just listened, commenting, or asking questions on occasion. It eased him, but my heart was on fire. I burned for this man, and it was clear he didn't feel the same. At least, I thought it was clear.

Keeping my feelings to myself was going to be hard. If I wanted Wyatt in my life, even as a friend, that was what I had to do.

Wyatt

Fuck. I was blowing it with Elora. When she stripped down to her lime green bikini, my body went on alert. It was ready for action. Her toned muscles and flat abs defined sexy in my book. Veronica had been soft, gorgeous in her own way, but she was never an athlete or even a casual jogger. Elora took care of herself. I'd wanted nothing more than to peel those small sections of fabric from her gorgeous body.

Then it smacked me into the boards headfirst. I'd compared her to my ex. Fucking Veronica. Two years of fake love. Two years of thinking I'd found the one to spend my life with. Two wasted fucking years. Elora deserved so much better than that. Than me.

When she touched my face and said we could be friends, the rage inside me built. Not at her, but at myself. How could she not see I wanted her? I felt like a fool. Elora seemed to know my reaction wasn't good. Instead of demanding I take her home, she laid back down with her head on my lap and told stories about her childhood.

It was almost one in the morning when we finally left the steam room and redressed. It broke my heart, and my dick, to see her cover herself again.

"Do you want to go get a coffee or something?" I asked as she pulled her coat on.

A long yawn was my answer. "Yes, but I'm exhausted. Maybe we could meet for coffee in the morning or lunch."

I smiled, or I think I did. "I'd like that. Lunch would be nice. We're heading out at two for a game."

She reached forward, straightening the collar of the light jacket I'd brought. Her fingers lingered, and it took all my power to not pull her against me. She deserved better than my fucked-up head. "How about an early lunch, like at eleven. You can tell me about the team you're facing. I plan on watching it at the student union this time."

"You're going to watch?" I thought she'd only seen the two games she'd been to with Melody.

"I haven't missed one yet. But I don't want to go to the bar again. It was too crowded, too loud." She let her hands fall, a small frown appearing on her face. My breath froze in my chest. I hated seeing her unhappy. "I think I like hockey better than baseball." She laughed quietly. "Just don't tell my dad."

"I promise." Reaching for her hand and weaving our fingers together, I started leading her back toward the exit.

"Thank you." She tugged my hand to stop me before we stepped outside. "For tonight. This was perfect."

I smiled, and this time I knew it was really there and not some phantom bit of happiness I'd constantly imagined. "You're welcome."

She pressed her lips together, and I wanted to kiss her. More than anything else in the world. In that moment, I wanted her to know I wasn't some dumbass mental case who couldn't get his head on straight. I wanted to show her that this was real between us. At least, it felt real. It felt *right*. Instead, I stood there like an idiot.

Her hand left mine, and she pushed open the door. I followed her outside, getting to the passenger door before she did and opening it for her. When we were back in the truck, I reached over for her hand again. I needed to feel her close to me. She didn't notice my not-so-slick move. I glanced over at her, and one hand was in her lap while the other propped her chin up as she stared out the window. Her jaw clenched tight, her lips hard against each other.

Chapter 10

Elora

Talk about a hurricane of confusion. One minute, it was almost like we were on the same page. The next, we weren't even in the same book. I had no idea what to think. He stared at me like he'd wanted to kiss me. Yet, my lips were still untouched. Well, by Wyatt's. I'd told him stories of my childhood just to get him comfortable again after I made my intention clear.

Were they, though?

Jesus, this whole dating thing was hard. Then it hit me over the head like a runaway library cart. That wasn't a date. We hadn't actually had a date. It was just two people hanging out... in a very romantic setting.

He tried to touch me in the truck, but I kept my distance. I couldn't go through the confusion again. So, I made a decision. I wasn't going to play his games. If he wanted me to be more than a friend, it was his move. I'd done my part. He hadn't even touched me other than holding my hand.

The truck slowed and pulled into the visitor parking lot behind the dorm. He shut off the engine.

I didn't want to climb out, but I had to stick to my guns here. "Goodnight." I kept my voice cheerful and upbeat, but I wanted to curl into myself. "Thanks again."

The door squeaked when I opened it, and I sort of slammed it shut. I started toward the front of the dorms at a fast clip.

"Elora, wait up," Wyatt said behind me. His door creaked as he closed it just has hard as I had closed mine. I stopped, but I really just wanted to run into my room and collapse. No way I was going to turn around. "Let me walk you to your room."

I snorted out a laugh but didn't start walking again until he was beside me. "That's not really necessary."

"I want to. Is that okay?" His voice took on that sultry, sexy quiet tone I loved so much. He put his hand on my lower back, and I involuntarily stepped closer. "Did I do something to upset you?"

Hysterical laughter bubbled in my chest, and I forced it down. I didn't say anything, just kept walking. After I swiped my card to get into the building, I kept going, taking the stairs to the third floor and avoiding the elevator. Wyatt stayed beside me. I hurried down the boring white walled, tan carpeted hallway to my room at the opposite end of the stairs. There was another set I used at my end of the hallway. Music and laughter could be heard coming through the doors of people who stayed in or where back from a night out. One very distinctive moaning sound came out of Catie's room. I practically ran past it. That was the last thing I wanted to hear at the moment.

I stopped outside my door. There was a note from Claire and Deidre for lunch Sunday on the dry erase board. And a message from Catie for Melody about drama.

"Well, this is me." I felt like an idiot. The fact that my name was on the door in bright neon letters was enough. I faked happiness, brightness when it was the last thing I felt inside. "Thanks again."

"Elora?" Wyatt's voice had a hint of frustration.

I unlocked my door and pushed it open, so I had a quick escape before I looked up at him. "Yeah?" I hated how hopeful I sounded, but I needed to squash that. Fast. "Wyatt?"

"I'm sorry if I upset you." He took my hand and squeezed it once. "I really ... I enjoy hanging out with you."

My heart melted a little, but he only meant as friends. If he meant more, he'd say so. Right? I didn't know. "I enjoy hanging out with you, too." *A lot*, I wanted to add.

His sexy smile returned, and he stepped back, glancing over at the door before turning his gaze back to mine. "Goodnight, Elora."

"Goodnight, Wyatt."

I watched him walk backward for several steps before I closed the door. A sob built in my chest, and I couldn't hold it back even if I didn't know where it was coming from. There wasn't any reason to cry other than my complete and utter disappointment. That and the rejection. I'd been rejected before, but that was totally different than this. I was just a girl, and the men who'd rejected me were too old for a girl who didn't know the first thing about how relationships worked.

Tears spilled down my cheeks. I wasn't that little girl anymore. My one experience with a man was enough to teach me how I should be treated, and it wasn't the way Wyatt treated me. He was so sweet, but he was so cold. Even though I was fairly certain he liked me, he didn't like me enough. I had to accept that and move on. It would be hard to be around him as long as Melody dated Damon, but I could do it. I steeled myself to that possibility when a soft knock sounded on my door.

I wiped my tears and tugged the end of my hoodie down as if that would make me more presentable. Not bothering with the peephole, I turned the knob expecting to see Claire or Deidre.

Instead, I came face to face with the reason for my tears.

"I'm screwing this all up, aren't I?" he asked as he reached for my face. His thumbs brushed away the tears. He stepped in and pressed his forehead to mine. "I'm sorry. I'm so terrified of screwing this up that I'm doing just that. Please be patient with me."

I grabbed onto his wrists, keeping us together. When he started to pull away, I looked into his eyes. There was so much emotion swirling in his head. I wanted to take a little of it away. Just a little, only what I could. Nobody can take all the pain from someone, but I could ease it. I rose on my tiptoes and pressed my lips to his cheek.

Wyatt sighed, then turned his face toward me.

His lips met mine in a gentle, chaste kiss that left me weak in the knees. I wanted nothing more than to open up to him, but that wasn't what he needed. He needed to know I'd be patient.

And I was going to do everything in my power to give him that.

He pulled back a little, our bodies still so close together.

"Patience is my middle name." I wrapped my arms around him, hugging him tight. His arms encircled me. I sighed into his chest.

"I'm... I have... I don't..." He didn't finish his sentences and just held me for a long moment. "Are we still on for lunch tomorrow? Before the team leaves?"

"Yeah, I'd like that." I let go, knowing he had to head home. Stepping back into my room, I felt his absence and shivered at how cold I suddenly was.

He pressed a soft kiss to my forehead. "I'll see you tomorrow."

Hope filled my chest as I watched him walk down the hall. It almost lifted me off the floor. I closed my door the minute he was out of sight, and I danced alone in my room. Then I emailed the only person who would understand how I felt. My brother.

A minute later, my phone rang. I opened the video call. "I wasn't expecting you to call me. Where are you?"

"We just docked in Miami, so I actually have service." He lounged in bed with the sheet pulled up. It moved, and I knew he wasn't alone. He reached over to the body next to his and tapped it. "I have to start helping to unload the luggage in an hour, but I have a minute. Tell me about this guy."

I grinned, and I just couldn't help the giddy excitement. "He's... I don't know. I can't describe him. I just know I feel alive when I'm with him."

The body next to him shifted, and Carlos put his head on Apollo's shoulder. He glanced at my brother with love, then he noticed me. "Oh, hi, E."

"Hey, Carlos." I loved Carlos like family. It had been two years since they'd met. He'd become another brother to me.

"Elora met a guy," Apollo told him before kissing his forehead. "Apparently, he's a hockey player."

"Oh?" Carlos rolled over, keeping his head on Apollo's chest. "Spill the beans, sister."

And I did. I told them both everything. They listened as the story spilled out. When I was exhausted and done, Carlos and Apollo both wrinkled their eyebrows.

"What?" I demanded, suddenly feeling like I was under their very observant microscope.

"Just ..." Apollo glanced at Carlos.

"He doesn't want to hurt your feelings, but you know I won't hold back." Carlos took Apollo's phone. "Listen, E, be extra careful with this guy. He's on a cliff. Whatever happened in his last relationship, which you don't know anything about, pushed him there. It could've been his fault. It could've been her fault, but he's walking that cliff for a reason. He could go over."

"And we don't want him taking you, too," Apollo said over Carlos' shoulder.

"We love you too much," Carlos added.

"I love you guys, too." My bubble had just been deflated out of existence.

"We're not saying he will," Apollo was quick to add. "We just want you to be careful, sis."

"I will be." I tried to smile, but their warning resonated. They were right, and I knew it. I just didn't want to see it. "Now get ready to unload that ship. I need to get some sleep. I have a paper due Monday."

"That paper is done," Apollo said, pointing at me. "I know you've finished it already."

"Doesn't mean I can't make it better." I grinned for real this time. "I miss you both. Can't wait to see you."

Apollo and Carlos glanced at each other. "Maybe you can sneak away in the spring. Meet us somewhere. Vegas would be fun."

"I'd love that. I'll drag Melody with me. She's a blast." I laughed at the idea of Carlos and Melody judging everyone's outfits on the strip. "You'll love her."

"Great. We'll make plans." They both blew me kisses, then ended the call.

Their concern tumbled through my thoughts. Wyatt *was* on the edge of a cliff. He was still trying to decide if he wanted to go over or if he wanted to walk away.

I wanted to help him, but I wasn't sure I could. So, I would do what he asked and be patient.

And I would do what Apollo asked me to do; I'd be careful.

Chapter 11

Wyatt

She kissed me. I hadn't kissed anybody since Veronica, and that brief moment was so much better than all of the ones with Veronica combined. Elora's lips electrified mine. It was like being hit by lightning and sticking my finger in an electrical socket at the same time. I felt it in each nerve, from the top of my head to the tips of my toes.

What would it be like to open up to her, feel her tongue slide over mine?

Jesus, I had to adjust myself. Stepping into the cool night air wasn't even close to the cold shower I needed to tune my body down. I wanted to say goodnight to her again, just a quick text to tell her I was thinking about her. When I pulled out my phone, my dumbass realized how stupid that was. I stopped short of my truck, staring at my screen. How could I have forgotten to get her number?

It was too late now. There was no way I was knocking on her door again and leaving. That wasn't a good idea. Even if it felt like the best idea.

I drove two blocks to the apartment I shared with Damon and T.J. It was almost two in the morning, but I knew they'd be out partying for at least another hour. Damon would stay out forever with Melody. T.J. would get as many puck bunnies to suck his dick as he could. He never had sex with them, just voluntary blowjobs. It hit me then that I knew way too much about my roommates' sex lives.

After I parked in my usual spot, I went inside and grabbed a bottle of water. It was too early for bed, and I was too wired. I'd almost screwed everything up again. The therapist coach insisted on had actually helped me this past week. I'd seen him twice, and I had made another appointment for next week. When Elora had said goodnight the first time, I thought it was for the best if she believed I didn't want to be more than friends.

Then my therapist's words shot into my head. "You've held onto this anger for so long, you don't know how to be happy. Why is that?"

I hadn't answered him. He pointed that out at the end of the session and asked me to think about it. That was two days ago. I'd finally found my answer. Unless I was on the ice, there wasn't a lot to be happy about until I met Elora. She made me feel alive again. She'd found that darkness in me and infused it with her sun. I put the water back and grabbed a beer. Fuck, I was turning into a lovesick puppy.

The thing was, I didn't want to turn this into a rebound situation. It wasn't like I had been chaste since Veronica's bombshell. I went home to North Dakota for a few weeks, hooked up with my high school girlfriend for a night, and then another. Neither time did I kiss her on the lips. Other places, but not once on her mouth. The second time she told me she'd missed me and was glad we were back together. I shot that shit down fast. The sting of her hand on my face didn't match the pain of seeing the woman I thought I loved being fucked by my best friend.

The sting of Elora's heart breaking in front of my eyes was worse than Veronica. I couldn't walk away from her. Without thinking about how she felt, I'd tried to stop myself from taking things too far, and I'd hurt her. Damned if that wasn't a tough pill to swallow.

I finished the beer and drained a second one, then grabbed two more from the fridge. The door opened, and a drunken Damon stumbled in. No Melody behind him. It dawned on me that she was the only reason I stayed up. If Melody came home with Damon, I could've gotten Elora's number from her. I closed my eyes and sank into the couch. The therapist was right. I needed to stop lying to myself about my actions.

"Hey," Damon said, plopping on the couch beside me. He took my unopened fourth beer and popped the cap. "Where'd you take off to?"

"I'm an idiot." I took a long pull from my third beer. My head started spinning.

"No shit. But why this time?" Damon reached for the remote, but I pushed it down.

"Elora." I felt like talking, and that wasn't a good idea. My last roommate knew everything about Veronica because of my loudmouth. And he fucked her and knocked her up.

"Tell me something I don't know." Damon tossed the remote on the coffee table, then put his feet on it.

"I don't trust you."

He spit his beer all over his feet. "What? Why?"

I just glanced at him out of the corner of my eye.

"Oh," Damon said and sat forward. He grabbed a discarded dish towel someone had left on the coffee table, probably T.J., and wiped down the spit beer. "I don't know what happened with—"

"Don't say their names," I snapped and closed my eyes. "Sorry."

"All I know about that sitch is from the rumor mill." He sat back with his beer, toeing his shoes off. They made a loud clunk on the floor. "Since you don't want to talk about it, I'll tell you what I heard. You can correct it or not. The former chick banged our former captain slash roommate, told you the last week of school, and you moved in with me until you headed home. Sound right?"

I laughed. "No. The former captain didn't sleep with her once. He'd been fucking her all year." I shook my head as the anger rose. Breathing in and out for ten counts calmed me but not by much. The image I tried so hard to keep out of my head emerged as vivid as the day it happened. "She asked me to get ice cream for dessert. I left, forgot my wallet, and walked back. When I opened the door, she was bent over on the kitchen counter buck naked. He fucked her on the kitchen counter, D. Where I ate my fucking breakfast."

"Damn. That's way worse than ... I'm sorry, man. That's fucked up." He set his empty can on the coffee table.

"That wasn't the worse part." I kept my eyes closed and fast forwarded through the fight to the point Veronica told me she was pregnant. With his kid. "He knocked her up. She's due around Thanksgiving." I opened my eyes, looking for an open beer, but there wasn't one. "Bitch sent me a wedding announcement over the summer. They took off to Vegas. Mom got a baby shower invite a month later. Who the fuck does that?"

"She was always selfish." Damon shook his hand and clamped his hand on my shoulder. "That's all pretty fucked up, Wyatt."

I turned my head to him. "I don't trust you. Or T.J. Or anyone else."

"You have good reason, but I can promise you that I'd never do something like that to you." He patted my shoulder twice then let go.

"I like Elora." It just flew out of my mouth. I hadn't meant to confess that to him. It felt good, though, like the moment after a puck bounces off your chest. It hurt like hell to say all that, but it felt good that it was over.

Damon snorted and stood. "I say again, no shit. That was pretty obvious from the way you took off after her in the parking lot. Left a lot of puck bunnies disappointed."

"You saw that?" I watched him walk into the kitchen and take two beers from the fridge.

"Yeah, we all did." He handed me one, then sat back down. "She's not Veronica, man. She's not the type to fuck around. Melody told me she's only ever had one boyfriend. The way she grew up, that's insane."

I smiled and thought back to the stories she told me in the steam room. "Makes sense why she's always cold, doesn't it?" I popped the lid and took a swig. The cheap ass beer Damon bought tasted better by the minute. "I took her to the steam room at Hugh's gym. I thought she'd like to warm up."

"Don't get pissed at me, but is she as hot as I think she is under all those layers?"

I glared at him.

"I'm just asking. Dude, I'm so fucking in love with Melody that Elora could walk naked through my bedroom, and I wouldn't give a shit." He grinned from ear to ear. "I'm just curious."

I finished my beer and stood. The anger simmered, but I didn't let it boil over. I answered Damon even though I didn't want to. "Hotter. She's toned, muscular. Sexy as fuck. Stay away from her."

Damon laughed and raised his still full bottle. "You have my word as a forward and a friend. I will never hit on Elora even if you guys are not together."

"Good," I snapped. "Sorry. I'm working on it. The anger thing."

"Yeah, I get it, man. Don't let that shit with Veronica eat you alive and ruin any chance with Elora. She's great. And she likes you, too." He grinned like a moron. "She's too good for your ass."

"Like you said twice, no shit."

Chapter 12

Elora

The water had been the perfect salve this morning. Despite how Wyatt left last night, I had my doubts. It wasn't easy to get up at six, but I did it. I needed it. Growing up on a boat, swimming was a necessity. Mom and Dad made sure Apollo and I both learned early on, but once they bought the yacht, we went through a survival training. Over the years, we also learned to scuba. I missed that, too.

I took a quick shower when I got back to the dorm. Both to warm me up from the cold air outside and to clean the chlorine off my skin. Walking through campus this early on the weekend was almost like walking through an abandoned city. It was eerily quiet, alive and not. My imagination went wild thinking about the number of couples who had fallen in love under the elm trees or by the fountain. It was a romantic place in its own right. I let my mind wander to Wyatt until my skin pruned. My heavy black robe tight around me, I walked back to my room and kept drying my thick hair.

A package propped against my door. I wasn't surprised that Melody hadn't heard anyone knock, if they even had. She was dead to the world. I heard her stumble in close to three this morning.

I picked up the brown paper wrapped box. It had my name in huge block letters across the top. I didn't recognize the handwriting. After opening my door quietly so Melody could sleep, I sat on the bed with the package on my lap. Something made me nervous. Like this was a bad thing. Or maybe a good thing. I never was a fan of surprises.

Except for the little surprises from Wyatt.

The hand warmers were sweet and thoughtful. So was the steam room. I shook myself out of those perfect little moments and turned my attention back to the package. A small piece of paper on the end was loose. I pulled at it, tearing it louder than I expected. Melody groaned and stirred. Who knew paper could be that loud?

I tossed the paper aside and opened the box. My heart almost stopped beating. In big letters, Wyatt's last name sprawled across the back of the material. On top was a yellow piece of paper with scratchy handwriting. I set the note aside and freed the jersey from the box. Wyatt's number 55 took up most of the back. The front had the Ridder U Beaver logo. I brought it to my nose and inhaled the scent of laundry detergent covering his warm smell. I loved it. It was perfect. Clutching it to my chest, I picked up the note.

I'm sorry. I can't do lunch as planned. We have a team meeting before we leave. Coach likes to drop them on us at the last minute.

I hope you wear this tonight. I'd rather you have my name on your back than anyone else's. If you want to.

Like an idiot, I never got your number. I'm sorry. I'm trying so hard not to screw this up. Text me.

His number was scrawled under the last line, followed by his name. As if he needed to sign it. I smiled and stood, dropping my robe onto the floor and pulling the way too big jersey over my shoulders. Damon wasn't as big or broad shouldered as Wyatt. His jersey had fallen mid-thigh. Wyatt's went to my knees. It was like wearing a dress. I pulled my hair up into a messy bun, then stood with my back to the mirror and took a selfie.

I typed out a quick note and sent the pic.

Wyatt

I should've known coach would call a last-minute meeting before we got on the bus. He did it every single time we had an away game. He also loved making the team get up for breakfast before the bus pulled out. Most of the guys needed the pick-me-up to get over their hangovers. I hated that he took our phones so we could focus on eating and listening.

It was almost ten before we got them back. The steak and eggs breakfasts had done the job. Like most of the guys, I'd take a nap on the bus for the three-hour drive to our next game. We'd get there about one, each lunch, warm up, and finally have another team meeting to go over the game plan again. Then it was go time.

Our equipment stored, we boarded the bus and got our phones back once we were in our seats. I tried not to be too eager, but I wasn't the only one. Damon grabbed his and didn't hide the look of disappointment on his face.

He glanced at me. "She's probably still sleeping."

I huffed out a laugh. He hadn't gotten home until a little after three. If he had his way, he'd still be crashed and rattling the walls with his snores. I unlocked my phone to see several messages waiting for me. Swallowing hard, I opened the app and looked for a number I didn't recognize. Mom, Dad, and one from my sister. Four from my little brothers and several from the group team text.

Then I saw it. An unknown area code, unknown number. I opened it, and my entire body turned to molten lava. Elora in my jersey and nothing else. At least, that's what it looked like. She could've had shorts on underneath it, but her perfect legs were bare, and she wasn't even wearing socks. Her hair was up in a bed-head bun, and her smirk as she looked over her shoulder put my dick on red alert.

"Damn," Damon said beside me. "That's fucking hot."

I glared at him, and he lifted his hands in self-defense. T.J., sitting behind me, whistled. Linden popped his head over Damon's seat before I closed the phone fast. "Damn."

"Do you mind?" I snapped, not bothering to let my fury show.

"No, let's see the hot chick again." T.J. laughed until I turned my anger toward him. "Whoa, sorry, man. I was just joking. But she is hot. That Elora?"

That deflated me. I didn't answer him, just turned back around. I wanted her to be.

"Yeah, that's Elora," Damon hissed. "Stay the fuck away from her."

Nobody said anything for several minutes, and I whispered to Damon, "Thanks, man."

"Text her back, Wyatt. They'll leave you alone." He leaned in. "But save that photo, because damn. I wish Melody had sent me one like that."

I smiled. He was right there. That pic was perfect. I glanced around to make sure nobody else was looking over my shoulder. They were wisely avoiding my glare. I opened my texts again and saved the photo to my cloud. Then I read the message.

Elora: *Thank you. I love it. Does it look good? It's so huge! I could sleep in it. Would that be weird? It would, wouldn't it? I'm sorry we didn't get to have lunch together. Maybe tomorrow? If you're available. Have a great game. I may curl up in my room and watch it on my laptop. Or I may go to the student union. I'm rambling. Sorry. Good luck.*

I smiled so wide my cheeks hurt. Her rambling text was cute. I started to type back, when Damon nudged me. He held up his phone so I could see the message and photo. *"Wyatt gave Elora a jersey? She's smiling like she won the lottery."* Under the text was a pic of Elora on her bed, staring out the window, still wearing it. That was just as hot as the one she sent me.

"Send that to me, then delete it." I pointed at it, then at Damon. He just grinned and did as I asked. "Thank you."

"Anytime." He went back to his conversation with Melody.

I downloaded the second picture and set it as my home screen. It wasn't nearly as sexy as the one she sent. She still had her hair up. Her legs curled under her as she leaned against the windowsill. The morning sun touched her upturned face, and the smile was one of pure joy. I wanted to see that smile more often. Hell, I wanted to be the reason she smiled. My overthinking brain tried to come up with the perfect response. Finally, I just winged it.

Me: *That looks much better on you than on me. I'm glad you like it. It wouldn't be weird if you slept in it. I kinda like the idea. And I'd love to have lunch with you tomorrow. And the next day. And the day after that.*

I closed my eyes, the image of Elora lying in my bed in nothing but that jersey lulled me into a deep sleep.

Chapter 13

Elora

I took a morning nap. It wasn't like me to do that. Once I was up, I was wide awake. But I did exactly what I told Wyatt I'd wanted to. I slept in his jersey. Not once did I feel cold, either. I woke up at noon.

Melody sat on the loveseat with her laptop propped on her lap desk. Books spread around her. One of the things I loved about her was her dedication to school. She partied, sure, but she was determined to get her degree.

"Long night?" she asked with a smirk.

"You're one to ask." I sat up, pulling the sleeves down. "What time did you get in? Three?"

Her smirk turned into a full on smile. "About. Damon and I were... busy." She moved her laptop onto the floor and leaned forward. "Spill the beans. What happened last night? Did you and Wyatt get busy?"

I laughed at that. "No. Not even close." My face heated as I remembered the soft, sweet kiss. "He took me to a steam room, of all places. It was... perfect."

"A steam room?" She raised her eyebrows. "Didn't he give you those hand warmers too?"

I nodded enthusiastically.

Melody smirked, adding a wink to her mischievous look. "He wants to *warm* you up."

My eyes widened, but I started laughing anyway. "He knows I'm always cold. It was sweet."

"It actually is. And romantic." She pointed to my chest. "How'd you get that if you didn't spend the night with him?"

I looked down at the Ridder U logo and mascot. "It was propped against the door when I got back from my swim this morning. He left me a note and his number. I sent him a picture." A horrible idea hit me. "Should I have? God, I don't know what I'm doing here, Mel. I like him a lot, but I've never actually dated before."

"Yes, you totally should have." She stood up and showed me a picture on her phone. "I sent this to Damon in case you didn't send one to Wyatt."

"Thanks." I actually liked that photo a lot. It gave me an idea. "Can you send that to me?"

Melody looked skeptically. "You're not mad at me?"

"Well, it is a little creepy that you took a picture of me without my knowledge, but your intentions were somewhat honorable. And it's a great picture. So, not mad."

She relaxed and sent the photo. "Did he text you back?"

"I don't think so." My phone was lost in the comforter. When I finally found it, the battery was dead. "Uh, I never do that. Guess my thoughts were somewhere else."

"Yeah, like on a hot hockey player who's clearly head over heels for you." Melody took my phone to put it on the charger. "So, are you going to tell me all the dirty secrets or leave me hanging?"

"There aren't any dirty secrets. He only kissed me once, and it was very ... sweet." My entire face burned at the memory of that simple kiss, and the confusion that led up to it. "He's fighting something, Mel. I'm not sure what it is, but I think it has to do with his past relationship. He kept telling me he didn't want to screw this up. But he kept pushing me away. He walked me to the door, and I was under the impression he just wanted to be friends. It hurt like crazy. Then he knocked on my door and kissed me like I was breakable. It was slow, sweet, and very... chaste."

"Wow, that's kinda romantic. Then he sent you this." She pointed to the jersey. "Be patient with him, E. It sounds like he wants to try being with you, but he's got some demons to battle."

"That's what my brother and Carlos said." I shrugged and climbed off the bed. "I'm starving. Want to go to get something to eat?"

"Yeah, but are you going to wear that all day?" She smirked.

"I may never take it off." I hugged the material to my body, loving how it felt against my skin.

"Well, at least put on pants."

Wyatt

Elora responded to my text with two little words that set my world on fire. "Me too." My mom always told me words have power. I finally got what she meant. We were going to try this.

I wanted to send her a long message about how I couldn't wait to see her again and just hold her. That was too sappy, even for me. Especially if it was true. Something like that would probably scare her off. Instead, I just sent her a quick note that said I was thinking about her and turning my phone off, but she could text me if she wanted. I'd get back to her after the game. Before I was able to shut it down, she sent two more words. "Focus. Win."

Damn straight.

It almost didn't work out that way. We played hard, but the Warriors did the same. T.J. was like a brick wall in the net. Nothing was getting past him. Unfortunately, their goalie rose to the challenge.

In the third period, we got our chance. Damon scrambled against the boards with one of their guys. Finally, he got the puck out and passed it down the ice to where I was breaking away. It was just me and the goalie. I deked left, watching the way his body shifted to guess my move. Just as I pulled my stick back for a quick wrist shot over his stick side, I went down hard. My entire body ended up in the net with their goalie on top of me.

He wasn't light.

"You okay, man?" he asked as he used my body to push himself upright.

My neck ached from twisting at an odd angle. "Good. You?"

"You were going stick side." He smirked and his eyes twinkled behind the mask. "I had you."

I shook my head and skated back to center. The refs finally made the official call. Two-minute hooking penalty, no penalty shot, which was bullshit, and Coach let them know. Didn't matter. We had the power play.

Coach waved us in, but I shook my head. This was my goal. I'd only been on the ice for thirty seconds. I wanted to stay in. He nodded and pulled Reeves back in. This wasn't my normal penalty kill line, but I didn't give a shit.

Elora drifted into my head. Her long legs coming out of my jersey and that teasing look in her eye. Her last message. Focus. Win.

It was time to do just that.

"Davis," I said, skating by him. "Get me the puck."

He nodded once and pointed to Linden. They had been on the line together since last season. Whatever silent communication they had worked. Linden won the faceoff. I plopped my ass in front of the goalie. After several seconds of passing, Linden sent it to Davis. He pulled back for a slapshot, and their defenseman went down to block. Then Davis slipped around him and put a hard shot on goal. The goalie was ready, but he couldn't handle the rebound. It landed right in front of my stick. I spun and slicked it over his shoulder, stick side.

Tapping my glove to my chest, a humble celly, but I was too tired to go big, I high fived the bench before sitting down. There was just over a minute left in the game.

Coach leaned down. "That's what I'm talking about."

I smiled up at him, then refocused on the game. It was pretty much over for me. I doubted I'd get another shift. The clock wound down, and we won by that goal. T.J. had his first shutout of the season. It was a great defensive game.

It took us about an hour to get showered and back on the bus. I was high on life. I couldn't remember the last time I felt this good. It wasn't just the win, but it was the girl waiting for me.

I climbed onto the bus and took my usual seat. Damon joined in. They wanted to talk about the game, but all I wanted to do was turn my phone back on.

There were eight messages from her.

Elora: *Good luck. I'm getting a lot of stares. I think it's the jersey. Melody says the girls are jealous. I don't know why. Lawrence is with us. He keeps talking, and I keep shushing him. Melody forced her way in between us so I didn't have to sit with him. Or listen. He's a nice guy, but he's driving me nuts. I just want to watch you play.*

Elora: *Sorry, Melody said I shouldn't have mentioned Lawrence. I just wanted you to know he was here. I don't want to hide anything from you. You played great in the first period. I loved that little spin move on your skates. I'd fall on my butt.*

Elora: *Okay, I know you're okay because you kept playing, but that guy slammed you into the boards hard. Are you okay? I know you won't answer until*

Elora: *after the game, but are you okay? That looked like it hurt. I'm surprised you didn't punch him.*

Elora: *Their goaltender is hot.*

Elora: *OMG. I meant hot as in not letting any pucks through. Not as in attractive. I'm sorry. Please don't be mad at me. I wasn't thinking. Melody says that might piss you off. That's the last thing I want. You had some great shots that he stopped, and I couldn't believe he stopped them! Sorry. You're the only hot guy on the ice.*

Elora: *And by hot, I mean hot. Sexy. I'm blushing. You can't see it, but I'm blushing. Is that too forward? Or too soon? I mean, it's not like you don't know that you're attractive. The puck bunnies are talking about your ass and having sex with you. It's kind of making me mad.*

Elora: *How was that not a penalty shot? I don't know a lot about hockey, but everyone is screaming at the screen. I'm not going to lie, I Googled. That should have been a penalty shot.*

Elora: *GOAL! That was beautiful! I loved it. You're amazing. You looked so eloquent and then just tapping your chest afterward. It was perfect. I can't wait to see you tomorrow. Oh, we just won! YAY!!!! Get some rest on the way home. And I'm sleeping in your jersey tonight. Just so you know.*

My brain ricochet around so much at those texts. Elora's honesty was sexy as fuck. I loved it. Every word, even the ones she said that might have pissed me off. I read through them twice. It was like she had a conversation with me, even though she knew I would be able to respond. Like I said, I loved it. Veronica never texted me during the games. I settled into my seat, hoping she wasn't asleep.

Me: *I'm glad you told me about Lawrence. Do you want me to make it clear that you're spoken for? You are, right?*

Elora: *Are you asking me to be your girlfriend? No dating anyone else? Just us. Together. Because if you are, the answer is yes. If you aren't, will you be my boyfriend? I'd really like that.*

My heart speed up faster than if I raced down the ice on a long shift. My hands shook as I started a response, but Elora beat me to it.

Elora: *Was that too forward? Maybe we should talk about that in person. I'm sorry. I don't know how to do this, and I just like being honest.*

Me: *Yes, I want you to be my girlfriend. And I want to show the world you're with me.*

Elora: *Everyone at the student union thinks we are because of the jersey. And, in all honesty, Mel told them. I didn't tell them we weren't. I just left it a mystery. Except Lawrence. He asked multiple times. He even asked me out again. I turned him down, but I don't know if he really gets it. So yes, please make it clear to him that we're dating. Is that what we're doing? I mean, you just said we're a couple and couples date, right? Or are we in a relationship? Is there a difference? Sorry, rambling again.*

I smiled too wide.

"Elora?" Damon asked as he leaned over to peek at my phone.

I pulled it back. "Yeah. Stop snooping."

Damon laughed and showed me a pic of Elora and Melody together at the game in our jerseys. In the background, several people gawked. "Mel said she can't stop talking about you and asking advice on how to be a hockey girlfriend. Then she backtracked and said you guys aren't official."

"We are now," I said, still sporting that huge grin. I pushed his face away when he tried to look again.

Me: *You tell me how you want to define us, Ellie. I'm all in.*

Elora: *Ellie? I like that. And I'm all in, too.*

Me: *Glad to know we're on the same page. As much as I'd love to talk until I get home, I'm exhausted. I'll meet you at noon at the student union for lunch, okay?*

Elora: *I'll be the one in the sweaty Wyatt Birch jersey. Goodnight, W.*

Me: *You really like it? I love that you like it. Sleep well, Ellie.*

I started to turn off my phone when another text came through. This time a picture of her in bed with a sleepy expression. Her dark hair was spread out over the pillow. Her eyes were half closed, and her mouth opened slightly, like she was in mid-yawn, but that's not where my mind went. My dick twitched at how sexy she fucking looked. I wanted to be with her, right then and there. Damn, she was beautiful. More than beautiful. Undefinable in her perfection. I was one lucky sonuvabitch.

Snapping a quick selfie, I attached it to a message that read, *Tomorrow seems like a long time to wait.*

Chapter 14

Elora

I only took off Wyatt's jersey when the classrooms were too hot. Claire and Deidre flanked me on the way to my first philosophy class. It was entry level, but I loved it. My psychology classes interested me, but philosophy was more than that. It made me want to change my major. Maybe I'd minor in it.

The late October air was cold, but the sun was warm. I sat on my usual spot at the fountain to wait for Wyatt. I'd saved the selfie he sent me and made it my lock screen. His hair was messed like how I imagined it would be if I ran my fingers through it. He's eyelids drooped, and I knew it was from the physical exhaustion of playing. But I imagined it more as a satisfied look. Just the thought of Wyatt made me giggle.

I felt a presence more than saw a body, then he was beside me. Inhaling deeply, I turned to face Lawrence. His eyebrows crashed together, and he glared at me.

"What's wrong?" I asked. He didn't need to stare at me like I was the devil reincarnated.

"You're still wearing that?" He pointed to the jersey.

I smiled as I glanced down. "Yeah. I told Wyatt I would. He didn't get to see me in it last night."

"Why?" Lawrence snapped, his glare intensifying.

"Why? I don't understand. Why what?" Confused, yeah, but this didn't make sense. Riddles were not my thing.

"Why him?" He turned toward me, gripping my hands into his with vice-like strength I hadn't known he possessed. "I thought I made it really clear how much I like you, Elora. I wrote you songs, invited you out on dates, and you came. I thought we were going somewhere."

I pulled at my hands, but he didn't let go. "You never asked me out. I mean, you invited me to that poetry slam and open mic night, but that wasn't a date. You wanted to share your music." I pulled again. His grip tightened, crushing my fingers together. "Let go of me, Lawrence."

"Then go out with me." He squeezed and rubbed his thumbs hard over the back of my hands. It wasn't at all sweet or romantic. It creeped me out. "Let's have lunch now. I would be so much better for you than him. Let me show you."

"No." I pulled at my hands again, but he wasn't letting go. My heart raced and my chest tightened until I couldn't breathe.

Lawrence bent toward me, his eyes closed and his mouth open for what I only assumed was preparation for a sloppy kiss. I leaned away and turned my head.

"Stop it, Lawrence." I pulled hard with my hands again, and he fell forward. I closed my eyes, praying this wouldn't happen. "No. Just no."

The air around me changed, and Lawrence's hands were ripped from mine. I looked up quick to see Wyatt standing beside me. Damon stood behind Lawrence, and another player I didn't know held Lawrence by the scruff of his neck.

"No means no, motherfucker," Damon snapped in his face. "You're lucky I won't let Wyatt whoop your ass."

Lawrence turned toward me, real fear in his eyes. I leaned against Wyatt's legs, and he wrapped his arm around my shoulder, holding me tight. His body shook with rage.

"I thought you were a nice person," I said to Lawrence. "I thought we were friends."

His gaze turned cold. "You're just like the rest of them. Chase the athletes and gain status. I'm sure you'll be happy sucking his dick for your notoriety."

"Linden, take this fucker away before I let loose on him. Or I'll let Wyatt beat his ass." Damon's hands curled into tight fists. Lawrence winced as the other guy tightened his grip.

"Touch my best friend again, and you'll have to deal with me," Melody said. I hadn't even seen her show up. She stepped around Damon and slapped Lawrence hard. She leaned in. "If you think these guys will hurt you, just know I fight dirty, asshole."

Linden pushed Lawrence into the grass. "Fucking rapist. When a chick says no, it doesn't mean yes, dickweed." Linden glanced at some girls walking by. "Watch out for this guy, ladies. He tried making the moves on a friend of mine, and she said no. He doesn't understand what the fuck that means."

I stopped watching and turned my gaze up to Wyatt. His anger radiated off him as he watched the scene Linden made. Melody knelt in front of me.

"Elora, are you okay?" she asked, concern lacing her words.

I glanced at her and nodded, turning my attentions back to Wyatt.

"That was hot, Mel," Damon whispered near her. "I fucking love you."

The air went downright icy, and even Wyatt broke out of his mood. We both looked at Melody as her eyes widened. Damon just grinned like a hyena. He had no idea what he'd just said. I knew from my conversations with Melody that they hadn't said those words to each other. She wasn't even sure if he felt that way, but she was having fun and didn't want to ruin it with emotion.

She turned toward him. "You love me."

Damon's eyes widened, but he nodded. "Yeah, pretty sure I do."

Melody jumped into his arms and kissed him hard.

"I think we're lunching alone now," Wyatt said as he smiled down at me, but that haunted look still filled his eyes. "Is that okay?"

"I'll take every minute with you I can get." I gathered my books and stood next to him. My neck still strained as I gazed into his face. "Literal minutes. Even if it's a quick hello as you walk by me."

Wyatt grinned and wrapped his arm around my shoulders. I snuggled against him. We fit so well. He kissed the top of my head, and I thought I would melt into the ground.

"You can have all the minutes, seconds, hours, days, you want, Ellie."

Wyatt

I stood in line to get our food. It made me nervous to leave her alone, especially after that shit by the fountain. If I saw that guy anywhere near her again, I'd knock him out cold. That would get me benched, but it would be worth it. If Damon, Melody, and Linden hadn't been there, I would have put a world of hurt on him.

Just the image of him trying to force himself on her infuriated me. I couldn't stop myself from going back to my apartment in May when I watched my supposed best friend fucking Veronica. Even though I knew Ellie wouldn't do that to me, I couldn't stand the possibility. She wasn't Veronica. I had to keep telling myself that.

I had to stop comparing the situations. Deep down, I fucking knew that, but it was hard. I didn't trust easily. Elora hadn't given me a reason not to trust her. If anything, she'd done the opposite.

When I glanced over at her, she had company. Two girls sat with her, a hot black chick with braids down her back and a perky blonde. I'd never seen them before, but they looked like they adored my Ellie. My Ellie. I loved that.

I grabbed two trays and strode back to our table. The girls both sat on the opposite side, so I had no choice but to sit beside my girl. Good. I liked being close to her.

"Hey," she said as she looked up at me. The look of pure happiness, pure adoration in her eyes set me on fire. I kissed the top of her head again and settled in beside her. "Wyatt, this is Deidre."

The hot black girl waved. Her smooth skin practically glowed and her eyes were olive green.

"And Claire."

The blonde blushed and held out her hand. "Nice to meet you. We live down the hall from Elora."

"And if you hurt her, you'll deal with me." Deidre leaned in so I would hear every word. "My dad's a homicide cop. I know how to get rid of bodies."

The table went icy and silent. That was not an idle threat. Even if she smiled after she said it.

I leaned toward Deidre. "If I hurt her, there's a lake off highway fifty-nine that's remote and icy. That's a good place."

Deidre and Claire laughed, but Elora didn't. She reached for my hand. I glanced at her.

"Deidre isn't kidding. Don't give her ideas." Her eyebrows tightened into a V. I reached out and pressed that spot. She relaxed and a small smile tickled her lips.

"Jesus, you two are too much. Come on, Claire. Let's go find hot hockey players. Or basketball players. Hell, I'd just take a frisbee player right now." Deidre stood and glanced between us. "Too damn perfect."

I couldn't agree more. My gaze settled on Elora's, and I just stared at her. I couldn't believe she was my girl. Her eyes widened, and a blush covered her cheeks.

"What? You're staring," she said, doing the exact same thing to me. "Do I have something on my face?"

I leaned in, pressing a kiss on her forehead. "No. You just captivate me, that's all."

Ellie laughed and ran a finger along my jaw. "Same." She dropped her hand and her gaze followed it. "I'm sorry about Lawrence."

I tilted her chin up so I could look into her eyes. "You have nothing to be sorry for, Ellie. I heard you tell him no. Everybody did. He's the one who should be apologizing to you."

"I still feel bad. Like I should've known he was a jerk." She sighed but didn't shy away from me. "When I first came to here, he was nice. We had a lot in common, I guess. He just seemed like he wanted to be my friend, and I'd never really had a real friend before." She tried to smile and failed. "As luxurious as it seemed living on a yacht in the Caribbean, it was pretty lonely. Especially after Apollo left."

"Where'd he go?" She'd told me a little about her brother, but not much about his life after leaving the yacht.

"He works on a cruise ship now. Remember? I showed you the video of the cast singing Happy Birthday." She turned from me and pulled out her phone. After a few swipes across the screen, a man with the same hair and eyes appeared along with another man. "That's Apollo. And that's his boyfriend, Carlos. They're pretty great."

"Tell me more about them," I said, suddenly desperate for every bit of information she wanted to share.

We settled into a deep conversation about family, mostly hers, until it was time to go to our afternoon classes. I didn't want to leave, but I also had practice after my ethics course. Honestly, I didn't care about my class. I walked her to the liberal arts building and kissed her forehead again.

There was something about his woman I didn't want to let go.

Chapter 15

Elora

"He gave you a key?" I asked as Melody and I stood outside Damon's apartment later that night. The white door with a small gold 4 above the peephole intimidated me. Wyatt didn't invite me over. Damon told Melody she could stop by any time. This didn't feel right. We'd only just become official. "I don't think I should be here."

"Don't be silly." She unlocked the door and stepped inside. "Come on. Just text him that you have a surprise."

Actually, I already had texted him about Melody's idea. Well, most of it. He hadn't gotten back to me. I took a leap of faith and stepped inside with the four grocery bags in my arms. Melody turned on the kitchen lights, and I froze. It was the most disgusting thing I'd seen in a long time.

I set the bags down on what little counter space I could find as Melody went to the living room to turn on more lights. The kitchen was a decent size. A counter separated it from the living room, which was not as dirty but not exactly clean either. The kitchen needed a hazmat warning.

Cleaning needed to be done before we could get down to business. I put all the dishes in the dishwasher and started it. Well, all that would fit and then I hand washed the rest. Melody joined me and cleaned the counters off. She neatly stacked the errant textbooks on the coffee table in the living room and sanitized the counters. We didn't really talk, just cleaned. It took us fifteen minutes to get it done. Melody quickly swept and mopped the floor while I got out the ingredients.

"Jerk chicken?" she asked as she set the all-spice on the counter. "You sure you can make this?"

I started mixing the spices for the rub. "One of the cooks at a resort showed me a quick way to make it for our guests on the yacht. It normally takes much longer for authenticity, but we don't have the time." I pointed at a few plantains I'd miraculously found in the produce section. "Can you slice those about a quarter inch thick?"

Melody found a small cutting board while I rubbed the chicken and preheated the oven. "I'm glad I thought of this."

"You're just glad I can cook," I said with a grin. The roux for gumbo would take longer, but like the jerk chicken, a cook had taught me a shortcut for yacht life.

"Yeah, that too. I mean, I can cook but not to your level." She turned on some music and started singing along while we worked.

It was nice to do this. I loved cooking, but it's not something easily done in a dorm. The motions, the smells, the simple feeling of accomplishment, all things I missed. Once the chicken was seared and in the oven to roast, I made a quick jerk sauce and started the roux for the gumbo. Melody prepped rest of the ingredients and prepared baked potatoes to steam in the microwave.

Once the food was all cooking, we cleaned our mess, took out the trash and set five place settings on the counter. We couldn't leave T.J. out, and they didn't have a table. I couldn't sit still while we waited for them to get home after practice. Being in Wyatt's apartment without his permission, it made me feel all stalker-ish. I snooped around, which made it worse, until I found a vacuum cleaner.

"They're going to shit when they see how clean their apartment is," Mel said as she started picking up the living room. It wasn't nearly as bad as the kitchen, but a good dusting and vacuuming would make it a whole new world.

"They live like pigs." I wiped the dust off the gaming systems, the TV, and an old school DVD player.

The living room had a large sectional couch in dark chocolate facing a gas fireplace with a flatscreen TV hanging above it. Several gaming systems sat on the shelves beside the fireplace along with a cable box and old school DVD player. There were two bedrooms off the living room, and a short hallway led off the kitchen to a half bath, the washer/dryer closet where the vacuum had been stored, and what I assumed was the third bedroom. I didn't snoop back there.

I'd just put the vacuum away when the door opened.

"Holy shit. What's the smell?" T.J. asked, dropping a large bag on the floor. He blocked the door as he inhaled.

"Get out of the way," Damon said, shoving T.J. inside. He stopped inside the door like T.J. had and inhaled deeply. "Damn."

I waited for Wyatt, but Damon closed the door behind him. He zeroed in on Mel and lifted her up in a big hug.

"Wyatt got held up by coach," T.J. said softly. He was way too close, and I took a couple of steps away. He smelled like sweat and more sweat. Not pretty. A sad smile curved his lips, and he closed his eyes for a moment. "Sorry. I'm often told I don't know boundaries."

"Okay. You just kind of smell... stinky." I smiled and relaxed as he chuckled. He was Wyatt's friend. There wasn't any reason to be hesitant around him. "Do you know if he got my text?"

T.J. just shrugged, then picked up his bag. "Thanks for cleaning too. The place looks great."

Melody pulled her lips away from Damon's long enough to reply. "You guys are slobs."

T.J. laughed and went into one of the rooms off the living area, closing the door softly behind him.

"Wyatt will be here in a minute." Damon walked into the kitchen and took a beer from the fridge. "You guys want one?"

"I'm good," I said. My stomach couldn't handle a beer at the moment. I focused on the food. The chicken was almost done, and the gumbo simmered in the large pot on the stove. Mel and I tried to time it perfectly. I found a skillet and started frying the plantains. The plantains sizzled in the oil, and I started removing them as they browned. I'd just put them on a platter—presentation was everything with food—when the front door opened again.

I set the plate down and turned to face Wyatt alone. Mel and Damon had disappeared while I finished the food. Wyatt's confusion broke my heart. I wasn't sure what to do so I did what I always did. I rambled.

"Damon gave Mel a key, and she wanted to do something nice for him, so she asked me to come along, and I wasn't sure if I should. I texted you, but you didn't respond. She was going to make some baked chicken, but I thought I'd spice it up and so I made dinner. I hope you don't mind." I bit my lip to shut myself up.

Wyatt dropped his bag and his keys, then he stalked around the counter. I waited for him to tell me I shouldn't be here. I opened my mouth to apologize when he put his hands on my face and kissed me softly. My body relaxed against his, and I opened up to invite him in. He took the invite, still kissing me gently as his tongue slowly explored my mouth.

He pulled away and put his forehead against mine. "Hi."

"Hi," I said breathlessly back to him.

"I've been waiting all day to kiss you like that." He kissed my forehead and let go. "This is a nice surprise."

I put my hand against the counter to support my weak knees. That was more than nice. It wasn't just my knees that were weak. My entire body sagged from the quick heat and sudden loss of his mouth. I wanted to climb on his lap for a repeat.

The oven timer beeped. Quickly, I started the microwave for the potatoes, my mind so not on cooking anymore. I pulled the chicken from the oven, almost forgetting the mitt on the counter. I wished I could've said the heat from the oven made my face burn, but I knew better. That kiss stayed with me, even when it was gone. The smell of sweet and spicy, mostly spicy, filled the air. I inhaled deeply, letting that bring me back down to earth.

"That smells delicious," Wyatt said, as he sat at the counter.

I smiled over my shoulder and stirred the gumbo. "You're not mad at me? For just breaking in?"

"Never." He held up his phone to show me the black screen. "I didn't get your text. Obviously." He plugged it in to one of the outlets on the corner. I'd untangled all the cords, wrapping them neatly. Wyatt's eyebrows furrowed and then he looked around. "Did you clean, too?"

"Mel and I did." I shrugged, but my embarrassment returned. "Is that okay?"

"The place looks great," he said, but his voice was strained.

I turned to look at him. Wyatt wasn't with me. He was somewhere else, and that somewhere wasn't good. He clenched his fist tight on the counter, lost in whatever my comment stirred up.

Wyatt

I'd seen the therapist earlier before practice. This whole talking thing was helping, and we talked about Elora and my stupidity. Comparing Veronica and Ellie. Everything about them was different, and I couldn't stop my mind from going there. Veronica hated it when I'd called her Ronnie. She never cooked for me, unless she was hungry. She'd never been much of a hockey fan, either. Elora said she liked it when I called her Ellie. And she made this delicious meal for me, but also for T.J. and Damon, too. And she wanted to learn more about hockey.

How could I not compare them?

He said if I kept doing it, it was because I was trying to figure out when Elora was going to hurt me the way Veronica did. I was just prepping myself for the worst.

I had to tell Elora everything, even the lowest, dirtiest part of it all.

After dinner. Not until we were alone.

"You didn't have to do that," I said as I opened my eyes. The terrified look on her face broke my heart.

"I'm sorry. I ... You practice so much and study, I just thought this would be nice, and Melody wanted to do something nice for Damon, so she thought we could just make dinner, and it would make both of you smile, and we had to include T.J. because we'd be jerks if we didn't, but she wanted to make some boring chicken meal, and why do that when we can have jerk chicken and gumbo. The cleaning part was just..." She tossed the mitt down. Her mouth pinched in frustration. "Well, it was more for me. You guys are too messy."

I laughed and the tension left my body.

A small smile played at her lips. "I rambled again."

"I enjoy your rambles." I stood and walked around the counter, taking her in my arms. "And I appreciate all of this. Even if it was Melody's idea."

Elora playfully slapped my arm. "She was going to surprise Damon with fast food. Then I said she could cook. That's when the chicken dinner came in, and I couldn't subject anybody to chicken with just gravy poured over it." She lifted on her toes and kissed me quickly. "It's ready, by the way."

I didn't care about the food. Lifting her by her waist, I set her on the counter and enjoyed the little squeal she let out. Her face was even with mine, and I kissed her gently, savoring every inch of her lips pressed against mine. It didn't last nearly long enough, but my stomach grumbled.

"You need to eat." Her face flushed a beautiful dark pink.

"Hang out with me tonight?" I asked, wanting nothing more than to just be with her. "We can watch a movie, or I could teach you about hockey, or we can study. Just stay for as long as you can."

Her fingers slid down my temple and over my jaw, her thumb grazing my lips. "I'd like that. A lot."

Giggling interrupted our moment. Melody and Damon came out of his bedroom, clearly having had dessert first based on Melody's hair alone. I leaned in and kissed Ellie one more time, just to taste her lips again before helping her off the counter.

"Get T.J.," she said softly.

"You amaze me." I wanted to kiss her again to show my appreciation, but she started plating the food.

After T.J. came out of his room, a little dumbfounded that he was included in dinner, we sat down to eat. The food was five-star worthy. Damon and Melody were lost in their own little world of conversation, but Elora wouldn't do that to T.J. I wasn't a fan of the way he looked at her, or the way he avoided looking at her.

"What's T.J. stand for?" she asked without looking at him.

"Tanner Jonathan." He stared at her, something like a real yearning in his eyes. I wanted to punch the shit out of him. "Dad insisted on naming his only son after him. Mom wanted to name me Zeus, so I won."

"My brother's Apollo, and I'm sure he would've preferred Tanner." Elora smiled politely and glanced at me. "I know Wyatt's got an older sister and two younger brothers. What about you?"

His eyebrows furrowed. "Three older sisters. Why?"

"Why what?" she asked, totally confused.

"Why are you asking?" He tilted his head, exploring her face with his intense stare. I didn't fucking like it one bit. Elora reached for my hand and squeezed it gently.

"Haven't you heard of conversation?" She sat back and shook her head. "You're Wyatt's friend and roommate. I'm just trying to get to know you. I don't really like you, not after the way you treated me at that party. So, consider it an olive branch, T.J. If you don't want to talk to me, you don't have to."

I almost choked on my chicken. She just drew the line in the sand and dared him to step up to it. Not over, just up. She might as well have said 'Man up.'

"Most people don't have conversations with me," he said with added menace in his voice. "Especially chicks."

"Well, maybe if you took the time to try, you'd get more than a casual blowjob when *chicks* are into you."

Damon roared on the other side of T.J., and I did my damnedest not to laugh along with him. T.J. had issues, none of which he shared, but I had an idea about what had made him such an asshole.

Most of us knew his dad was a failed pro goalie who only made it as a backup for an NHL team. There was tension there, but there was more to the story. It wasn't a theory I would share with anyone, not even Elora. T.J. had to tell us when and if he was ever ready. I didn't think that would be anytime soon.

He glanced over Elora's shoulder and glared at me. "You should keep your woman leashed, Birch."

I stood, knocking the stool over. He crossed that fucking line. But Elora put her hand on my arm, holding me back.

"I'm not some animal to control, T.J.," she said softly. She met his angry gaze with defiance and pride. "I'm a human being who deserves respect and kindness. Just like you do. Maybe once you learn that, you can grow up." She turned back to her food, ending that conversation.

But T.J. wasn't about to let it go. He leaned in too close to my girlfriend and said something that made her blush. Damon and Melody just stared at him. When he was done, he grabbed his plate and took it into his room. I wanted to follow him and beat the living fuck out of him, but the blood drained from Elora's face. I picked up my stool and sat as close to her as I could.

"What did that fucker say to you, Ellie?" I asked.

She turned toward me, tears skimming her eyes. Then dropped the bomb. "Who's Veronica?"

Chapter 16

Elora

T.J.'s words rattled around in my head. After I asked Wyatt who Veronica was, his face went pale and the joy in his eyes dried up. Even when he was angry at T.J., he still looked at me with happiness underneath his anger. That didn't exist anymore.

"Fuck," Damon said under his breath. "Come on, Mel. They need to talk."

Melody protested, but I couldn't hear what she said. I could still hear T.J.'s words echo in my head. That was more than enough.

"Never mind," I whispered as I gathered the empty plates. "It's none of my business."

Wyatt stood and followed me to the kitchen, taking the plates from my hands and leading me gently to the couch in the living room. I sat on the soft microfiber, but the comfort of the couch did nothing to ease the tension. Wyatt turned on the gas fireplace, then sat on the coffee table in front of me. His head hung toward my knees, his hands clenched together so tight I could see his veins, and his entire body stilled.

"Veronica was my girlfriend," he said softly. He didn't look at me, but he kept talking. "We met during freshman orientation and started dating shortly after that. I thought... it doesn't matter what I thought. Last May, I caught her fucking my best friend, who also happened to be our team captain."

I inhaled sharply and covered his fists with my hands.

"I'm not being metaphorical either. She'd asked me for some specific ice cream, so I went to the store, but halfway there, I realized I'd forgotten my wallet. I went back and walked in on them having sex in the kitchen." He finally glanced up at me, tears rimming his red eyes. "You can't imagine how much ... Anyway, I spiraled after that. Veronica was pregnant by that asshole, not me. She kept me around just for her amusement, not because she loved me. They got married over the summer. Baby's due any day, if she hasn't already had it." He paused, his gaze focused on his shoes for a moment before meeting mine, when he started his story again. "Like I said, I spiraled. I didn't go to classes for the last two weeks, not that it mattered. My grades dropped a half a point. When I got back home for the summer, I was drunk most of the time. I had a brief fling with my high school girlfriend. My dad threatened to kick me out if I didn't clean up my act, so I quit drinking because that man's opinion means more to me than anyone's."

I squeezed his fists, and he loosened them, curling his fingers around mine. They were so cold, so steely. Nothing like the touch I'd felt from Wyatt before. Something told me this wasn't the end of the story.

"The fights at the games, those were because of the anger I hold inside." He rubbed the back of my hand with his thumbs. "Coach insisted I go to a therapy session with the school's shrink, or I'd get benched, so I've been doing that twice a week. I'm still angry, Ellie. At her, at him. But mostly at myself, because I can't for the life of me figure out why I wasn't good enough to keep her." A tear slid down his face. "But I'm so fucking glad I wasn't, because I never would've met you. And you mean more to me in three weeks than she meant to me in the almost two years we were together. I'm fucking scared as shit I'm going to screw this up too."

I scooted forward and pushed my knees in between his. It was hard to let go of his hands, but I wanted him to look at me. I put each of my hands on either side of his face and forced his head up. "I'm not her."

"You're so not her." He leaned in to kiss me, but I moved back. The pain across his face killed me.

"I'm not her," I said again, so he understood. There had to be no doubt in his eyes, in his heart. I wasn't the type of person to use someone for my entertainment. It wasn't who I was. I wondered if it was who Veronica was deep down or if she just didn't want to hurt Wyatt when she fell for that other guy. "Wyatt, I need you to know that." I pressed my hand over his heart. "Here."

He covered my hand with his own. "You're not her." He lifted my hand and kissed the back of it, some of the light coming back into his eyes. "I'm sorry. I didn't want to tell you about her. I didn't want you to judge me or think I was less of a man."

I put my hand over his mouth to shut up that ridiculous crap. "I think you're sweet and kind, but you hide that side of yourself for some reason. You care deeply, even though you don't show it. That first game, you defended Melody's honor just because some guy ogled her in the stands. I'll admit my relationship experience is limited, but I think I know enough that honesty is important. You don't have to try to be someone else to be with me. Just be you. Because you are pretty awesome."

He smiled and a twinkle lit his eyes. "I didn't fight Mesher because he was ogling Melody." He leaned in, and I didn't pull back. "He ogled the hot girl next to Melody, who I mistakenly thought was a puck bunny. I was pissed for two reasons. One, he even looked your way. And two, that this gorgeous woman wasn't going to be picky about who she slept with."

I started to protest, but he pressed his lips gently over mine.

"I'm sorry about the puck bunny thing," he said before he kissed me again, slower, longer, and a little more urgently. "I'm not sorry about kicking Mesher's ass."

A laugh bubbled, and I just let it go. "Me, too."

Wyatt moved to the couch and settled in beside me. "Ellie, I don't want to push you into anything or make you feel like ... I'm not ..."

"We take our time." I snuggled into his shoulder and inhaled the clean scent of his soap mixed with his natural sexy smell. It was hard not to climb onto his lap. That wasn't what I needed, and as much as I was sure he'd like some sexy times, it wasn't what he needed, either. "One day at a time, one moment together. Okay?"

He kissed the top of my forehead. "You tell me what you need from me and when."

I snuggled closer. "This. Right here, this is perfect."

"Yeah, it is." He picked up a remote and turned on the TV. "Now, let's learn some hockey."

Wyatt

We watched video of the next team we faced, and I explained the calls. Elora caught on fast. She got angry at a bad hooking penalty. It was sexy as fuck. T.J. and Damon both came out of their rooms. I threw T.J. a dirty look, but it didn't faze him. Not much did.

Melody joined us a few minutes later, her hair wet from a shower. Damon watched her like a tiger as she sashayed into the kitchen in one of his t-shirts and a pair of boxers. I started discussing the tape with him and T.J., and Ellie jumped in with her opinions. T.J. was quick to explain why her ideas wouldn't work, but he didn't talk down to her. I appreciated that, even if I was still pissed at him.

"Oh, wait," Ellie said, grabbing the remote from T.J. and rewinding it. His gaze darted to where her hand grazed his. Or maybe that was my imagination. I needed to let this shit go, but it was hard when Ellie was so close. "What's that called?"

The player had a breakaway and triple deked right before the goalie. A quick wrist shot sent the puck over the shoulder for a goal. I explained it to her, and she looked at T.J.

"Why didn't he just lift his shoulder?" she asked, truly curious.

"It was a good fake. He indicated that he was going to go glove side, and the goalie overcommitted that way. His momentum took him out of the play." T.J. took the remote from her, rewinding it again. He leaned too close for my liking and pointed at the screen. "See? Right there? He does try once he knows the play's going stick side. He's just too late."

"Oh. Okay, I think I get it." She smiled at my soon-to-be former friend. "That makes sense."

T.J. tapped her leg twice with the remote. "Anytime you want to learn more, let me know. Wyatt's good with the on ice, but when it comes to goaltending, nobody beats me." He fucking winked at her.

"Except when they score," Damon chirped up. He raised his eyebrows at T.J., then dropped his gaze to where his legs were pressed against Elora's.

"Nobody's perfect," T.J. said before standing and heading into the kitchen.

"Thank you," I said to Damon.

Ellie turned toward me, concern on her face. Then she smiled brightly and kissed me on the cheek.

"What was that for?" I asked softly.

"I've decided whenever you get that dark expression on your face, I'm just going to kiss it away." Her smile lit up the damn room, and it definitely lifted my mood. "Is that okay?"

"More than okay," I said. Her smile didn't waver until a yawn took over. "You should probably get back." *Unless you want to stay.*

"Yeah, it's getting late." Ellie stood, stretching her arms above her head. Her Ridder U tee lifted above her waist, revealing smooth, kissable skin. She offered her hand, and I let her help me up. Leaning in so only I could hear her, she whispered, "I think Melody's staying here tonight."

"I think Melody's moving in," I said lightly. "I'll walk you home."

"I'll be fine. You should get some rest." She pressed her hand over my heart again. "It's only a block."

"I'll walk you home." I wasn't letting her walk even a step alone this late at night. Anything could happen to her between our place and her dorm.

She just nodded. As soon as we were outside, I took her hand. She shivered from the cooler air. It was getting closer to November, and it wouldn't be long until she got to see her first snow. That made me smile. I loved winter. The snow, the skiing, the outdoor rinks, there was so much to do.

"T.J. pissed you off," she said bluntly when we were a few steps from my place.

"Yeah, he doesn't understand boundaries." I wanted to rip his face off when he leaned in too close to her.

"Maybe, but he's not going to do anything to me. Or to you. He's just going to tease and flirt because he doesn't know anything else." She stopped in the middle of the sidewalk. I couldn't see her expression, but her lips found mine. This wasn't like the sweet, gentle kisses we'd shared before. Ellie kissed me like she wanted to feel every bit of me. I sank into it, wrapping my arms around her waist and lifting her. Her legs wrapped around my body. Then she pulled away and kissed my nose. "I needed that."

"You didn't have to stop," I said as I set her down.

"Yeah, I kind of did. We're taking this slow, remember?" Her tone suggested that she didn't want that. Neither did I, but I wanted her to set the pace. If I had my way, we'd be back at my place in my bed. "Plus, we're outside. Anybody could see us."

"You're in charge," I said, taking her hand again. "We don't have to have sex either. We can just hold each other."

Ellie laughed and bumped against me. "We can. I'd like that."

It hit me then. I was a failure as a boyfriend. "Will you have dinner with me tomorrow? On a real date? We haven't actually had one yet."

"Lunch counts, right?" she asked as we stepped inside her dorm building.

"We weren't alone." I opened the door to the stairs and led her up the flights.

"True." She turned around after she had two steps on me and was eye-to-eye. I loved how short she was. "I would love to have dinner with you, Wyatt."

"Great. Tomorrow after practice. I'll pick you up and we'll be officially dating." I pulled her against me. "But I want lunch tomorrow too."

Ellie smiled. "Lunch tomorrow, too. And the next day."

"And the next day."

I kissed her like she was water and would slip through my fingers any second. That fear laced through me. I didn't want to blow this.

Chapter 17

Wyatt

I stepped out of the therapist's office and headed toward the rink. This time, I didn't make another appointment. My anger was totally under control. If it wasn't, I would've beaten the pulp out of Lawrence when he tried to force his lips on Ellie. It still makes my blood boil, but I can keep myself in check.

The locker room was crowded, as usual. Guys boasted about their latest conquests. That's always bothered me until I figured out most of it was bullshit. T.J. hadn't had his dick sucked nearly as much as he claimed. Linden slapped my shoulder and nodded.

"That guy sniffing around your girl again?" he asked. Linden was a brute, nothing more, nothing less. He knew who and what he was on the ice. Off the ice, I didn't know him that well, but I liked that he had my back.

I shook my head. "I think he got the point."

Linden smirked and showed off the gap in his mouth where a tooth used to be. "Text me if he does. His face is punchable."

"Thanks, man." I popped open my locker and started to pull out the equipment from my bag. As I changed, I listened to the chatter surrounding me. It was a balm to my anger. These guys got it. A few of them talked about their girlfriends. Others talked about the pros and what they needed to do to get there. It was never really on my radar, but I'd always asked myself what if?

"How'd she take it?" Damon sat beside me while I laced my skates. When I got back to the apartment last night, he'd been a little busy. And I was out the door before he crawled out of bed.

I shrugged. Even though Ellie seemed to take it well, it was hard to tell. She was too honest to hide anything from me, but that didn't mean she wasn't still thinking everything over. "She kept telling me she's not *her*."

Damon snorted and slapped my shoulder. "She's nothing like Veronica. Don't treat her like she is." He pushed off me, standing on his skates. "Melody said she's naïve, to a point, but she's also very open-minded. I don't think Elora would bullshit you. If she had any issues with your history, she'd tell you and she wouldn't pull any punches. Unlike you on the ice."

I glared at him. "I do not pull my punches."

"Yeah, you do," Linden said as he walked by, totally oblivious to the main point of the conversation. "But you don't need to hit anybody. I got your back. Just point at the culprit."

I liked that guy more every day.

Damon grinned. "He rooms with us next year. T.J. can take his moody ass back to the dorms."

"He didn't have to throw that out there." I stood on my skates and stretched my arms high. God, there was nothing better than the moment before a skate. Knowing I'd be working my body to the brink of exhaustion, then getting that skating high. Kind of like a runner's high, only better.

"He's got issues." Damon shook his head before shoving his helmet on. "I think he's got a thing for

Elora, to be honest. The way he looks at her, the way he leaned into her last night." Damon glanced at me as he pulled on his gloves. "I'll have a talk with him."

"I can fight my own battles." I pushed my helmet down and grabbed my stick. "She thinks he's misunderstood and a little creepy."

"Because he is." Damon started toward the hall.

Ellie didn't like T.J., so I wasn't worried, but it bothered me that my roommate had a thing for my girl. He needed to understand that she's not a toy for him to play with. And I wasn't about to watch him try.

I warmed up with the rest of the guys, skating slowly around the rink until I saw T.J. in front of me. Speeding up, I slid up next to him.

"What's up, Birch?" he asked, too casually to hide the tension.

"Why'd you tell Ellie about Veronica?" See? I didn't pull my punches. That was a solid shot to the face.

He snorted and kept skating toward the goal. "You weren't going to tell her."

"That's my decision, not yours." I stopped in the blue paint.

T.J. pushed his face guard back and glared at me. "She's too good for you. You'll just fucking hurt her. She had every right to know about your ex and your issues. Don't fucking hurt her, Birch."

"I'm with Ellie. We're good, strong, *together*. So stay away from my girl." I shoved his shoulder harder than necessary. "I'm not kidding."

"I'm not an asshole, and I'm not Lucas," T.J. said, pulling his face guard down. He started stretching between the posts.

I opened my mouth to tell him where to shove his fucking stick, but Coach called me to center ice. "Is there a problem?" he asked with his whistle in his mouth.

"No," I snapped. Then I remembered who I was talking to. I'd done that therapy to avoid getting benched. The last thing I needed was to piss him off, so the benching happened anyway. "No, sir. Just a little roommate to roommate chat."

Coach nodded and pointed to the other end. "Make Wilkson work for his start on Saturday."

I raised my eyebrows, but I didn't question that decision. "Yes, sir."

T.J. worked on the opposite end, taking slapshots from the defensive line. The centers and forwards took shots at Wilkson. He hadn't started a game yet this year, but he was due. T.J. would be pissed. He'd have to get over it. I sent a pretty pass up the left side where Waldmann was supposed to be. He sped in at the last minute and centered the puck for Reeves. The little rubber disc bounced off Wilkson's left shoulder, but I was there for the rebound and sent it right through the five hole.

God, I loved hockey.

I glanced down at the ice. The perfect idea formed in my head for tonight. Dinner wasn't enough for her. Ellie needed something special, something to show her I was all in. Really all in.

And I knew exactly what we were going to do.

Elora

I didn't know what to wear. Wyatt had texted me to dress warm. That was never a good sign. And I was never really warm. Melody tried to help, but her idea of warm was a short skirt and a tight shirt. That was not going to fly. I ended up with jeans and an oversized sweater from Mel's side of the closet. The temperature was killing me, and we weren't quite to November yet.

The possibility of snow loomed in the dark clouds, and I was excited to see it. Mel said it wasn't cold enough. She would know. Her dad was a meteorologist in St. Paul. I just wanted to add snow to my list of experiences, and I would soon enough.

A soft rap on the door drew my attention from the mirror. I brushed my hands down my clothes to smooth them, but really it was to calm my nerves. Taking a deep breath, I pulled open the door.

Wyatt's crooked smile greeted me, and all the nerves disappeared. He had his light leather jacket on and jeans. At his feet by his sneakers was a picnic basket, complete with red and white gingham around the lid.

"Hi," he said, kicking the basket. "Ready for dinner?"

I bit my lip and nodded. "Is that dinner?"

"It's a surprise." He picked up the basket, nodding down the hall. "People are staring."

I leaned out to catch Claire, Deidre, and Melody ducking back into a room. "Goofballs. They're desperate for romance."

"Even Melody?" His eyebrows furrowed. "Damon doesn't romance her."

"I don't think either one of them know what romance is." I smiled and grabbed my parka from behind the door.

"That's a shame." Wyatt took my hand, leading me down to the stairs. Once the door closed behind us, he turned and pressed a soft kiss on my lips. "How was your day?"

"Okay, but it's better now." I smiled. We strolled down the steps, then out into the chilly evening air. "How was yours?"

"Good. I racked my brain to come up with a good idea for tonight, then it hit me." He turned the corner of the building and headed toward his truck. "I think you'll like it."

"I have no doubt." I climbed into the passenger side and closed the door. Once Wyatt was in with the picnic basket between us, I got up the courage to admit something. "I'm nervous. I've never really been on a date before."

"Seriously?" He hesitated before starting the engine. "None of the guys on the islands asked you out?"

"I wasn't really any place long enough to date." I shrugged, nervous for a different reason. He'd told me about his ex-girlfriend, and I'd told him about my one fling. I hadn't dated that guy, though. We hung out, fell in a summer love or lust, and then went our separate ways. "When I was with that guy, it wasn't like being in a relationship ... It's hard to describe. We knew our time was limited. Mom and Dad rarely stay anywhere more than a month, so this was different, but we were still going to leave. We spent a lot of time together, but we never actually went on a date."

Wyatt bobbed his head, but there was a silence between us that felt too tense.

"That's the closest thing to a relationship I've had." I shrugged, embarrassed by my lack of life experience.

Wyatt's hand covered mine and squeezed. I glanced back toward him. He had reached over the picnic basket to get to me. His arm was at an odd angle. I raised our combined hands and set them on top of the basket.

"Sounds like it was harder than you let on," he said in his perfect timber that made my knees quake.

"It was at times, but it was all I knew. Honestly, I don't think I could have adjusted to being in an actual school after the first two years. Sometimes it's a struggle now." I stared at the window as I opened up this side of myself. "I get little panic attacks when I'm in a classroom for too long. They aren't bad, they just are."

"What helps them?" There wasn't any judgment in his tone, just concern and curiosity.

"Getting outside and breathing." I glanced at him with a grin. "Even if the cold air burns my lungs."

Wyatt chuckled and pulled into a parking lot. When I finally tore my eyes from him, I saw the sign in big blue letters: Ice Rink. That was it. My eyes widened and one of those panic attacks started. I breathed through it, and I reminded myself that this was why I was here. New experiences.

I raised my eyebrows at Wyatt, who just grinned.

"You know I can't skate," I said pointedly. "I've never even been on the ice."

He leaned across the basket. "Good thing you have me. I'm an excellent skater."

When we got inside, the place buzzed with excitement. I wasn't sure if it was mine or Wyatt's. I wasn't even sure if what I felt was excitement or fear. Maybe they were one and the same.

Then I saw the shortest hockey team ever. The kids wobbled on their blades, but most of them were steady as they skated down the ice in a scrimmage. Wyatt led us to the long wooden benches behind one of the teams. It was freezing, but I actually didn't mind it so much. The little kids were cute in their equipment.

Hugh Helmsly turned around and waved at Wyatt. Several of the parents also turned our way. It wasn't long before the kids started to notice him and begged him out onto the ice.

"Sorry," he said softly after he begged off. "I thought they'd be done by now."

"Don't be. Go out there. It will make them happy, and I can sit here contemplating how I'll die in these soon." I held up the rental hockey skates and shook them.

Wyatt grinned before kissing my cheek. The kids all teased him with aws and ews. I just laughed. It didn't take Wyatt long to lace up and get out there. He played mock referee and stopped them when he needed to correct something. Each of the kids looked at him with adulation.

A woman plopped down beside me and held out her hand. "Hi, I'm Bea Helmsly. That goalie is mine."

"Nice to meet you," I said, a little overwhelmed that this woman would just make herself known to me. It was blunt. I respected that, even if it was a little scary. I was nervous enough about skating. "I'm Elora."

"Wyatt's a great teacher. The kids all love him." Her gaze stayed on the action in front of us. "He's been through a lot."

"He has." I didn't know how much this woman knew, but she had a clue as to why Wyatt was on the edge. "He told me."

She raised her eyebrows. "My cousin was an idiot to do that to him."

It was my turn to be shocked. "Your cousin?"

"Yeah, Lucas was an idiot. Now he's stuck with that horror of a wife." She shook her head, but she didn't look at me. "He's the one who introduced Wyatt to Hugh. I'm just glad Wyatt doesn't hold any grudges against my husband for it. I wouldn't blame him if he did."

"Wyatt never mentioned ... He said he started helping with the team." The words wouldn't settle in my mind. I took a deep breath and exhaled slowly. "Wyatt never told me his name. I don't think he can say it."

"That's not a surprise." She turned to me and smiled genuinely. "Just do me a favor, don't do what Veronica did to him. If another guy turns your eye, be honest with him. You're young, beautiful. It's clear he's crazy about you. I'd just hate to see him get hurt."

"He's crazy about me?" It was hard to believe she thought that or noticed.

Bea laughed and drew the attention of the others around us. "It's so obvious." She held out her hand as Hugh blew the whistle, calling an end to the practice. "It was nice to meet you, Elora."

"You too," I said before she walked back to her group.

I watched Wyatt as he knelt down on one knee and talked to a smaller player. The kid took off his helmet, wiped his eyes, and nodded. Wyatt just kept talking until the boy smiled. Then he made the kid laugh. Wyatt grinned and pointed toward the bench. When he looked up into the stands, his gaze met mine.

There was no way another guy would turn my eye.

Chapter 18

Elora

I made my way down toward the ice through some of the families still lingering along with their kids. The boy Wyatt had cheered up sat on the bench with his skates on. His head hung low, and he swung his feet back and forth. I sat beside him. He glanced up, his wide brown eyes staring at me.

"Can I ask a favor?" I smiled and lifted the rentals. "I don't know how to do this, and you seemed so good on the ice. I don't even know how to put them on. Can you help me?"

"How come you're staking if you don't know how to put skates on?" His dark eyebrows slammed together to form a small V.

"We all have to learn sometime, right?"

"Yeah, I guess, but I thought everyone in Minnesota knew how to skate." He shrugged, then took one of the skates from my hand.

"I'm not from Minnesota. I grew up on a boat in the ocean." I leaned over to take off my shoes as he inhaled sharply.

"Like a real boat?"

I sat up and nodded, smiling at the shocked expression on his face. "Yep, a real boat. So you can understand why I don't know how."

His shock switched to a smile, and he handed me the skate. "Tie it tight or your ankles will hurt."

"I got that, buddy." Wyatt knelt in front of me and gently slid my foot into the boot. He glanced at the boy, whose eyebrows still hadn't returned to normal. "What?"

"Did you know she grew up on a boat and doesn't know how to skate?" the boy asked, still confused and awed by the entire concept.

"Yep, that's why I brought her. You want to help me teach her before you leave?"

I grinned at Wyatt, grateful and something more. Just that small act of kindness to this kid set my pulse racing.

The boy turned around to look at a woman, who chatted with Bea and Hugh. A larger boy sat near them with his phone in his hands. Wyatt lifted my other leg and put the second stake on me. I loved the feeling of his hands on my ankle. It was almost erotic. The thought choked me, and I refocused on the world around us.

"Mom? Can I skate with Wyatt and his girlfriend?" the boy asked.

The woman nodded, then went back to her conversation like the kid didn't even exist. I doubted that was how she really felt, but it bothered me. My parents would've at least had a brief conversation with me before agreeing. But not everyone was raised the way I was.

"Great," I said as I tried to stand. My legs almost gave out on me. The boy caught my arm, steadying my balance. "Thanks. What's your name?"

"Louis. What's yours?" After I told him, he wrinkled his nose. "That's a weird name."

"So I'm told." I turned to Wyatt, who couldn't stop laughing under his breath. It was so sexy to see him relaxed and enjoying himself. I wanted to pull his lips to mine. "What do I do now?"

"Skate." He held out his hand, unable to control that laugh still. I shook my head, and he tried to school his face into a mask of seriousness. He failed.

I took a deep breath and whispered to Louis. "Don't let me fall."

"We won't." Louis ducked under Wyatt's arm and skated a circled on the ice before coming back to me. "Come on, Elora. You can do it."

I wanted to laugh, but the sincerity on his face kept me from doing so. He really wanted to help, and I don't think anybody had ever asked him for advice or help before. Louis was going to do his best for me. It warmed my soul.

Wyatt shook his hand, raising his eyebrows. "He's right, Ellie. We won't let you fall. Too much."

I took a tiny baby step forward. My balance was normally excellent. Years of self-taught yoga on the yacht helped in that area. I took a larger step, more confident I wasn't going to fall.

Then I put my skate on the ice and it went out from under me. Wyatt hooked his arms under my elbow, keeping me mostly upright. Louis was there too, grabbing my hand. Fear laced through every ounce of me.

"Wow, you've really never done this before," Louis said as Wyatt righted me. My skates slipped until I could control them. "I thought you were half-joking."

"You okay?" Wyatt asked in my ear. His hot breath made me think of other things not ice related, and I melted against him. "Do you want to keep going?"

I nodded, unable to speak. The combination of the fear and the desire doing things to my head, and I didn't know which way to go. I needed to do this, though. Wyatt was giving me exactly what I came to Minnesota for—new experiences. This was not on the list to try, but why not?

Louis squeezed my hand. I smiled down at him. To be honest, in those brief moments, I'd forgotten he was there. I squeezed his hand back.

"Wanna race?" Wyatt's tone was flat, but I knew he had to be joking.

Responding to *that* wasn't a good idea. I needed to focus on not falling. "How do I do this?"

"Push off and glide," Louis said, then demonstrated. He stumbled a couple of times, but that didn't stop him.

"Louis struggles sometimes," Wyatt said beside me. "His mom's more focused on being seen rather than seeing him."

"That's so sad." I tightened my grip on Wyatt's arm. "He seems like a good kid."

Louis skated back to us, his cheeks red from effort and a little bit of joy. Skating clearly made him happy.

"He is. Don't get me wrong, his mom's nice enough, but Louis wants her to watch him, and she doesn't." Wyatt shook his arm, making me loosen my grip. "You try it. I'll hold onto you. Glide your left skate forward and push off with your right."

Nodding, and swallowing that giant lump that suddenly appeared, I let my left foot move forward. When I thought I was going to lose all sense of balance, I pushed off with my right like Wyatt instructed.

"Good. Now repeat," Wyatt said. Louis settled in on the other side of me. "You got this."

"Yeah, Elora, you can do it." Louis turned around, skating slowly backward. He stared down at my feet. I thought it was weird until I glanced at Wyatt who did the same.

We went to the other end of the rink, and I didn't even stutter a step. My short glides were smooth. Pushing off was simple. It was much easier than I thought.

"Okay, guys," I said when we stopped by the boards. "Let me go back without your help."

"Are you sure?" Wyatt wrapped his arm around my waist, pulling me close. "I don't want you to get hurt."

I kissed his nose quickly, eliciting a small ew from Louis. "I can do it. Just pick me up if I fall, okay?"

"Don't fall." He kissed my forehead and let go.

"Okay, Louis, stay close by," I ordered to my little instructor.

Then I pushed off, gliding slowly. I kept repeating it and my confidence soared. This was amazing. I loved the feel of the blade under my feet, slipping over the cold surface. I loved the breeze on my face, created solely by my own movement. It was a new kind of freedom.

Of course, some freedoms don't last long.

I pushed off too hard to gain speed and discovered how solid the ice was under my butt. The shock of impact shot up my spine, rattling my head. Wyatt was there in an instant with Louis not far behind.

"Ellie? You okay?" Wyatt's frantic voice set me off.

I fell all the way back, laughing hysterically. Ice chilled me to the bone, but for the first time since coming to Minnesota, I didn't care.

"I think she knocked herself silly," Louis said. He stared down at me like I was crazy.

"That's exactly what I did." I couldn't stop, but I held up my hands so they could help me to my feet. Once I was steady, I finally controlled myself. Well, except for the smile that wasn't going anywhere. "That was amazing."

"Falling was amazing?" Louis asked, but Wyatt just grinned at me.

"The falling was just a byproduct of the amazing." I glanced at Wyatt before turning my focus back to Louis. "We all have to take falls in life to get to the amazing." I turned back to Wyatt. "I see why you love it so much."

"Wait until tomorrow. You're going to be sore." His shoulders shook as he laughed. "You might change your tune."

"Louis, get over here," his mom called from the bench. "We have to go."

His chin fell to his chest. "Bye."

Louis slowly headed to the bench, and I decided to follow. The kid didn't need to be yanked down so fast. I heard Wyatt mutter behind me, but I didn't catch it. Louis stepped off the ice and into the bench area. I stopped along the boards.

"I'm sorry he bothered you," the woman said in a tone that bordered on sincerity and sarcasm.

"He didn't." I perked my voice up. "He was so great with helping me. I don't think I would've been able to skate alone without his encouragement."

"You fell," Louis said sourly.

I laughed and threw my hand out in the universal gesture of whatever. "Yeah, but I fall all the time. Like I told you, to get to the amazing, sometimes you have to fall. And sometimes the ones you love have to let you."

"The ones you love, huh?" Wyatt said in my ear. His hands settled on my hips.

I didn't respond because I didn't mean it that way. Much. Maybe I did, but I wasn't going to let him in on that.

"Thanks again for helping, Louis. I appreciate it," I said before turning to Wyatt. My cheeks burned, but I hoped that they were already red from the cold. His gaze heated, and I wanted to kiss him again, but this was not the time or place for what I had in mind. "Let's go again."

He took my hand, and we started gliding around the rink. I kept a slow pace so I wouldn't fall. Wyatt didn't say anything until he stopped us near the penalty box. He turned toward me and kissed me softly.

"I like *like* you," he teased.

A giggle escaped my lips, and I loved the high those four words gave me. "I like *like* you, too."

It couldn't have been a more perfect first ever date.

Chapter 19

Elora

"It was so romantic," I explained to Claire outside the student union the next morning. She sat beside me on the fountain with two oversized physics books on her lap. "I've never experienced anything like it before."

Lawrence walked by. When our gazes met, he ducked his head and scrambled away. I felt horrible. He made a mistake trying to kiss me, but he didn't need to be persecuted over it. I'd have to be the one to smooth things over, make it clear that I like him, but not like that.

Claire sighed loudly. Then her eyebrows wrinkled, and she stared at me like I had two heads. "But you didn't sleep with him?"

"No." I rolled my eyes. "He didn't even ask me back to his place. He was a complete gentleman." I shrugged, and if I was totally honest, I wasn't sure I was ready to sleep with Wyatt. My body wanted to, but my mind wanted to take it slow. "I like that he's taking things slow and not pressuring me into anything."

"All the good ones do," Claire said. She tapped my knee, then pointed in the opposite direction.

"Those guys look lost."

I followed her finger to see two very tan men with a campus map. One wore a bright orange Nevis t-shirt and shorts, while the other had his back turned to me. But I didn't need him to turn around.

Dropping my bag beside her and taking off at a sprint, I jumped and landed on Apollo's back. He screamed like a girl. He always did that. Carlos just started laughing.

"I can't believe you're here!" I jumped off his back and pulled him into a bear hug.

"I wanted to surprise you," he said, lifting off my feet. "You weren't kidding about how cold it is here. Jesus, we need sixteen layers of blankets."

"Heated blankets," Carlos added, hugging me once Apollo let go. He shivered, and I totally knew how that felt.

"Let's get inside." I grabbed both of their hands and dragged them over to Claire. "If you see Wyatt, will you tell him I'm taking these idiots inside?"

Claire raised her eyebrows and pointed at Carlos. "Cold?"

"Freezing," he said, rubbing his hands up and down his arms.

"Come on, goofball." I hurried inside and found my usual spot empty. After scooting the chairs a little closer to the fireplace, I went to the coffee cart and order three hot cocoas.

"Whipped cream today, Elora?" Tommy, the barista, asked. He smiled at me like he did with everyone. His blue-green eyes reminded me off the sea of the Virgin Islands. When I'd first met him, I thought he was sweet, funny, and kind, but most of all, cute in that nerdy way guys can be. His thick frames and not-stylish messy hair were endearing.

"Better make it a double." I pointed over my shoulder to where my brother huddled with

Carlos. They totally looked like tourists. "I think they need the comfort as much as the warmth."

"Just like when you got here." He glanced up at me through his thick lashes. "You know them?"

"Yeah, that's my brother and his boyfriend." I smiled at the mere mention of them. "They just surprised me."

"That's pretty cool." He steamed the milk in the stainless-steel jug. The sound echoed in my ears, but I loved it. To me, it signaled warmth and comfort. I was starting to like hot drinks. "So tell me something, how serious is it with the hockey player?"

"Um," I wasn't sure how to answer that. Actually, I wasn't sure why he'd even asked. It wasn't like Tommy and I had talked outside of the coffee cart. Yeah, he was cute, but that ship had sailed once I met Wyatt. "Like our relationship?"

He nodded and handed me one of the cups.

"We're a couple, if that's what you mean." My comfort level had dropped. Tommy was a nice guy, and he wasn't being a jerk. I was sure of it, but why did he care? I'd shown him a little interest in the beginning, and he had totally ignored me.

"Cool." He set a second cup on the counter. "I knew I should've asked you out months ago." Tommy shook his head and put the third cup on the counter. "Guess the chickenshit loses again."

"You wanted to ask me out?" I had a hard time believing that. "Why?"

"Seriously?" He laughed, throwing his head back a bit. "Not only are you gorgeous, but you might be the nicest person I've ever met. Wyatt's a lucky guy."

"Yeah, I am," a dead voice said behind me.

I spun around to see a thoroughly furious Wyatt glaring at Tommy. My eyes widened, and I didn't like the murderous look in his gaze. I turned back to Tommy. "Thanks, Tommy. I'll see you later."

"Sure. No problem. Take care, Elora." He stared hard at Wyatt for a beat before softening when he looked back at me. "Be careful."

I took the cups, balancing them precariously in my hands until Wyatt took one. Frustration shook through me. I wanted to address it, but I didn't want to deal with it either.

"You're mad," he said softly, taking a second cup from me.

"Yes." I stopped and stared at him. At least he had the guts to appear embarrassed. "Tommy's a nice guy. You didn't have to be so cold."

"He might be a nice guy, but he was coming on to you." Wyatt's shoulders fell. He closed his eyes and inhaled deeply. When he opened them, some of the rage had dissipated. "I didn't like it."

"He wasn't hitting on me," I said, far gentler than he deserved, but I got it. This wasn't about me or even about Tommy. This was about his ex and his trust issues. "He asked about us and said he wished he'd asked me out before I met you. Not once did he hit on me. We just had a conversation." I put my hand on his forearm, squeezing gently.

"There wasn't anything going on. Okay?"

"You're right. I'm sorry." He held up the two cups. "Why do you need three hot cocoas?"

I grinned and pointed to my crazy sibling. "Those two just showed up from Miami to surprise me. Come on."

Wyatt stared at Apollo and Carlos with a wary eye. When I set my cocoa down and gave one to each of them, I gripped Wyatt's arm and pulled him forward. "Apollo, Carlos, this is Wyatt." I bounced a little because I loved the fact I was introducing my brother to my boyfriend. And my brother's boyfriend to my boyfriend. "Wyatt, this is my
brother, Apollo, and my future brother-in-law, Carlos."

"Elora, we're not engaged," Carlos said as he stood. He glanced slyly at Apollo. In the last two years, Carlos and I had become close. I already considered him part of the family. Apollo, at twenty-one, wasn't ready to settle down that seriously yet.

"I know, but I wasn't sure if you wanted me to introduce you as my other brother." I turned to Wyatt, who was having a stare down with Apollo. "Stop it, you two. Play nice."

Apollo stood up and wiped his hand across his shorts before offering it to Wyatt. "Nice to meet you. Hurt my sister and you die."

"Yeah, we work on a cruise ship. We can easily sneak you on board and dump the body." Carlos's threat was way too cheerful considering what he said.

Wyatt raised his eyebrows, but I could tell the idle threat actually relaxed him. I was never going to understand men. "I'd deserve it if I hurt her."

I put my arm around his waist, hugging me against his warm body. Wyatt pressed a soft kiss to the top of my head.

"Sit down," Apollo said, pointing to the two seats across from us. "We need to know what clubs to hit tonight. Or any parties. I've never actually done that scene."

"Oh, a party would be great." Carlos finished his hot cocoa, so I handed over mine. "I haven't gone to a college party in years."

"You're the same age I am," Apollo said with a wrinkled brow. "When did you go to college parties?"

Carlos poo-pooed him. "When I was sixteen. They weren't carding anybody, even though they claimed to." He waggled his eyebrows. "Lost my gayginity at one. I also lost my virginity at another, but I didn't like it."

Wyatt choked on either a laugh or shock. I wasn't sure which.

"Too much information, Carlos," I said, not bothering to contain my own laughter. "I don't want to hear things like that about my brother."

Carlos glanced at Wyatt, then at me. He raised his eyebrows and sipped the second cup of cocoa.

"Wyatt has practice," I said to get Carlos's mind out of the gutter. "So does Damon, my roomie's boyfriend. He's on the hockey team, too. Mel probably knows of a party or club. If not, I'm sure Deidre will."

Apollo glanced at Wyatt, his eyebrows wrinkling. "Great. We've got an apartment for the week." He glanced at Wyatt again before pulling out his phone. "This is where we're staying."

"That's in my complex," Wyatt said when he saw the address. He half smiled at Apollo. "Two buildings over."

"You don't live in the dorms?" That underlying threat mixed with his words. Apollo's concern was sweet, but it was getting on my nerves. "Not in a dorm?"

"I lived in the dorms my freshman year." Wyatt didn't offer any further information, which drove my brother nuts.

"Stop it," I snapped at my brother. "He lives with Damon and T.J. My virtue is intact, even though you never had any to begin with."

Apollo glared at me. "According to most heterosexuals, I'm still a virgin, little sis."

Carlos choked on his cocoa. "Not this again."

"And I'm not, big brother." I crossed my arms and tried Mom's signature glare, but I failed. Apollo wasn't backing down.

"They do this a lot," Carlos added under his breath. "He's still mad about that guy in St. Marteen."

"Oh my God, I was old enough to make my own decisions. Why can't you get over that?" It was time for full pout mode. That usually shut him up. "You were sixteen. He was
twenty-two."

Wyatt choked this time, and Carlos raised an eyebrow as if to say, 'I warned you.'

"And you were sixteen, and how old was that guy?" I asked, knowing I'd thrown down the trump card. Apollo's lover was twenty-three. And he was furious when he found out how old my brother was. Apollo lied and said he was eighteen. He'd always looked older than his age, so the deception was easy. In Apollo's defense, he'd lied to get into a club. When the guy asked him, Apollo kept up the lie so he wouldn't get kicked out. It was stupid, childish, and he's regretted it ever since.

"Low blow, Elora." Apollo shook his head and glanced outside.

I reached across the table and took his hand. "You're right. That was low, but you have to remember I'm not sixteen anymore. I know what I'm doing."

Apollo glared at Wyatt, then back to me. "I hope so."

Chapter 20

Wyatt

I tapped Elora on the knee. "Ellie, I have to get to the rink. We have weight training today."

She tore her gaze away from her brother and nodded. "I have to get to class." She turned back to her brother. "I'll text you when I'm done, okay?"

"Yeah."

We all stood. Elora gave Carlos a warm hug and her brother a tense one. When I shook hands with each of them, Carlos' was a small squeeze, but Apollo tried to break my hand. Never one to back down, I did the same, and he winced visibly.

"Can I walk you to class?" I asked, not sure what ground I stood on with her at the moment. No doubt she saw the handshake issue. "Or are you mad at me?"

Elora didn't say anything as she slipped her hand in mine and led us away from her family.

I held the door open for her. We stepped outside into the cold October air. Elora still hadn't said anything until we were outside. She turned to me, glanced around, then pulled me around the side of the building.

"Why would I be mad at you?" she asked, concern etching unnecessary lines in her beautiful face.

"The thing with the coffee guy. Whatever I did to make your brother not like me." I ran a finger down her jawline. "Something I didn't realize I did. I don't know."

She melted against my light touch. "I'm disappointed about how you reacted to Tommy. You can trust me, Wyatt. Even if you don't trust other guys, you can always trust me. And Apollo decided not to like you before he even met you." She stepped closer, and I wrapped my arms around her waist while she snaked hers under my jacket. "Don't think I didn't notice the strongest man handshake, though, but I'm sure Apollo started it."

"He did." I kissed the top of her head, longing for time alone that we clearly weren't going to get. "He's just being protective. I can relate to that."

She sighed against my chest.

"And I'm sorry I overreacted about the coffee guy," I added, even though I wasn't really that sorry. He'd made a move on my girlfriend. Not cool. "I'm still working on it."

"I know." She leaned back and stared into my eyes. "You just have to trust me, okay?"

I nodded, totally mesmerized by her gaze and the loving expression I saw. Maybe it was in my imagination, but I didn't care in that moment. She chose me.

"Kiss me like you're going to miss me, Wyatt," she whispered.

I didn't hesitate. My lips found hers, and the heat was instant, all-consuming. I wasn't prepared to use the L word to describe how I felt about her. Not that it hadn't crossed my mind. It had a lot, more than I wanted to admit even to myself. It was definitely there, in my chest, waiting to burst free. I loved how she fit with me, against me, and how patient she was. And how her body felt pressed against mine. How she listened, really listened, and understood or at least worked to understand. I couldn't get enough of her kissing me like I mattered. We stayed like that for too long, but I really didn't care about anything but her.

My phone buzzed in my pocket, and I knew it was time to let go. I pulled back, kissing her forehead once before taking my phone out of my pocket. Great. I waved it at her before unlocking the text.

Get to my office. You have five minutes.

"Your coach?" Elora asked, as she stepped back and let one hand slide down my arm to link with mine.

"Yeah, guess he found out I stopped seeing the therapist." I shoved the phone back into my pocket. We started walking toward her class.

"You did? When?" Concerned laced her tone. "Why?"

I shrugged and squeezed her hand. "I agreed to go once, and I exceeded that. Since I met you, I haven't felt the need to go. I'm not angry all the time anymore."

"Oh" was all she said.

I didn't like that doubt in that one little syllable. "You think I should keep going?"

She lifted one shoulder, but I knew there was more. "I think it's a good thing to talk to someone, even about me." We stopped outside the entrance to Markings Hall where her next class was. "I actually saw the school's therapist when I first got here. I still do when I feel overwhelmed." Her face turned a pretty sunset pink. "I have an appointment this week because I have some things to sort out."

"What things?" The panic was there in my voice. Even as I tried to push it back down, it pressed through. "Things about us?"

She put her hand on my cheek and smiled. "Things about my major. About my feelings for you, and how they overwhelm me. I've never felt like this before, and I'm not sure if it's going too fast or not. Melody's not the best to talk to. She's all in or all out."

"I thought you were all in?" My chest tightened, and I was ready to fall to my knees in front of her, beg her not to leave me. Yeah, this was definitely the L word.

"I am, but I've never been in this position before. I just want to talk to someone who doesn't have an agenda. Someone who can help me sort out my fears and my hopes, so they don't collide." She sucked her upper lip into her mouth. "And I think I'm going to change my major. That scares me. I'm not sure what to do."

The panic seized every bit of my body. I didn't want to lose her over something a shrink said. That didn't seem possible or even probable, not that the full freak out mode cared. So I cut open my chest and bled it all out for her. "Ellie, I know this is fast, intense, and crazy, and I'm terrified I'm going to fuck it up. I feel like I'm drowning when you're not around. It's insane. I've only known you for a few weeks, but I can't help it. I don't want to pressure you into anything. Don't ... don't be afraid of this thing between us."

"Is this love?" she asked softly. Tears skirted around her eyes.

I could only nod. This wasn't how I wanted to tell her, but I fucking panicked like an asshole.

"Is that what this is?" She pressed a fist to her chest. "This feeling that I'm going to lose you when you're not with me? This feeling that I'm going to screw this up by saying the wrong thing? This feeling that I'm not good enough for this gorgeous guy who likes me for some insane reason? This feeling that the world is right when you're with me? That nobody could ever make my knees quake and my body burn with desire? Is that what this is?"

I nodded again, totally lost in her words, her emotions. My throat tightened as her tears slid down her cheek.

"I'm ... not ready to say... *it*." Her breath shook as she tried to control herself, but I didn't want her to hold back. "I care deeply about you. And I want to spend more time getting to know you. There's so much we still don't know about each other."

"I know how I feel, Ellie. That's not going to change." I took her fist and put it over my heart. As much as I hated what I was going to say, I told her what she needed to hear from me. It was the truth, but I didn't want to say it. Sometimes the truth isn't easy to say. "And I get it. Take your time. I'm in this for the long haul. If you have doubts, tell me now."

"Not doubts," she said, and the burden slid off my chest, but the pressure stayed. "Just questions. Can you understand that?"

"Yeah, I think I can." I brought her fist to my lips and kissed her fingers. "This is all a little overwhelming for me, too. I never expected to feel this way for someone else after what happened with *her*. And this thing between us is far more intense."

"I worry that we'll burn fast and then burn out, Wyatt." She opened her hand and entangled it with mine. "Kind of like this conversation."

That brought a smile to my lips. "That did escalate quickly, didn't it?"

"I'm sorry." She let go of my hand and wiped her tears from her cheeks. "I just ... I was surprised you stopped the sessions. And I wanted you to know it was okay to go."

I stared into her eyes and knew in that moment that I wasn't falling in love with her. I'd already done the falling part. This was love. Plain and simple. I bit my tongue to stop from telling her. It wasn't time. She wasn't ready. I respected that honesty, even if it hurt to hear. "Do you want me to go?"

"It's up to you, Wyatt." She smiled sadly. "I'm late for class."

"Okay, I'll text you after practice." I tucked a strand of her hair behind her ear. "If you're up to hanging out, let me know."

"Don't forget about Apollo and Carlos. They want to go to a club." She looked at me like she was hoping for permission and was ready to be defiant if I didn't agree. That was something I wasn't crazy about. She didn't need my approval to hang out with her own family. She didn't need my approval for anything.

"If you want me to catch up, let me know. I'll still text you." I kissed her forehead again. PDA wasn't really my thing, but I couldn't help myself around her. All I could do was contain it. "If you want to hang with your brother and Carlos without me, I totally understand."

"Sorry, it's just ... I wish we could sit down and finish the conversation." She glanced over her shoulder. "I feel like there's so much more to say."

"We'll get there." I hoped. No, I wasn't allowing myself to doubt her or this relationship. I'd done too much of that with Veronica, before, during, and after that disaster. Damn, I wanted her to know where I stood. "Ellie, I... I'm going to get my ass chewed and you need to get to class."

She nodded and hurried inside. Once the double glass doors closed behind her, she turned to give me a small wave.

My heart clenched in my chest, and I waited until she disappeared from my view. It was hard letting her go.

But something deep down told me I'd be letting her go again. I hated the idea of it more than I hated Lucas. Red flared in my vision, and I hurried across campus to work out the sudden rush of anger inside me.

That was what I needed, some intense exercise and to remind myself over and over that Ellie wasn't Veronica, and Lucas wasn't going to take her from me.

Chapter 21

Elora

"What's the deal with the hottie?" Carlos asked as soon as Apollo went to the bar for drinks. I took them to Zinger's, the local bar and grill, favored by some of the graduate students. Clubbing would come later. Maybe. I wasn't sure if I was up to it. "He seems pretty serious about you."

I couldn't stop the smile from taking over my face. "I think it's getting that way. It's all so new to me, you know?"

"Girl, I understand." Carlos glanced at the bar where Apollo smiled at the bartender, and I couldn't blame him. The bartender's broad shoulders and muscular arms were attractive. "Sometimes, I feel like he's waiting for something better." Carlos sighed, then shook his head to eradicate such thoughts. "Being with someone isn't easy. Especially men with strong personalities."

"You think Wyatt has a strong personality?" I wasn't even sure what that meant.

"Most definitely." Carlos set his water glass down and put his arms on the table. The conversation had been too serious, but Carlos wanted to get his point across. I valued his opinion on so many things. Over the last two years, I'd confided in him more than my brother. "Wyatt is the type of guy who will demand everything from you, and he'll give you everything back. But if there's a time when you're unsure, he's going to get frustrated. He's not the type of guy to put up with any bullshit or excuses."

"Is that a bad thing?" I asked, thoroughly confused about what Carlos meant. "He's sweet and gentle. Not overpowering." I cocked my head at him. "Don't I have a strong personality?"

"Exactly." Carlos leaned back with a grin. "That's my point. Two strong personalities tend to clash more. Just in my experience."

Apollo handed Carlos a pink mixed drink and sat down with a tall beer. "What did I miss?"

"I was just telling Elora my opinions on her boyfriend." Carlos stirred his pink drink with the tiny straw.

"That he's a dick." Apollo stared at me, a challenge in his eyes. "Guys that don't talk much are."

"You don't talk much to people you don't know," I pointed out.

Apollo opened his mouth, but our server finally arrived. "I am so sorry for your wait." He glanced appraisingly at Carlos, but his gaze snapped away once Apollo put a protective hand over his boyfriend's. "I see you have drinks already. Do you know what you'd like, or do you need more time?"

Carlos glanced at me, then back at the waiter. I knew that look. He was going to stir it up with Apollo. "What do you recommend, honey?"

As planned, Apollo's hand tightened over Carlos's. I just rolled by eyes and waited the little show out. Each time the waiter said anything, Carlos flirted back and Apollo got angrier. It wasn't nice, but I knew why Carlos did it. He'd sat back and watched my brother flirt with the bartender.

I thought back over my psychology courses, and I realized Carlos was right. Wyatt displayed all the signs of a strong personality. It wasn't a bad thing, but understanding it helped me understand him more. The only thing was Wyatt's confidence, his trust, his positivity had been wrecked by Veronica. He even had a hard time saying her name, and never did he mention Lucas. I only knew his name from my brief conversation with Bea.

"Why do you have to flirt with every waiter we meet?" Apollo snapped at Carlos.

He just raised an eyebrow and sipped his cocktail. "Why do you have to flirt with every bartender? And don't deny it, I saw your little side lean with a head nod. It shows off your pecs."

"Don't fight," I interjected. If I hadn't, it would go on all night, and I was fairly certain that was the point. "Just tell me why you don't like Wyatt."

Apollo tore his heated gaze from Carlos. "He's going to get possessive. Or he already is."

"He has his moments, but it's nothing I can't handle." *And it's for good reason.* I waved off his comment. "He needs to learn how to trust again. I just have to be patient and understanding."

"What about his patience with you?" Apollo smirked like he threw down a trump card to win the game. "Doesn't that matter?"

I stared down at my hands and thought about our earlier conversation. Wyatt *had* been patient then when I was honest about not being ready for certain things. He hadn't pushed me into anything. He hadn't even tried to touch me other than kisses. And I loved those. "I do matter to him. You're judging him after one meeting. Give it a chance. You'll see you're wrong."

Apollo snorted and rolled his eyes. "Or you'll see I'm right. Where's he at now? With his friends? Drinking?"

I hadn't seen Wyatt drink anything other than water, and Apollo's insinuation irritated me. "No, he had practice. And he had weight training before that."

Carlos must have kicked Apollo because the table jumped, and my brother grimaced.

"How long are you here for?" I asked, desperate to change the subject.

"Until Sunday." Carlos smiled, clearly glad to have something else to talk about. "We're going to hit the art scene in St. Paul tomorrow. Can you skip out and come with us?"

I probably could, but the thought of doing it made me nervous. "Not really. I have a big paper due in my adolescent psychology class. And another one due in my philosophy class."

"Why are you taking philosophy?" Apollo asked, his demeanor switched to calm and carefree now that we weren't talking about Wyatt. "I thought you had all your core classes done."

"I couldn't get into one psych class, and it was available." I shrugged, but it was kind of a blessing in disguise. "Do you think I'm crazy to change my major now?"

"Honey, you're nineteen." Carlos pointed his tiny straw at me. "You don't have to decide your life right this minute. Change your major. It's not like you or Apollo are ever going to want for cash. You could get your degree in both if you want."

Apollo cut a sharp glance at Carlos. "Even though I hate how flippant he is, Carlos is right."

The waiter arrived and wisely kept his gaze down. The topic changed again, and I listened to them regal me with tales and horrors of working on a cruise ship. Carlos loved every minute of crew life. Apollo was quiet, letting his boyfriend take center stage. They were so different, yet so alike.

My thoughts drifted to Wyatt. We both agreed we're all in, but what happened after graduation. Yeah, that was a long way off. Just under two years, maybe more, if I did change my major.

I shook that out of my head. Thinking that far into the future was futile. We never knew what it would bring and guessing seemed useless. He was falling for me, and I was pretty sure I was already in love with him. I just didn't know what that would mean in a month or two, or even six.

But I saw myself with him.

Just not in Minnesota.

Wyatt

Practice had been rough. That was an understatement. Coach rode my ass after I showed up three minutes late to his office. He just wanted to scream about the stupid therapy. I didn't hold back. He'd been on my case all year. And I was done.

"Damn it, Wyatt," he barked. The veins in his neck popped. "You agreed—"

"I agreed to *one* session." I held up my finger for emphasis. "And I did four."

"You need to go back. You don't have this under control." He glared at me; his hands planted on his desk. His thick upper body threatened to launch over the desk. "Get back there."

"No."

"What do you mean no?" His voice radiated a calm he didn't feel.

"I'm not going." I glared back at him; my hands clenched into fists behind my back. "I'm good. Got a new girl. I'm fucking happy. Why do I need to see a therapist?"

"Because you're still angry." He pointed to the chair, a silent order to sit down. With a real calm, he decided it was story time. "This doesn't leave this room."

I sat down and waited for the sob story. Wasn't that how this shit normally worked?

"I've seen this before," he said solemnly. "My college roommate lost all control after a tragedy in his family. He thought he was fine. It kept building inside him until a month later, he just exploded during a game. Player from the other team hip checked me into the boards. It was a clean hit, but I landed wrong and wasn't quick to get up. My buddy beat the living shit out of that guy. Sent him to the hospital."

I raised my eyebrows. Fights happened more in his day than mine, but they still happened.

"He punched a ref. Got ejected." Coach closed his eyes and swallowed hard. "He left the arena before everyone else. When I got back to our apartment..." His voice choked, but he opened his eyes and stared into mine. "He was hanging from his ceiling fan."

"What?" I heard him; I just had a hard time understanding.

"He lost control. His rage was a byproduct of his grief." Coach leaned forward, resting his elbows on the desk. "I'm not saying you're heading that way, Wyatt. My buddy had a lot of other problems in his life. It all exploded in that one moment on the ice. I just don't want to see you lose it like that. Or even a fraction of that."

I stared at him for a minute before I said anything else. "I'm not going to."

"Yeah, that's what he said." Coach slid over a piece of paper with dates on it. "Just go back until the end of the year. Appointments have already been made."

Bile filled my throat. "Or you'll bench me."

"No, not this time." He leaned back and crossed his arms over his chest. "I'm not doing this for the team this time. This is all for you. You're a good kid, Wyatt. That shit that Lucas did to you, that Veronica did, it's eating you up even if you can't see it. I don't want to see you make a mistake that will ruin your life."

I took the paper. It wasn't necessary to go. I was fine. Those names rang in my head, though, and I felt the rage inside me fighting to grow. It wasn't going to win. I wouldn't let it.

"Get dressed out." Coach pointed to the door, dismissing me. "We've got a lot of work to do and game tape to review. Copies are in your locker."

I nodded and stood, setting the paper down on his desk and walking out without it.

When we got back to the apartment, Melody was on the couch, crying. Shit. That was never good. Damon dropped his bag inside the door, and I had to step over it. T.J. kicked it out of the way behind me. I went straight to my room to avoid whatever was going on. No way I was getting sucked into any argument. By the time I showered, I had expected them to be in Damon's room, but they hadn't moved. He shushed her as she cried and repeatedly asked what was wrong.

I didn't need this drama shit. My phone buzzed in my pocket, and I unlocked it as I slipped out the front door. It was from Coach.

The appointment times.

That man wasn't going to give up.

Chapter 22

Elora

Wyatt texted me as Apollo and Carlos dropped me off at the dorm. I was exhausted. So was he, because he apologized.

Wyatt: *Just got in. Sorry. Hard practice.*
Me: *Understand. Breakfast?*
Wyatt: *You still with your brother?*
Me: *No. I'm in my room. Mel's not here.*
Wyatt: *She's here. Mind if I come over?*
Me: *No. I'll meet you downstairs.*

Our room wasn't messy per se, but I still did a hurried clean to get Mel's clothes out of sight. Wyatt's jersey hung over my headboard. I liked waking up and seeing it there. After a few minutes, I went downstairs just in time to watch him walking up the sidewalk. He looked dejected. His head stayed down, even as he got closer to the doors. With each heavy step, his wavy dark blonde hair flicked over his forehead.

I smiled despite my concern. I smiled because I knew in my heart that this was it. This feeling wasn't a maybe or a guess. All I wanted to do was to comfort him, take care of him. Love him.

"Hey," he said when I pushed open the door to let him in.

I lifted on my toes and pulled his mouth to mine. Wyatt kissed me back gently, slowly, as if he savored every minute. I was, and I didn't want to stop. His fingers dug into my waist. I needed more from him, more of his touch. We stood like that, just fused together until someone shouted, "Get a room!"

Wyatt pulled back, a small sigh escaping his mouth. "Sorry. I don't usually make out in public like that."

I smiled and took his hand, leading him into the dorm. We took the stairs to my floor. Thankfully, the hallway was empty even though it was clear some people were awake based on the music and *other* noises. Meghan's room, two doors down from mine, had loud music to cover up the other noises, not that it helped.

Wyatt chuckled under his breath. I let go of his hand to open the door. My hands shook for no reason. Well, of course, there was a very good reason, but I wasn't focusing on that. I just wanted to be alone with my boyfriend. As I fumbled, Wyatt's hands slid around my waist, tugging me back against his thick muscles. God, I felt so safe in his arms, so protected, so loved.

There was that L word again.

I finally got the door unlocked. Wyatt lifted me up, and I started laughing. This was not the time to laugh. Wyatt's laugh breathed in my ear. My thighs clenched tight, and I wanted him to keep doing that.

"I'm sorry," I said once he sat me down inside the room. Turning to face him, I saw that I wasn't sorry at all. Wyatt had a huge grin on his face. "What?"

"You're adorable." He reached for me, pulling me back against him.

"Me?" I pressed my hands against the hard muscles hiding under his shirt. "I'm clumsy, shy, naïve. And don't say I'm not naïve, because I know I am."

"You're beautiful, kind, open to anything. Nothing in this world matters more to me than seeing you smile." He tightened his arms around me and kissed me like he owned me.

My entire body quaked, and as much as I loved it, there were still things we needed to discuss. I pulled back and stared into his eyes.

Wyatt's eyebrows furrowed into a deep V. "Talk to me."

"You're right. My brother hates you." I bit my lip, hoping the next blow would soften it. "Carlos doesn't. He just thinks you have a strong personality."

"Strong personality?" His hands drifted up and down my lower back under my coat. He tugged at it. "Take this off. Unless you want me to leave already."

I stepped back, shrugging out of my coat. Wyatt did the same. He handed his to me and I tossed them on Mel's bed. I took his hand, leading him to the small loveseat in the corner of the room.

"I'm surprised you have a couch," Wyatt said as he settled into it. "These rooms aren't that big."

"Totally worth it, though." I sat stiff beside him. Wyatt reached for me, pulling me back into the crook of his arm. "I'm sorry."

"You can't make Apollo like me," he said, his fingers making small circles on my shoulder. "I like this shirt, by the way."

I glanced down at the thin white Key West t-shirt. "Why? This thing is so old. It's comfy, though. I normally sleep in it."

A small cough left his lips. "I won't be able to get that thought out of my mind."

I looked up at him. Wyatt reached for my knees, tugging them over his lap. "Talk to me, Ellie. What else is going on?"

His thumb made circles on the outside of my knee, and it was distracting. But I needed to power through this. "A lot." I didn't know what to do with my hands. They twisted around each other until Wyatt covered them. "Sorry. I just... What we were talking about earlier."

"That I'm falling in love with you?" he asked as he kept caressing my knee. His hand snaked in between mine, breaking their ongoing battle.

"Um, yeah." I squeezed his fingers. "I have... feelings. Like I said, and I'm not ready to define them."

He smiled, but he didn't say anything.

"I have concerns, too." There was the bandage, and I just ripped it off. Saying concerns was almost a knife wound to relationships. It was one step away from doubts. "We don't know each other very well. I know you have an older sister named Jane and two younger brothers, Virgil and Warren. I know you love hockey, and you play center but can sometimes switch to forward. I know you're from North Dakota and you're a junior."

"All true." His hand slid up my thigh. "And I'm impressed by that little hockey knowledge."

"I don't know your goals, your dreams. I have no idea if you want to be a pro hockey player or if this is just something you enjoy for now." Wyatt put his finger over my mouth. "What?" I asked through it.

"Ellie, that's part of being with someone, learning all those things." His finger traced my mouth, then he dropped his hand back into my lap. "But, in order, here are your answers. I'm a business major. After I graduate, I'll go home and help my dad with his hardware store chain, eventually taking it over. I'd love to be a pro player, but the chances are slim. I'm not in a D1 school, and I'm not big enough."

"You're pretty big." I glanced down at his large form taking up most of the loveseat.

"I'll take that as a compliment." His hand slipped up my thigh higher and I wanted nothing more than to feel his skin on mine, but that had to wait.

"And I haven't been scouted. That's a big part of going pro."

"What about your dreams? Goals?" I asked, trying to not lose my concentration. His finger heated my skin, even through the thick fleece leggings I wore.

"I've always wanted to travel. More than just going from rink to rink. I'd like to see other parts of the world." He shrugged and his demeanor changed to something more melancholy. "It may happen. It may not. I'm here on a scholarship. My parents aren't poor, but they aren't millionaires either. Plus, they have my little brothers to think about. Once I finish school, I have to start working and earning my own way."

"I know I'm lucky," I said, guilt welling in my chest. Most people would never have the opportunities I have already had. And, thanks to pure luck of birth, my parents had enough money and set both me and Apollo up with hefty trust funds. "I didn't even have to go to college, but I wanted to."

Wyatt tipped my chin up. "It's not your fault."

"I know, but I always feel bad. Like why should I be the one who is lucky? Why not Melody? Or Deidre? Or even Lawrence?" Wyatt cringed when I said that last name, and I regretted it. He was the last person I should've brought up. "I'm just saying, there are other people out there who are good people and deserve a lucky break."

"Maybe you were a saint in your past life?" Wyatt grinned and leaned in, kissing me until I thought I would pass out. He pulled away with a sigh. "What are your dreams, Ellie? What do you want out of life?"

In that moment, the only thing I wanted was Wyatt's lips on mine, but I knew that wasn't what he meant. "I want ... a house. Eventually. I want to have my feet on solid ground, but I want to travel. I want to experience the world before I put down roots." I took his hand and pressed it against my heart. "You know how I love reading biographies and memoirs?"

"You can't get enough of those." He spread his fingers across my heart.

"That's why I decided to major in psychology. I wondered why people did what they did in life." I shook my head, laughing quietly at myself. "I'm taking a philosophy class. Now I know that's actually what I'm interested in. The philosophy of everything. I'm always asking why and trying to learn more about it."

"Makes sense." He stared down at where our hands met on my chest.

"You don't think it's crazy to be a philosophy major?"

"I think it's crazy if you don't follow your heart." He tugged me onto his lap.

"What's your heart saying right now?" I asked softly.

"This." He pressed his lips gently against mine. "And this." He trailed tiny kisses along my jaw. "Some of this, too." I shuddered as he made his way down my neck. Then he stopped. "I don't want to stop, Ellie, but I know you're not ready for everything I want to do with you."

"Go slow," I said gently.

Wyatt's gaze burned into me. And he went oh so slow.

Chapter 23

Wyatt

I woke up pressed against the warmest, most perfect person I'd ever met. My arms cocooned her to me as she snuggled into my bare chest. I slept in my jeans. When Ellie asked me to go no further, I listened. But I didn't stop kissing her, caressing her. And she responded. Her chest was bare against mine, and I fucking loved the feel of her skin.

We'd probably only been asleep for a couple of hours. My alarm on my watch vibrated. That was the only reason my eyes cracked open. And, honestly, I was glad. Watching Ellie sleep set my body on fire. I wanted to wake her up, finish what we started the night before. But I also just wanted to look at her. She was so peaceful.

A contended sigh escaped her lips. Her breath tickled the hairs on my chest. I couldn't stop the smile. Then her eyes fluttered open, and she smiled back.

"What?" she asked through a yawn.

"You're adorable." I kissed her forehead. "I like waking up like this."

She responded by kissing my chest right over my thundering heart. "Me too, but this bed is too small."

"Mine's bigger."

Ellie giggled and stared up at me through her thick dark lashes. "Is it softer?"

"Why don't you come over tonight and find out?" I didn't care if she had morning breath or not. Leaning down, I kissed her with unbridled passion. Cheesy term but it was totally applicable.

The door opened, and a disgruntled voice interrupted us. "Unbelievable." Something loud fell onto the floor, like a backpack full of books. "Elora?"

Ellie giggled, then lifted her hand to wave. I kissed along her neck. Her body quaked beneath me.

"I can't believe him," Melody sniffled. I heard the springs compress on her bed. "What is the problem with men? This isn't something to joke about." She paused for another sniffle. "Whose jacket is this?"

"Um, Mel," Elora said, still grinning at me but I could see the concern in her eyes.

"I tell him there's a chance..." Melody trailed off when I lifted my head and met her gaze. "Oh, shit."

"Hey, Mel. You okay?" I asked as Ellie peeked over the comforter.

She glared at Elora. "Why wasn't there a white towel on the door? You know there's supposed to be a white towel!"

Before either one of us could respond, Melody grabbed her backpack and ran out the door, slamming it behind her.

"White towel?" Elora glanced up at me, clearly puzzled. "I thought that was a movie myth."

"Not a myth." I stared at her lips. My hand slid up her sides, caressing her skin. I loved how soft she was. "I know you have to go after her, but I really don't want to move."

"I could stay in bed all day," Elora agreed, rolling onto her back. I pulled the comforter down. Her perky breasts made my mouth water. I filled one hand, and Ellie moaned at my touch. "I need to make sure she's okay."

"I know." I kissed my way down her chest, showing her how much I enjoyed touching her everywhere. "Give me a minute."

Her hands snaked into my hair. With each press of my lips against her flesh, she breathed harder, faster. I kept going until I was at her waistband. When I started to move back toward her chest, she pushed my head down and lifted her hips.

"You sure?" I asked.

"Yes."

I waited a minute, giving her a chance to say no. When she nodded again, I reached for her waistband and pulled her leggings down. Ellie spread herself for me, and I gave her everything. There wasn't an inch of skin on her body I didn't kiss or suckle. She responded to my every move, crying out into her fist.

After making sure she was fully satisfied, I laid beside her. My rock-hard dick wanted more, but I still needed to give her an out. Ellie cured that need when she rolled on top of me. Her mouth devoured mine, demanded me to open for her. I gave her everything of me. Pausing only long enough to put on a condom, I showed her how much I loved her.

Neither one of us made it to class.

Elora

I felt horrible. Well not horrible, really. Not after making love with Wyatt. That's what it was too. When I lost my virginity in St. Marteen, and every time after that, it was sex. This wasn't just sex. I wanted to share myself with him. I wanted to experience everything with him. I gave myself to him, and he gave himself to me. It was sweet, sensual, and beautiful.

And I loved every minute of it.

The only regret I had was waiting until the morning. But once I woke up with him, I knew. I just knew. There was more to it than the physical act. There was an emotional connection I'd never experienced before. And I wanted more of it all.

Neither one of us wanted to leave my room, but we had to eat. It was close enough to lunch, so we got dressed and walked to the student union. Wyatt held my hand as we walked slower than necessary. When my stomach growled, he just smiled.

"What?" I asked, playfully poking his arm.

"Worked up an appetite, didn't you?" He tugged my hand, and I fell against him. Then he put his arm over my shoulder and tucked me to his chest.

"Goof." I nuzzled into him. "One of the many reasons I love you."

Wyatt stopped cold. I had kept walking, so I ended up spinning into his chest. He stared at me like he'd never seen me before. His gaze turned white hot, and he kissed me like we were back in my bedroom. I lifted onto my toes as he pulled me tighter against his chest.

"Wow," I said as I tried to catch my breath. "What did I do to deserve that?"

His face fell, and he looked like I'd just kicked his puppy. "You didn't mean it?"

"Mean it?" I fell back on my heels. "You mean..." It dawned on me then. I'd said the L word. I'd meant it too, but I hadn't meant to say it out loud. Not yet. The universe clearly had other ideas for me. "That I love you? Of course, I meant it. I just... I wanted to tell you in a romantic way, not just blurting it all out there."

Wyatt smiled slowly. "You blurting it out there is one of the many reasons I love you."

I was totally taken off guard by how happy that made me feel. My family was always telling each other that we love one another. Every night, even after I turned eighteen, my mom would kiss my cheek and say, "I love you," and my dad would do the same. But to hear it from Wyatt, that was entirely new. And I wanted to hear it again.

"Say it again," I whispered, just in awe that this man could feel that way about me.

"I love you, Ellie," he whispered back. "I am head over heels in love with you."

I grabbed his shoulders and leapt into his arms for another R-rated kiss that drew some whistles and "get a room" shouts, but I didn't care. I pulled back long enough to see it in his eyes. He loved me.

"Wow," he said with his hands firmly on my backside, holding me up. "What did I do to deserve that?"

"You being you is enough."

Chapter 24

Elora

Wyatt took off for his afternoon class, but I stayed with a very irritated Melody. Throughout lunch, she mumbled under her breath and glared at Wyatt. He didn't say much, but he never really did. Wyatt observed, listened, and he spoke when he felt it was necessary.

"Okay, stop mumbling and tell me what's going on," I said, putting my fork down.

Melody did the same, then the tears slid down her cheeks.

Oh, no. I switched seats to sit beside her and pulled her into a hug. "It'll be okay. Whatever it is, it'll be fine."

Melody shook her head, but her tears increased, followed by a sob. We sat there for ten minutes, and I missed the start of my afternoon class. Melody finally pushed off me and wiped her tears with a used napkin.

"Sorry," she said. "Shit. I missed class. *You* missed class. You never miss class."

I shrugged like it wasn't a big deal, but I couldn't lie to myself. There was some serious anxiety about it. This morning had been totally worth it.

And making sure Mel was okay was totally worth it, too. "What's going on? Wyatt said you were at his place last night, and you were upset."

Melody took a long inhale, held it a beat, then let it out. "I think I'm pregnant."

All other thoughts and concerns shot out of my head. This was huge. "You're not sure?"

"I'm late." She shook her head, sniffling into her napkin. "I took two tests yesterday. One positive. One negative." She lifted her head. "I didn't know what to do, but I knew I had to tell Damon."

I took the nasty napkin out of her fingers and set it on the table. Then I held her hand. "What happened? I mean, I *know* what happened, but what did he say?"

"He fucking proposed." She laughed, but she didn't find it funny. Neither did I. "How old school is that? I'm not even sure. I shouldn't have told him anything. I should've just waited."

"Waited for what?" I asked gently.

"I'm going to the clinic today." She dropped her head into her hands. "What am I going to do, Elora? I'm too young for a baby."

I rubbed her back like Mom did for me whenever I was upset. "You'll do what you think is right." She snorted, but I continued. "One step at a time, Mel. First, we go to the clinic and find out for sure. Then we'll worry about step two if we need one."

"We?" she asked, a tiny bit of hope in her voice.

"I'm not going to let you go through this alone." I smiled sadly. "I may not have known you that long, but you're the sister I never had, remember?"

Melody hugged me, tears starting again. "Thank you."

"What time do we need to go to the clinic?" I asked when she let go.

"My appointment is in thirty minutes. Thank God they had a cancellation, or I wouldn't have gotten in for another three weeks." She sat back and stared at me. "We were safe. I'm on the pill, and he used a condom. I don't understand how this happened."

I immediately thought about this morning. Wyatt and I had been safe, too. Before I flew to Minnesota, Mom and I went to the OBGYN. I never wanted to take the pill or anything chemical, but Mom insisted. We decided on an IUD, which was ninety-nine percent effective, but there's always that five percent.

"Oh, God." Melody's eyes shot open wide. "Jesus, I just realized. You and Wyatt..."

I smiled, because how could I not? It had been beautiful. "Don't worry about me. Let's focus on you."

"But you and Wyatt... He was in your bed this morning." She smiled a real smile. "Well? How did it all happen?"

"We are not having this conversation in the midst of your crisis." I rolled my eyes, but I couldn't help the little giggle that escaped.

"Oh, this is totally the distraction I need." Her expression dropped for a moment, but she pulled herself back together.

I took a deep breath before I launched into the events. Well, most of them. "He came over last night after practice. We talked, made out, and only went so far. But this morning... Waking up with his arms around me..." I sighed and smiled. "I knew."

"That's so much more romantic than how Damon and I ..." Her expression darkened. "Anyway, I'm happy for you. Wyatt's one of the good ones."

"Yeah, he's great." I mentally swooned as I thought about our bodies intertwined. Shaking myself out of it, I glanced at my watch. "We should go. Find out for sure."

Melody nodded, all the tiny joy she'd tried to show for me. I wanted to hug her again. Melody shot away from me. I wondered if she was preparing herself for the worst or praying for the best. Either way, I wasn't going to let her go through it alone.

Wyatt

I smelled the Ridder U Athletic Department tee. It was nasty. As much as I hated doing laundry, it was well past time. I grabbed a different shirt. When I did the smell check, Elora's scent was all over it. I glanced down at the t-shirt I had on last night. The memories were still at the front of my mind. I'd had a hard time concentrating on anything after I left her for class. Her soft skin, her hot mouth, her fingers drifting over my body. Damn.

"Hey." Damon tapped my arm. "You talk to Elora today?"

I turned to tell him I had, when I froze. Damon looked worse than when someone had beat his ass on the ice. His eyes were swollen and red, plus the dark shadows underneath and lines around his mouth. Dude looked like he hadn't slept either. "What's up?"

"She tell you?" he asked, his lips twisted into a knot. "About the baby?"

My knees buckled out from me, and I sat hard on the bench. Not again. This wasn't happening again. I clenched my fist to my chest, trying to get it to slow down. Damon was still talking, but I heard none of it. My ears clogged. Why hadn't she told me? Jesus, whose was it? We'd only just had sex this morning, so there was no way.

"Wyatt," Damon snapped. I looked up at him. "Are you listening, man? I asked you a question. Did Elora tell you Mel's pregnant?"

The relief that washed over me was almost better than a good orgasm. Almost. I couldn't talk so I shook my head. Damon sat beside me and leaned forward, resting his elbows on his knees. It was selfish to be relieved. Damon loved Mel. Of that, I had no doubt. Mel's the one I doubted. She was flighty at times, and she definitely was aloof at others. She flirted with a lot of guys. Damon didn't seem to mind that, but it was a red flag in my book.

"That's why she was over last night. To tell me." Damon clenched his fists. I knew that feeling of anger oh so well. "She said one test was yes, and one was no."

"Wait a minute. You're telling me she's pregnant, but there was a negative test?"

Damon nodded, his gaze still on the tiled floor. "She's pretty sure."

I clasped his shoulder and squeezed.

"She said no."

"To what?" I asked. This wasn't easy on him. Damon came from a huge family of ten kids. It only got bigger as his older siblings started having babies of their own. Being the seventh, he lived in hand-me-downs and donated hockey gear. He wasn't the first to go to college, but he was the first to go on mostly scholarships and full-time status.

"I asked her to marry me." He finally looked at me. His expression showed exactly what he was feeling. She'd destroyed him when she said no.

"She seeing a doctor?" I had to change the subject. He was beating himself up for the rejection, but I got it. Even if Damon was sure marriage was the right thing, Mel wasn't. She also wasn't the type to buck to any old school traditions. Damon was raised with them.

"Yeah, she's calling one today." He pushed himself up, and I stood beside him. "She hasn't called to tell me when."

"She probably needs time." I tugged at the collar of my shirt. A wave of Elora's coconut and sea water scent wafted to my nose. It was hard not to smile.

"Hey, get your asses out here, now," Coach yelled from the door.

Damon didn't say anything else as he hurried out to weight room. It was a light workout day.

We'd end up on the ice for a couple of hours, but the weight room was short day. I looked forward to getting on the ice. The sooner I was done with my workout, the sooner I was back with Ellie.

I worried for Damon and Mel. And I wondered, and it was fleeting, but it was there, what Elora would do if we were in this situation. It was way too soon to think about that, but we definitely needed to talk about making sure we didn't put ourselves in that position.

Coach yelled at someone, and I hurried out into the weight room before I was the next victim. Then I lost all thoughts of babies, marriage, and Damon. I lifted my sets, thinking of nothing but Ellie's soft lips and warm body.

Best workout I had in a long time.

Chapter 25

Elora

Apollo texted me, then freaked out when I told him I was at the clinic and called. Thankfully, Carlos took the phone so I could actually talk. The rapid-fire fifty questions my brother threw at me were impossible to answer. I kept Melody's secret, though. It wasn't my place to tell her story.

"Dinner?" Apollo had snatched the phone back from Carlos.

"Sure. How much longer are you going to be here?" We hadn't even talked about that. I was so excited to see my brother that I didn't think about him going back to Miami.

"We're driving to Milwaukee tomorrow for a couple of nights, then we'll be back for the weekend."

"And parties," Carlos shouted in the background.

I giggled at him. "He's nuts. The hockey team has a game here Friday night. You can see Wyatt play." I loved the idea of showing off my boyfriend, plus I wanted them to like each other. "Then we can go to the after party."

"Perfect." Apollo yawned loudly. "We're going to nap."

"Okay, old man." I laughed again and got a few odd looks from the other people in the waiting room. "I'll see you tonight."

Just as I hung up, Melody stepped out from the back. Her smile was infectious, and I grinned back at her. I stood and waited for her to say something, but she only linked her arm through mine and tugged me outside. Once we were free of the building, she let go and danced in circles with her arms high in the air.

"I'm not pregnant," she finally said, then pulled me in for a big hug. "Thank God. I'm so not ready for that." She let go, unable and unwilling to stop smiling. "And I have an appointment in three weeks to get an IUD instead of the pill. The doc thinks my prescription is too old and not strong enough and that was part of the problem."

"You used protection, right?" I asked, thinking back to this morning. Wyatt hadn't hesitated to put on a condom. There wasn't a question or a doubt that it was going to happen.

"Except for one time." She blushed and glanced around. Softly, she added, "We went for a drive and ended up in the middle of nowhere. Damon had brought a blanket."

"Wasn't it cold?" I shuddered visibly. The idea of being naked outside in fifty-degree weather wasn't one I found appealing. Eighty degrees on a beach had happened in St. Marteen. Other than sand in weird places, it had been romantic and amazing.

"We warmed each other up." She waggled her eyebrows. "Anyway, the condom broke, and I was impatient." She shrugged, but it made me nervous how blasé she was being. Melody wasn't normally so flippant. "It was perfect. We were so in sync with each other. But it won't happen again. I'm not sleeping with someone without protection."

We started back toward the campus when my phone buzzed in my pocket. I pulled it free, and I grinned. It was a selfie from Wyatt. He was sweaty and bare-chested. Without thinking, I pulled Mel in close and sent him one of the two of us. Melody smiled, but when I looked at it after hitting send, I could see the tension in her expression. And she was too quiet. Her normally gregarious self was muted, despite her good news.

"What's wrong?" I asked, bumping her shoulder. "I thought you'd be happy."

"Damon."

That was all she said, and I needed more information. "What about him?"

"When he thought I was pregnant, he proposed." We stopped and Mel stared into the sky. "If I'm too young for a baby, what made him think I'd want to get married?"

"He probably thought it was the right thing to do." I waited for her to look at me. "Or do you think he was serious?"

"I'm nineteen." She glanced across the street to where a mom pushed a stroller. At least I thought it was a mom until a small poodle poked its head out. "I don't want to get married."

"You don't have to do anything you don't want."

Melody stared at the sky for a moment. Then she shook her head and took off at a full sprint down the street, shouting, "I'll catch up with you later."

The dog barked, and I stared at her retreating form, wondering what in the world had caused her to take off so fast. I started along the same path and debated about pulling up a ride share app when my phone vibrated an incoming call in my pocket. I pulled it free, and the smile burst on my face.

"Hey, guys," I said as soon as the video chat pulled up my parents' faces crammed into the tiny screen. "Where are you?"

"Antigua." Dad pushed Mom's face out of the frame. "Remember Cleo?"

I nodded enthusiastically. Cleo had taught me to cook fungi.

Mom pushed Dad out. "She's leaving the island. Can you believe that? After twenty years, she's moving back to Miami. I tried to call Apollo to let him know, but he's not answering."

"He's here." By the shocked expression on Mom's face, I wondered if I should've kept that little tidbit to myself. "You didn't know?"

"No, is Carlos with him?" Mom glared at Dad, who kept peeking over her shoulder.

"Yeah, why?"

"No reason." She tried to force a smile, but I knew this game too well.

"Lie." I pointed at the screen. "Put Dad on. He'll tell me."

Dad didn't wait for Mom to hand him the phone. "Your brother is leaving the cruise ship. He's trying to find a way to break it to Carlos. He told us he'd meet us in Jamaica in November. I think he's got a job at a resort, but he's not really saying much otherwise."

Mom took the phone. "We're surprised he took a trip with Carlos. Maybe they're working it out."

"Wait, so Apollo's breaking up with Carlos? After all this time?" I wanted to sit down, but there wasn't a place and I needed to get back to campus. It wasn't easy to keep walking and talking with this conversation.

"I guess. He's been vague." Mom looked off screen. "What, honey?"

Dad mumbled something. Mom nodded, then turned back to me. Her face hadn't lost that sour expression.

"What?" This was really getting old. "What else?"

Mom inhaled, a sure sign she was going to give bad news. "We can't make it up for Thanksgiving. The Winchesters booked us for the week to take them to Belize. Your *father* wasn't paying attention to the dates when they emailed. I'm sorry, honey."

I shrugged, but I was disappointed. Not that I wanted them to see that, so I smiled widely. "It's okay. I'll be fine. Claire and Deidre mentioned they were staying on campus already. I just wanted you to meet everyone, especially Melody." *And Wyatt.*

"Hey, Elora," a vaguely familiar voice shouted a block from campus. I glanced up to see Lawrence jogging toward me. "Wait up?"

"Honey? Are you okay?" Mom asked.

I glanced at the screen, faking another smile. "Fine. Just a little startled."

Dad laughed in the background. "Always the jumpy one."

"If you're sure?" she said, tossing a nasty glance over her shoulder.

"I'm sure." Even though I wasn't. Lawrence had avoided me, even in class when I wasn't near Wyatt. He smiled as he stopped a few feet from me.

"Well, we'll let you go, honey." Mom did her own version of the fake smile. "Call us later tonight, okay?"

"I will. Promise." There was more to talk about, and I planned on ambushing my brother at dinner. I glared at Lawrence. There wasn't any reason to make this easy on him. I hung up the call, missing my parents immediately. It felt like forever since we had any real conversations. There just wasn't enough time on the phone.

"Um, hi," Lawrence said, wisely keeping his distance. "I ... uh... I wanted to apologize. Actually, I've wanted to apologize for a while, but that brute told me if he saw me anywhere near you on campus, he'd beat my ass. So I've stayed far away."

"And now?" I crossed my arms and kept a firm grip on my cell.

"Technically, we're not on campus." He had the sense to look sheepish. "I'm really sorry. Jealousy got the best of me, and I shouldn't have acted like that."

"You really shouldn't have." I relaxed and let my arms fall. "I liked you as a friend, Lawrence. Nothing more."

Lawrence's face fell as he nodded. The kindness I liked originally disappeared completely. He scowled at me, his gaze drifting down my body. Anger radiated off him, and I took a step back. My hand shook as I clutched my phone tighter.

"Because a girl like you wouldn't date a guy like me?" Venom seeped through each syllable. Who was this guy? This wasn't the guy I met in class. This wasn't the guy who played guitar and wrote terrible poetry. This wasn't even the guy who'd just apologized. "What is it with girls like you? Always acting like you're too good for guys like me?"

"What're you—"

"Gotta fuck the athletes instead, the one percenters?" Lawrence stalked toward me, and I kept walking backward. "What's that guy got that I don't?"

I didn't answer him. There wasn't an answer that would satisfy his anger. I couldn't risk taking my eyes off him either. My heart raced in my chest as fear gripped me. I fought all the *I'm gonna die* thoughts repeating in my head, but they weren't stopping, and I didn't know what to do. I couldn't even think. Panic tripped my feet.

"What's the matter, Elora?" He sneered and tilted his head like a predator about to pounce on his prey. "Scared?"

He took a misstep, falling off the sidewalk. It was enough to put him off balance, and enough for me to run. I turned on my heel and took off. My feet slapped hard against the pavement. I wasn't much of a runner, but my early morning swim session kept me in excellent shape. Footfalls echoed behind me. I was still half a block from campus, but that wasn't going to be good enough. Just because I set foot on Ridder U property didn't mean Lawrence was going to stop. He was never going to stop now.

I pushed myself harder, my phone still clenched in my fist. Lawrence wasn't far behind me. I could feel him gaining ground. Sweat streaked down my face as I reached the parking lot behind the admin building. I didn't stop. I couldn't stop.

And I don't remember what happened.

Chapter 26

Wyatt

I hadn't heard from Elora since that selfie she took with Melody. Coach put us through the ringer, too. We did line sprints, full length speed drills, and so many passing drills that I lost track of all sense of time. My legs were mush, and all I wanted was a shower and my girl.

Selfishly, I texted her that I was home and invited her and her brother over to my place for a movie or something. It wasn't fair to encroach on her time with them, but I also wanted to show Apollo that I wasn't some random asshole who only wanted to get in her pants.

After a few minutes, I couldn't wait anymore. The stench rolling off my skin was offensive. I jumped in the shower and let the water roll down my sore muscles. The heat soaked into my skin. I would've stayed in longer if a knock wouldn't have echoed off my bathroom door.

"What?" I shouted as I turned off the water. The knocker hammered again. "Jesus, just a minute."

I dried off quickly and wrapped a towel around my waist. When I pulled the door open, Damon stared at me. His face was pale, and his cell was in his hand.

"What's wrong?" I asked, tightening the towel.

He held his phone to me with a shaking hand. I didn't like his expression or the way his hand jolted. My stomach rolled as I took the phone.

"Hello?" My voice was tentative, to say the least. I had no idea who was on the other end.

"Wyatt, it's Melody. Elora's in the hospital."

My body froze in place. "What?"

"Elora's in the hospital. Carlos just came by to get me. We're heading over there now." Her voice shuddered with each word.

"On my way." I threw my towel off and tossed Damon his phone. "Get dressed. We're going."

Damon ran out of the room, shouting at T.J.

Five minutes later, I ran out the door with both of them on my heels. T.J.'s long strides overtook mine and he unlocked the black SUV he rarely drove. Nobody said a word as we climbed inside until T.J. started the engine and asked what hospital. Damon told him. I heard nothing but vocal sounds from each of them. My head swam in the ocean of silence taking residence between my ears. T.J. drove like a bat out of hell. He took a corner, and my head cracked against the passenger window.

"Sorry, dude," T.J. said as he sped down the street and blew through a hard red.

"Don't kill us," Damon said from the backseat.

T.J. ignored him, but he slowed to a stop when the next light changed. He rubbed his finger under his nose.

I turned toward him, the one person who I knew wouldn't lie to me. "Is she going to be okay?"

T.J.'s hand fell, and he glanced at me. "I don't know." He looked at Damon in the mirror. "Did Mel know what happened?"

Damon didn't say a word, but T.J. slammed his hand into the steering wheel. "Damn it." He pulled forward, glanced both ways, then ran the red.

Lights flashed behind us, but T.J. didn't stop. "Fuck em. We're only two blocks away."

Another cop car pulled up behind him. He blew through the next light as it turned yellow and turned hard onto the street where the hospital was. Just outside the ER, he slammed on his breaks and put the SUV in park.

"Fucking run," he shouted. Then he took his keys out of the ignition and held his hands outside the window. "Go."

I opened the passenger door and ran into the waiting room. It took me two seconds to find Melody, Carlos, and Apollo. They stared at me with wide, scared expressions. I started toward them, when someone tackled me from behind.

The air shot from my lungs. A heavy body fell on top of me, hands yanked my arms behind my back as cold handcuffs snapped around my wrists. I closed my eyes and waited for his voice to tell me not to move or issue my Miranda Rights.

"Why'd you run, kid?" a high feminine voice asked in my ear.

I looked over my shoulder. Wide blue eyes stared back at me. Her lips pursed in a thin line. The sharp features screamed, "Don't fuck with me," and I wasn't about to let that little bit of shame I felt at being tackled by a woman get me down.

"His girlfriend's in the ER," Melody said. She wisely stayed several feet away. "I'm sorry. I called him and told him to get here as soon as possible." Mel glanced at me. "What did you do? Steal a car?"

The officer sighed and got off me. I rolled over onto my back side, hands still firmly cuffed behind me. "T.J. didn't pull over after the cop turned on his lights," I said to Melody with my gaze firmly on the cop. "He didn't stop until we got here."

The officer stepped away from me and talked into her walkie. After a couple of very tense, very uncomfortable moments, she walked back over and hefted me to my feet. Without a word, she unlocked the cuffs. I turned around to face her, rubbing my wrists. That shit hurt.

"Your friend's going to be locked up. The driver. Your other friend is on his way in." She shook her head.

"He was just trying to help," I said softly. T.J. was an asshole most of the time, but he gave a shit about his friends. He'd do anything for us.

"Yeah, I get that, but he still broke the law." She glanced over my shoulder. "Hope your girl's okay."

"Thank you." I held out my hand, and she shook it with a firm grip.

Damon rushed in as the cop sauntered out. He glanced at the officer once, then again. "Dude," he said, pointing at her retreating form, "that's who tackled you? Damn."

Melody laughed half-heartedly. "She took him down hard."

"It was kinda funny," Apollo said as he stepped up to Melody and put an arm around her. He held out his hand to Damon. "I'm Apollo, Elora's brother."

"Damon." He glared at Apollo's arm around his girlfriend, but he was smart enough to shake his hand anyway.

Carlos appeared from behind Apollo and held out his hand. "I'm Carlos, Apollo's boyfriend."

Damon relaxed, but I noted something strain in Apollo's face. It wasn't important at this exact moment. I was almost killed by T.J. and tackled by a cop half my size. Still, nobody told me what happened to Ellie.

"We don't know," Melody said softly. She stepped out of Apollo's shadow and forced me to sit down. "Apollo got a call from her cell. It was a cop who said there had been an accident and Elora was on her way to Central Baptist. That's all we know."

"Nobody's come out to tell us what's going on." Apollo sat beside Mel, and Carlos took a seat by him. Damon paced in front of us. Apollo dropped his face into his hand. "She's just a kid."

I stared at the doors to the rooms. I'd been to Central Baptist's ER before. My freshman year, I'd taken a nasty hit headfirst into the boards. It scrambled my brain, and I went in and out of consciousness. Next thing I knew, I woke up in the ER with an elderly nurse who treated me like her own grandson.

So I could only imagine what Ellie was going through. If she was even awake. Jesus, what if she was unconscious? What if she was bleeding out alone back there? What the fuck was going on? I started to stand up to demand answers when Melody started talking.

"This is my fault," she whispered. Tears started streaming down her cheeks. "I shouldn't have left her. I should've walked back to campus with her."

"What're you talking about?" Apollo asked. That comfort toward her was gone. He was cold, angry.

"She went with me to the clinic." Melody turned toward him, facing his wrath head on. "We were on our way back when..." She glanced past me toward Damon. "I had ... It doesn't matter. It could have waited, but I was only thinking about myself." She turned back toward Apollo. "I'm so sorry. I didn't think anything would happen to her."

"No, you just didn't think," Apollo said. Carlos put his hand on Apollo's shoulder, but he shook it off.

"That's harsh," I said, even though I agreed with him. Whatever Melody had to suddenly do, it wasn't as important as their safety. I took her hand and squeezed. "She'll be okay, Melody. Don't worry."

Melody's dam broke, and she burst into tears. Damon pushed me aside. I got up, taking over his pacing duties. Yeah, I was pissed at Melody. She wasn't the most considerate person, but she had a good heart. Whatever reason she took off and left her had to be a good one. Maybe it was something to do with the baby.

"Mr. Castellanos?" a tall, slightly overweight doctor in faded blue scrubs walked out in the lobby. He was the type of doctor you wanted working on a loved one, dedicated. He recognized the family resemblance between Elora and Apollo. "You're her brother?"

Apollo could only nod.

The doctor glanced at each of us, assessing our involvement in Elora's life before focusing back on Apollo. "Your sister is going to be fine. She's got a sprained left ankle and a nasty bruise on her thigh from the impact. She also hit her head pretty hard and has a mild concussion, so we're going to keep her overnight for observation. You can see her while we prep a room." He nodded to each of us. "Sorry, but family only until she gets to her room. Visiting hours are until eight."

"Thank you," Apollo said, the relief evident on his face.

"Wait," I said before the doctor turned. "Do you know what happened? All we were told was that she was here."

The doctor's eyes narrowed. "She was hit by a car."

Chapter 27

Elora

Apollo walked up to my bed. I'd know my brother anywhere by his casual gait with a hint of swagger. He took my hand and sat on the edge of the mattress, bowing it toward him. Deep lines etched into the corner of his eyes. His lips pressed into a thin line. The room was so dark that he almost looked like a shadow.

"Elora are you okay?" he asked softly.

"Yeah, but my leg hurts. So does my head." My voice was scratchy, and that hurt too. I desperately needed water. Apollo sensed that and put a straw to my lips. "Thank you."

"What happened?"

The question made me cringe. The only thing I knew for a fact was Lawrence chased me, and I ran like hell. Then I was here. It was just one big blank. The door opened again, and another person stepped inside with the doctor. The bright light of the hallway burned my eyes. The headache throbbed more. The doctor turned the overhead light in the room, but he turned it down until it was almost like dusk.

"Miss Castellanos, Officer Martin has some questions for you if you're up to it. If at any time you feel you need to stop, then the interview will end." Dr. Adams glared at the cop. I liked him even more. "Do you understand, Officer Martin?"

She rolled her eyes, but she nodded. I liked her, too. But I wasn't a good judge of character. That much was clear. I'd liked Lawrence and look where that had gotten me. Officer Martin stared down at me with kindness. Her dark skin and gorgeous braids reminded me of a girl I'd hung out with in Martinique one time. She'd wanted to be a police officer in the United States. When we went back to the island, I couldn't find her. I just imagined that her dream had come true, and she was in the US somewhere.

"What do you remember?" she asked gently with her pen poised above her notepad.

"Nothing." The entire accident was a big black hole in my memory.

She jotted that down. "Let's start before the accident, Miss Castellanos. Tell me everything that led up to it."

I took a deep breath, and my chest hurt from it. The wince must have been visible because Apollo leaned over me.

"What's wrong?" he asked, his eyes tight with concern.

"She has a couple of bruised ribs," Dr. Adams said. "Nothing to worry about. No punctures. That's the least of her injuries."

"I'm fine," I told my brother. Then I looked Officer Martin in the eye. "I was walking back from the clinic with my friend Melody. She's a freshman and can't have a car. I don't have a driver's license, so we walked." My words were soft, but I put all of my energy behind them to give them strength. "Melody had something to do and took off. I walked alone for a couple of blocks and talked to Mom and Dad on my phone."

My body froze in a tight ball of tension. It was the next part that I didn't want to remember. My heart raced, and the monitor beeped louder beside me. Dr. Adams rushed over. He muttered something to Officer Martin, and she started toward the door. But I didn't want her to leave. I didn't want to be left alone again. I didn't want to tell her. I didn't want *not* to tell her either.

"Don't go," I blurted out hard and fast. My lungs burned from the effort. I reached for my brother. Apollo grabbed my hand with both of his. "I'm okay, I think. Please, let me finish."

"I'm going to order something to help with the panic attacks when this is over." Dr. Adams shoved his hands in his pockets.

I nodded slowly because that's totally all that was, right? A panic attack. I've never had one before, but it made sense. My body, my mind didn't want to remember how much Lawrence had scared me. I knew enough from my class on trauma's effect on the psyche to understand it. Not that the knowledge helped.

"Are you sure?" Officer Martin asked, her pen still poised. She wanted this information as much as I wanted to share it.

I took a deep breath, again wincing at the pain, but it gave me a weird strength. "Lawrence approached me. He ... he said he could talk to me off-campus because Wyatt wasn't around. He claimed he wanted to apologize for what had happened. When I told him I only ever liked him as a friend... he... he turned ugly. I didn't feel safe, and we were still a block from campus. I backed away from him. When he tripped, I ran. That's all I remember until I ended up here."

"Why was he afraid of Wyatt?" Her pen sped across the paper, and she flipped the page.

"Wyatt's my boyfriend. Lawrence tried to kiss me, and Wyatt, Damon, and another one of the hockey players stopped him. I guess they told him to stay away from me on campus. We weren't on campus, so Lawrence thought we could talk." I looked up at Apollo, whose fury showed clearly on his face.

"What's Wyatt's last name? I'd like to talk to him about the incident," she asked.

"He's in the waiting room," Apollo said, barely containing his anger. "So's Damon. I'll take you to them."

The officer nodded but her gaze never left my face. "You felt threatened by Mr. St. John?"

"How'd you know his last name?" I stared at her with complete confusion. My brain was tapioca, but I knew I hadn't said his last name.

"Mr. St. John was on the scene after you ran into Dean Stuart's car." Officer Martin didn't elaborate.

"Wait, I thought she was hit by a car." Apollo squeezed my hand a little too tight, and I winced. "You just said she ran into the dean's car."

I closed my eyes. Of all the people involved, it had to be Dean Stuart, the head of student affairs.

"I'm afraid I can't say anything else." Office Martin's expression softened. "Dr. Adams wants to give you a day to remember. After that, I can tell you anything you want." She turned her attention toward Apollo. "Can you introduce me to Wyatt and Damon?"

Apollo nodded and pressed a kiss to my forehead. "I'll be back."

"I'm glad you're here, big brother." I forced a smile despite everything I'd been through. At least I had my brother here. What would I have done without him? "Can Carlos come back?"

"Only if he's—"

"Family," Apollo and I said together. The love in his eyes for his boyfriend swelled my heart. There was no way he'd break up with Carlos. I just couldn't believe it.

Dr. Adams nodded, then he took out his stethoscope to check my heartbeat. I waved at Apollo as he led Officer Martin out of the room.

"Miss Castellanos, this is sensitive, but I have to ask." He stared grimly into my eyes. "Did anyone rape you?"

"God, no." I cringed at the thought, then I said the one thing I didn't want to admit out loud. "I... I think he might have, though, if I hadn't ... I don't know. I was scared, so I ran."

"Okay." He patted my shoulder. "Rest now. Your room is almost ready. Dr. Wells will be your floor doctor. Let me know if you need anything else."

"Thank you." I settled into the bed and stared at the ceiling. Thoughts ran through my head, all of them what ifs. What if I hadn't hit a car? What if Lawrence had caught me? What if he had.... No, I wasn't going to dwell on any of that. I didn't want to. I couldn't. It wasn't going to do any good. And I didn't like how it made me feel.

The door opened and Carlos came in. His worried face broke my heart. I'd caused so much heartache by judging Lawrence to be a kindred spirit. Carlos hurried to my bed and sat on the edge. I sat up the best I could. He wrapped his arms around me.

Then I did the only thing I had left in me. I cried.

Wyatt

I paced opposite Damon. Melody cried by herself, not wanting Damon's arms around her. Probably part of the reason he paced. Apollo strode out with a short female cop on his heels. He nodded to Carlos who shot through the doors. I tried to follow him, but Apollo put his hand on my chest.

"You can't go back. Family only." His tone was firm, but he wasn't being a dick about it. At least I didn't think he was. "Officer Martin has a couple of questions for you."

"Me?" I glanced at the cop then back to Apollo's worried expression. "Carlos isn't family."

"He's close enough." Apollo nodded to the cop, then stepped around me. I didn't see where he went, but I figured he took my spot in the pacing parade.

"Can I get your last name and phone number for the record?" Officer Martin's pen was poised over her notepad.

I rattled off my number without thinking why. "Birch. What's going on? Does this have something to do with the cop who tackled me earlier?" I glanced toward the automatic doors in case she came back in.

Officer Madison pointed her pen at me. "No, but I'd love to hear that story." She dropped her pen back to the notepad. "Do you know Lawrence St. John?"

"St. John?" That name didn't ring a bell. I went through my mental Rolodex, then it hit me. The anger that surged through me made Officer Madison drop her hand to her taser.

"Mr. Birch? Calm down, okay." Her tone was soothing, non-threatening. Perfectly trained to deescalate the situation.

I closed my eyes, counted to ten, and only reopened them when I knew I wasn't going to flip out. I'd save that for later when I beat that motherfucker's ass. "Sorry, Officer. I know him. I don't like him. He tried to kiss my girl even after she said no."

Officer Madison raised her eyebrows and let her hand relax. "When was this?"

"A few weeks ago." I took a deep breath again, trying to keep the anger to a slow simmer. "Ellie was nice to him, and he has a thing for her. She told him no. Pissed me off because it's common knowledge she's my girlfriend. He'd seen us together before then." Officer Madison jotted down something on her notepad. "What does this have to do with Ellie's injuries?"

Office Madison didn't answer me. "Did you threaten him?"

"I didn't." She already knew someone else had, namely Linden and Damon, but I wasn't going to rat them out. All they had told him was to stay away from my girl. "I didn't say a word to him."

She eyed me like she believed me but didn't at the same time. "Anything else you can tell me about Mr. St. John?"

"Not really. Ellie's not into him, but she's a trusting person. She doesn't judge people." I wished like hell I'd been with her. "Is she okay? Can you tell me what happened?"

"I'm sorry, Mr. Birch. It's an ongoing investigation." She closed her notebook and pointed at Damon who paced past us. "Is that Damon?" I nodded, then her finger moved over my shoulder to where Melody sat crying. "And is that Miss Castellanos' roommate?"

I glanced at Melody. "Yeah, that's Mel. She's pretty torn up."

"Why do you say that?" She raised an eyebrow and flipped her notepad open.

"Ellie was with Melody before whatever happened." I glanced at Mel again. "She thinks it's her fault."

She closed the notebook again, but I saw doubt in her eyes. Or a shrewdness only cops had. I wasn't sure which. "Thank you for your time. If I have any further questions, I will call."

I nodded, but my focus shifted to the nurse who made a beeline for Apollo. He pulled his phone from his ear, and I stepped over to him so I didn't miss a word.

"Mr. Castellanos?" the nurse said. Dark circles made her eyes look sunken. "Your sister is being moved now. Room 423. She'll be settled in about thirty minutes."

"Thank you." Apollo forced a smile, then got back on his phone. "Mom, she's fine." He paused. "Yes, I will keep you posted." He finished his conversation while I waited patiently. "Let's go upstairs," he said after he hung up and checked his screen. "Carlos is on the fourth floor in the waiting room."

He interrupted the cop's conversation with Melody to let her know what was up. I wanted to scream at her, and I wanted to comfort her. Without really knowing what happened, it was hard to know what to feel. I just wanted to see Ellie, make sure she was okay.

And I also wanted to beat the living fuck out of Lawrence St. John. He was behind all of this. I knew it in my gut.

It wasn't until I was alone in the elevator with Apollo that I finally found out what happened to Ellie.

Oh, yeah, Lawrence St. John was in for a world of hurt.

Chapter 28

Elora

The nurse woke me up as soon as I was wheeled into a room. I wasn't sure how long I'd been asleep, but I wasn't all that happy about being woken up, either. My body ached, and my head felt swollen to the point of bursting. I wanted to shove a sharp object through my skull to break it like a blister. My stomach rolled worse than being on the ocean during a storm.

"Thanks," I said as he helped me get into the bed. "The room's spinning."

"That's not uncommon with concussions, even mild ones." He wrote something on a dry erase board on the opposite wall. "You won't get a lot of sleep tonight. One of us will be in every few hours to wake you up." He glanced over his shoulder with kind brown eyes. "Standard protocol."

I struggled to sit up, and he stepped over to adjust my bed. Panic seized my chest. I couldn't stop the sudden fear exploding inside me. His eyes narrowed, and I saw Lawrence's face.

"Please," I begged.

The nurse held up his hands. "I'm not going to hurt you, Miss Castellanos."

I shrunk back from him, from this person who was just doing his job. My logical side knew he wouldn't hurt me. Deep down, I knew better than how I was reacting. But that didn't matter. He hovered over me, too close, too damn close. I wanted to run, hide, get away.

He held his hands up and walked carefully toward the door. "I'll have someone else be your nurse tonight, okay?"

Then he was gone, but the fear, the panic, didn't ease. I stared at the door, praying he didn't come back. My body shook, tears streamed down my face, and I was too scared to move to wipe them away.

The door opened again, and a woman stepped inside. Her light brown hair was pulled into a messy bun, and her scrubs had cartoon characters on them. "Can I come in?"

I swallowed, trying to get the fear under control, and failing. "Yes."

"Elora, my name is Dr. Wells. Nobody's going to hurt you here, okay?" She stepped closer to the bed. "I'd like to give you a minor sedative to help. Is that okay?"

"Will it make this stop?" I asked. I didn't even sound like myself.

"It will help." She walked to the IV and quickly injected something into my tube. "I'm going to recommend no visitors—"

"No, please. My brother's here. I'd like to see him." I felt a wave of calm wash over me. "And Carlos."

"There are a couple of others here, too, or so I'm told." She smiled gently. "One happens to be a handsome young man who can't stop asking everyone who passes him if you're okay."

"Wyatt's here?" A different wave of relief washed through me. "Can I see Wyatt?"

"For a moment, but only one at a time. I'll send one of your brothers back first, okay?" Dr. Wells smiled and then her brow wrinkled hard. "Another nurse will be assigned to your room. If you feel uncomfortable, just press here." She held up a remote attached to the bed and indicated the button. "Same if you are in pain or if you have another panic attack."

"Okay." My voice sounded so small in my ears. It was as if I was five again and on the yacht for the first time. It was an entirely different world now. Instead of losing my home on land, I felt like I'd lost something else. I just wasn't sure what that was.

Dr. Wells left. After a few minutes, my eyes started to close when the door opened, and a hulking figure appeared. My heart shot into my throat, but it calmed as soon as I saw Apollo's face. He sat on the edge of the bed and took one of my hands.

"How are you?" His tone faked calm. The fear in his eyes couldn't be hidden.

And I didn't want to talk about me. "Are you breaking up with Carlos?"

"What?" He shook his head, then decided not to hide the truth. "Yeah, I think I am."

"Mom mentioned it. She said you're meeting them in Jamaica." I pushed the button that lifted my bed. That was a function I could get used to. "What's going on?"

"Are you sure you even want to talk about this right now?" He let go of my hand and started tucking the blankets around me. "Don't you want to rest?"

I glared at him hard. Well as hard as I could considering the circumstances. "A distraction would help. I know ... my head hurts, Apollo. It's killing me, and I don't want to think about it. So talk."

A ghost of a smile crossed his lips. "Some things never change, do they?" He glanced toward the door, then back to me. "Carlos wants to get married. And I don't." Apollo shrugged, but there was more coming. "When I signed my contract for my first two seasons, I had already decided that was going to be it. It's not that I don't love the ship or the life. I just want to live on dry land for a change. The few months in Miami, when I'm off ship, those have been amazing. But I'm trapped on that boat. Carlos ... he signed on for two more seasons when we docked a few weeks ago. He didn't even talk to me about it."

"What about Jamaica?" I prodded.

"The old cruise director bought into a private resort last year." He shrugged again. "We stayed in touch, and she offered me a job managing the pool. It's not ideal, but it's a start. The resort's exclusive and near Montego Bay. You'll love it there."

"Can I ask you a question?" I waited for him to agree. "Did you talk to Carlos about Jamaica?"

He shook his head. "I wanted to, but he was so excited about extending his contract. I didn't want to break his heart."

I snorted. "So you break his heart a different way. You need to tell him. Maybe he wants to go to Jamaica, too."

"I will, but I think I need a break. We've been together since I was your age. I feel like an old man already." He shook his head and stood as a knock sounded on the door. "I'll talk to him tonight. Our flight's leaving on Saturday. Unless you need me to stay."

A sadness washed over me. "No, go home. Mom said they were meeting you in Jamaica in a few weeks. Give them my love."

Apollo leaned in and kissed my forehead. "Okay, sis. I'll be by in the morning to pick you up."

The door had barely closed before my eyes drifted shut. Apollo felt like he was too young to be tied down. He had a point. As much as I loved Wyatt, it scared me to be stuck in one spot or stuck to one life. I wanted many lives. I wanted to travel more. I wanted to experience everything before my feet settled on dry land.

I wasn't sure I would get to do that if I was with Wyatt.

The door opened, but I didn't look up.

"Elora?" Wyatt's voice washed over me like a soothing balm. "Ellie? You awake?"

I kept my mouth firmly shut, and I tried not to cry. Doubts filled my chest. His soft lips pressed against my temple. Even that tiny touch made my heart soar. Still, I needed to think. And I needed a clear head to do that. It wasn't going to happen with a mariachi band using my skull for maracas.

"I'm so sorry he did this to you. When you get out, I'm going to take you to my place. I'll sleep on the couch if that's what you need. I just need you to be safe."

God, he was too perfect. And that stopped me from opening my eyes. I thought Lawrence was a nice guy, kind, sweet. We had so much in common. There was nothing in common with Wyatt except how we made each other feel. Maybe I was fooling myself. I'd always thought I had good judgment in people, but that foundation had been rattled. Hard.

"Get some rest, Ellie."

When the door opened and closed again, I let the tears free. He was everything I ever dreamed of in a boyfriend. There had to be something wrong. There had to be a reason his ex cheated on him. There has to be some hidden secret of his that will destroy us.

It was clear that my judgment in people sucked.

How poorly had I judged Wyatt?

Chapter 29

Wyatt

Apollo texted me the next morning from Ellie's phone. He was at the hospital and would stay until she was released. There wasn't any reason for me to come by. There were a million reasons to go, but I wasn't sure if this was Apollo's decision or Ellie's. He was being protective, and I could respect that. Ellie might not want to see me for whatever reason. I hated that, but I had to wait it out.

I hadn't slept well. I replayed my conversations with the cop, Apollo, Carlos, Melody, and even my one-sided conversation with Ellie. That was the one I got hung up on. She wasn't asleep. I knew it by the way her eyelids *didn't* flutter. If our one night together taught me anything, it was Ellie was an active sleeper. She moved a lot, and it started the minute she fell asleep. Maybe that was just a fluke, but I didn't believe that. She was awake when I was in her room.

Damon slapped my shoulder as I ate my oatmeal at the counter. We'd done better keeping the kitchen clean since Mel and Ellie had scrubbed it down.

"Skipping class?" He took a bowl from the cabinet.

I shook my head.

"Really? I thought you'd be at the hospital this morning." He poured some nasty ass sugar filled cereal and started eating it. Without milk. It reminded me of my older sister. She used to do that all the time. Still gross.

"Apollo's there." I dropped my spoon into the bowl and leaned back. "I don't think she wants me there."

Damon's spoon stopped midway to his mouth. "Why do you say that?"

I told him about my trip to Ellie's room. "I just have a bad feeling, man."

"Like she's going to dump you over something someone else did? Elora's not like that." Damon set his bowl down and crossed his arms.

"Maybe, but she's a deep thinker. She questions everything. She wants to learn everything. If she has even one doubt about me, she'll question everything else." I leaned my elbows on the counter and hit him with the biggest concern. "I overheard Apollo tell Carlos she wants to go home. If that happens, I'll never see her again."

"Or Apollo wants her to go home. To keep her safe. He's pretty protective of her."

I nodded. That was entirely possible. He'd put his wants before her own if that meant keeping her safe.

"She's also strong-willed, Wyatt." Damon pushed off the counter. His intense gaze stared down at me. "Think about it. She moved all the way up here. Didn't you tell me it was because she threw a rock at a map? That takes guts. She's gonna need time to get through this. Just be there for her."

"When did you become so smart?"

"I didn't. Melody's pushing me away. I'm just doing what she asked." He shook his head slowly. "She's not pregnant, but she's pretty freaked out.

I'm giving her space. I don't fucking want to, but I am. You need to give Elora whatever she needs."

"Yeah. You're right." I just had to prepare myself for the worst. And try to prevent it from happening.

Elora

I couldn't look at my phone. The screen was too bright. And I couldn't even watch TV or do homework. Reading was totally out of the question, and music made my head hurt worse. Despite all of that, I refused to stay with Apollo and Carlos even for a night. I wanted my own things, my own life.

After twenty minutes of annoying brother antics, they finally left my dorm room. I settled into my bed.

It smelled of Wyatt.

I glanced up at his jersey still hanging off my headboard. My heart swelled with love and with dread. He was so good to me, for me. Or so I thought.

What if I was wrong about him, about everything?

What if this really wasn't love between us, but just a new experience that would fizzle out in a matter of months? Did I want to put myself through all that?

What if he wasn't the man I thought he was? Was he really that loyal to his family? Did I want to be tied down to a life in North Dakota? Would we even make it that far?

My head throbbed, and I tried to drift off to sleep. The image of Lawrence's sneer haunted me. I couldn't sleep because I couldn't get that image out of my head. Wyatt wasn't like that. I knew it in my heart, but I just couldn't get that nugget of doubt away from me. It was like tapeworm.

The door opened and closed. Melody tiptoed around, probably assuming I was asleep.

Thankfully, she didn't try to turn on the light.

"Melody?" I said, hating how hoarse I sounded.

She jumped and put her hand over her heart. "Jesus, you scared me. I thought you were asleep."

I forced myself to sit upright. "Can't sleep. What time is it?"

"Almost noon." She sat on her bed and crossed her legs. "I was going to meet Claire and Deidre for lunch. Do you want anything?"

My stomach grumbled before I could answer.

"I'll get some soup." She didn't move to leave. "Are you okay?"

"No," I said honestly. My laptop sat on the edge of my desk. I reached for it and motioned her over to me. "Can you help me send an email? The screen hurts my head. Dr. Wells said it would take a few days before the symptoms ease."

Melody didn't hesitate. She moved swiftly to my side and sat on the bed with care. I appreciated her gentleness. "Who are we emailing?" she asked as she logged on.

"Miss Bostic." A blush rose to my cheeks, even though I had nothing to be embarrassed about. I'd seen her twice a month since I got to Ridder. The transition had been rougher than I thought. "She's a counselor at the student health clinic."

Melody nodded and pulled up my email account. She was extra careful to keep the screen away from my eyes. "Okay. Got it. What's the email?"

"Can you just tell her I need an emergency appointment and to call me to schedule it?" My ankle started throbbing in time to my head. It was time for my painkillers. Maybe that would help me sleep.

"Okay. I'm going to let her know that you have a concussion." Melody typed faster, so I wouldn't tell her not to. "Done. And I'll take you there. Whenever it is, I will make sure you get there."

My phone rang within two minutes. Melody answered it, then handed it to me.

"Hello?" I hated how small I sounded, but I wasn't sure who was on the phone, and I really wasn't ready to talk to Wyatt yet.

"Elora, it's Miss Bostic."

Relief washed over me. "Hi."

"Can you come in this afternoon? I have an unexpected opening at three." She paused and before I could agree, she switched tactics. "Or I can come to you. That might be best if you're concussed."

"You'd do that?"

Miss Bostic chuckled. "I don't normally make house calls, but I can in this case."

"Thank you." Tears slid down my throat. This was too much kindness. Then again, maybe she got paid by student. Or billable hour. Maybe this was why she wanted to fill that time slot. "Are you sure?"

"I'll be there a little after three. Get some rest."

I thanked her again and hung up. Melody raised her eyebrows. "She's coming here at three."

"Good. This is good." Mel's gaze lifted to the ceiling. "Do you need anything?"

"Water."

She reached into the fridge, jostling the bed. "I'm sorry."

"For what?" I asked after she handed the bottle over. After a quick sip, I reached for my painkillers and shook a pill out of the semi-clear brown bottle.

Melody didn't look at me. "For leaving you behind. I should've stayed."

Even though I didn't blame her, I also didn't understand why she just took off. Maybe I'd been misjudging Melody this whole time. "Where did you go?"

She looked me dead in the eye. "To meet someone who wasn't Damon."

I raised my eyebrows, but it hurt too much.

"I know." Her voice drifted down to a whisper. "It was stupid. I ... it wasn't a date or anything like that. It was a guy from my econ class. He mentioned he was going to be at the BrewHaus over off Tucker, and that he'd save me a seat. I ... Damon's great, and I care about him."

"But you don't love him."

"I don't think so. I mean, I thought I did." She met my gaze again. "Then I thought I was pregnant, and I realized that I didn't want to be tied to him like that. So after I knew I wasn't, I took off to meet Chase. Nothing happened. We just talked. It was nice, and it wasn't going anywhere, but the possibility that it might.... So yeah."

"Did you tell Damon?" I knew she hadn't. Just like I hadn't told Wyatt that I need some time to work out a few things, mainly my own brain.

"I'm trying to figure out how." She laid her head on my shoulder. "This is a mess."

"Just tell him, Melody. It'll be easier now than if you wait." I wasn't sure if that was true or not, and I needed to heed my own advice. Apollo hadn't told Carlos yet, either. I knew that was going to be harder since they'd been together for so long and lived together on land. "He deserves to know."

"Yeah, he does." She sniffled. "Do you forgive me?"

"There's nothing to forgive. Lawrence would've cornered me either way, eventually."

"You want to talk about it?" She sat up and met my gaze.

"Not really." I yawned as the painkillers kicked in. "I kinda want to sleep."

"Okay." Mel stood and walked over to her purse on her bed. "I'll be back before three to make sure you're awake and to bring soup."

I nodded slowly, but my eyes were already closed, and the sweet release of pain-free sleep overtook my body.

Wyatt

An idea hit me as I was on my way to class. It wasn't smart on my part to skip, but I really didn't give a shit. There were more important things in the world than an ethics course. I drove into town toward the main shopping district, past the dying mall. There was a team store for anything Ridder U that you couldn't get on campus, a chain bookstore, several clothing shops, and a jeweler.

I parked in the first spot I could find. As I hurried past the children's store, I almost slammed into a woman coming out with a stroller.

"Wyatt?"

That voice stopped me cold. For two years, it had whispered sweet nothings to me, told me lies upon lies. I looked into Veronica's eyes, expecting the rage. But I felt nothing. No hate, no anger, nothing whatsoever. For the first time, I didn't wish her out of existence. She simply didn't matter.

"Hi," I said.

She had the gall to look surprised and a little horrified. "You look good."

I almost laughed. "Thanks. This the kid?" I peeked into the stroller. A round pink face stared up at me. "Cute."

"Thanks." She glanced around, then pointed to a nearby bench. "Can we talk? Just for a moment?"

This was not a good idea. But I was full of shit ideas most of the time, so I sat at one end. "What's up?"

"We never .... Jesus, I'm an asshole." She put her hand on her forehead. "I'm sorry. I have wanted to tell you that for ... well, before everything happened. I didn't mean—"

"It doesn't matter if you meant to fall for him, Veronica. You did. Instead of telling me, you just fucked around behind my back."

She just nodded because how could she argue that.

I glanced out at the parking lot, then back at her. Her blonde hair was pulled into a sleek ponytail, and she hadn't even bothered with makeup. That wasn't like her. Or it wasn't like the Veronica I knew, anyway. This person was different. She was a mom now.

"Lucas hates himself," she said softly.

The anger erupted like a volcano. "He should."

"Wyatt—"

"No, Veronica. He should hate himself. He was like a brother to me. I loved him like family." The root, this was it. Miss Bostic told me I had to find the root to my anger, and running into Veronica had offered it up on a silver platter. "You hurt me. But he's the real reason I'm ... The only thing he could have done to me that was worse would have been shoving a real knife in my back. So, I give zero shits how much he hates himself. He can burn in hell." I stood and looked down at his spawn. "Have a good life, Veronica. I ... I mean that."

I walked past the children's store and into my destination. For the first time in months, I felt free.

Chapter 30

Elora

After my session with Miss Bostic, I stayed in my room. Melody, out of guilt or friendship, brought me the promised soup, a nice butternut squash. She also became my eyes, reading my emails and texts messages. My professors sent emails to assure me I could catch up and wishing me well. Apollo stopped by, along with Carlos, of course. They were solemn and didn't stay long, mainly because I kept dozing off. I felt horrible that my brother was going through such an emotional time, and I couldn't help.

Wyatt called. I didn't talk to him. Melody managed that for me too.

Three days of just sleeping, resting. I woke on the fourth day, Thursday, and got out of my room. Normal was what I needed. While I wasn't ready to swim yet, I was desperate for a shower. The spray burned my skin. I hadn't even realized I was so cold. My head ached, but it was dull and more annoying than anything. Thoughts rode each scrambled wave.

I thought of Mom and Dad, who were still unaware of my situation. They were somewhere on their way to Belize without cell or internet.

I thought of Apollo and Carlos.

I thought of Melody and Damon.

I thought of Wyatt. A lot.

He didn't deserve my cold shoulder. When I finally had enough of the shower, I went back to my room and picked up my phone. The back light didn't bother me as much as it had, but I still turned it down. Then I scrolled through all the messages from Wyatt. They were supportive, caring, and not at all pushy. My heart split, and tears rolled down my cheeks. He wasn't Lawrence.

I sent him a quick message. *Good morning.*

Elora? He shot back instantly.

Yes. You're up early. I added a smiling emoji that I didn't really feel. It was something I used to do all the time.

I have a paper due in Business Ethics. Kinda blew it off the last few days. Three little dots popped up to indicate he was typing again. *Are you feeling better?*

I think so. My head still hurts. I paused before I hit send. There was so much I wanted to tell him. *I'd like to see you.*

You say where and when, I'll be there.

I smiled and tried not to let the doubt sneak in. *Breakfast? Maybe Mel and I can come over there. I'm not ready for the student union yet. Too loud.*

Not sure Mel wants to come over here.

I started to ask why, when he sent me another message.

I'll bring breakfast to you. We can eat in the common room.

Okay, but why would Mel not want to come over? Bacon and eggs with toast and real butter, that sounded like heaven, so I added that to the text.

You got it. And she broke up with Damon. It wasn't pretty. He's been on a bender all week. It really fucked him up.

She never bothered to tell me.

Don't let her know. He's adamant he's over her, but we all know it's bullshit. Give me an hour and I'll call you when I'm downstairs, okay?

I sent a thumbs up emoji and laid back in my bed. Wyatt's jersey hung over me. I thought about putting it on, about how proud I was to wear it that first time. Then I saw Lawrence's face, angry and hurt. It was because I fell for Wyatt. And I still wasn't sure if I should trust him. Maybe he was just like Lawrence when he didn't get what he wanted.

My stomach rolled when I thought about sitting alone with him at breakfast. He'd never done anything to warrant that reaction. I just couldn't help it.

I forced myself to think back to the accident. Miss Bostic told me it would help, even if I didn't remember everything. I needed to look at it all again.

And I remembered everything now. Every night, I woke up in a cold sweat with the pain shooting through my body again as I ran into that car. My ankle was mostly healed since I'd stayed off it, and the massive bruise on my thigh had turned a nasty green. I was so lost in the memory that I hadn't realized how much time had passed by. My phone rang, and Wyatt's smiling face stared back at me.

"Hey," I said as I climbed out of bed. "I'll be down in a moment."

"I'll be waiting." His smooth voice washed through me. God, I missed him. He wasn't Lawrence. If I kept telling myself that...

I put on my favorite leggings, mentally thanking Mel again for doing my laundry, and my oversized Ridder U hoodie. Mel stirred in her bed and popped awake.

"Where are you going?" she asked.

"Downstairs. To have breakfast with Wyatt." I could hear the strain in my voice. This was a bad idea. Or a good idea. I wasn't sure of the difference anymore.

"Do you want me to come down?" She threw the cover off her and sat up.

"No, I'll be okay." I put my hand on the door and hesitated. "Why didn't you tell me you broke up with Damon?"

Mel yawned and stretched her arms above her head. "You have enough shit to deal with. I'll give you a ten-minute head start, then I'll be down."

"You don't have to," I said as I opened the door.

"Yeah, I do."

I shook my head slowly and closed the door behind me. Instead of taking the stairs like I normally would, I rode the tiny elevator to the main floor. The common room was mostly empty. The only traffic was the other students leaving for early morning study sessions.

Wyatt stood outside the glass doors with two bags. My stomach rumbled, and my heart picked up its pace. I missed him. So much. Then that doubt, that sword to my chest, took over. I couldn't curb it. It took all my strength to put one foot in front of another and open the door.

"Hey," he said with a gentle smile.

"Hi." This was stupid. This was Wyatt, not Lawrence. He wasn't... but he could. I led him to a small four-seater table near the windows. "Is this okay?"

"Fine." He set the bags down and pushed one toward me. "I wanted to get you something. In case you... Something to remember us by."

"Remember us by?" My brain had been scrambled pretty good, but I wasn't sure what he was talking about. "Why would I need something to remember us by?"

"Damon said Apollo was taking you home." He sat down, and the sadness seeped through the room. I reached across the table, then pulled back. "You don't have anything to be afraid of here. Lawrence... he won't bother you again."

"What did you do?" I asked, the anger in my voice surprised even me. "You didn't hurt anyone?"

Wyatt's eyes widened. "He chased you into a car. He put you in the hospital, Ellie." His nostrils flared. "But I didn't hurt anyone. And neither did anyone on the team, although it was hard to keep T.J. and Linden down. They wanted to beat his ass until he couldn't sit ever again. All I did, all we did, was make sure the entire school knew he wasn't the hero he was playing himself up to be. We told everyone what he really did."

"I just... I don't want you to get in trouble for me. I'm not worth it."

"You're worth everything," he said. There was so much emotion in his voice. I could barely even look at him. He pushed the small gift bag toward me. "Open it. Please."

I wasn't sure I wanted to. He'd done this for me, but ... I was so confused. So lost. I took the bag and set it in my lap. It was light. I reached inside and pulled out a small flat box. My heart raced. This time in a good way. I wasn't afraid of what was inside. It was anticipation. At least I could still tell that emotion from the others. I flipped the box open. On top of a black velvet lining was a silver charm bracelet. I lifted it from the box and stared at the way the sun glinted off the silver. There were three charms, a beaver, two crossed hockey sticks, and the number fifty-five.

"It's beautiful."

"If you leave, I'll never see you again. I just thought..." He inhaled sharply and hurt filled his eyes. I couldn't look at him. This was my fault. "Ellie, you know how I feel about you. I just... I wanted you to remember me when you're back home."

"I'm not leaving." I put the bracelet back in the box, my fingers tracing the chain. "Apollo's heading back tomorrow, but I'm staying here. I ... I like it here. I've never stayed in one place for longer than three months, so this is a change."

He reached across the table and took my hand. I thought about pulling it away, but I didn't. His touch warmed my skin. "I'm glad. I know you have a lot to work through. It takes a while before concussions really heal. Be patient. Don't push it, okay?"

I nodded, and my stomach growled as soon as the smell of bacon hit my nose.

Wyatt chuckled. "Let's eat. Then we can talk about nothing at all." He pulled two Styrofoam containers from the bag and handed me one. "I started reading that Jane Addams book you recommended."

"Really?" I nibbled on the crispy bacon, not sure if it was going to make me sick or not.

"Yeah, she was a fascinating woman." He handed me a fork and napkins. "How's Mel doing?"

"I don't know. She's been ... I don't know." I ate some of the eggs. They were bland with only a little pepper added. I wished I had some siracha. Wyatt slid a packet of hot sauce across the table. "How's Damon?"

"Like someone ripped his heart out and ground it into taco meat." Wyatt didn't touch his eggs or sausage. He kept his hands on his lap, and his gaze focused over my shoulder. "I ran into Veronica."

My gaze snapped to him, and he settled his eyes on me. This was the feeling I had. That something was going to fall on my head. It was Veronica. She wanted Wyatt back. My stomach shifted, and for the first time in my life, I wanted to punch something. "I don't want to know."

He put his unused fork down and moved to the seat next to me. "Ellie, I don't love her. I don't think I ever really did." He took my free hand and put it against his heart. "It was good that I saw her. We talked. And I realized ... the anger that I've been carrying around. It wasn't directed at her."

I set my fork down, turning to face him. There was nothing but truth in his eyes. And I needed to give him some of my own. I put my free hand on the side of his face. "That's good." My thumb drew circles under his eyes. "Wyatt, I'm ... I have to be honest with you. I'm... confused. And scared. I don't know ... I need time. I have so much to sort through and..."

"You need time from me?" His soft voice broke my heart.

"I have to figure things out and ..." I wanted to kiss him, to make him feel better. "I'm so confused right now."

He nodded and turned his head to kiss my palm. "You take the time you need, Ellie. I'll be waiting. And if you decide that things ... Just give me a chance to show you that you'll always be safe with me before you make any decisions about us."

I leaned in and brushed a kiss on his cheek. "I'm sorry, Wyatt."

"Yeah, me too." He lifted the bracelet from the box and secured it around my wrist. "Promise me something. Talk to me when you're ready. You know how I feel about you. If you decide this isn't what you want, then just tell me."

I nodded, regretting my decision almost immediately. Wyatt was sweet, kind, and angry. The angry scared me. It was never directed toward me, but Lawrence had seemed like a saint when I met him. I kept my gaze down, focusing on the black scratch one the white tile floor. Wyatt kissed my forehead.

My heart seized. It hurt more than humanly possible. If I didn't know better, I would've thought death was on me. I lifted my head, wanting nothing more than to meet his warm gaze and tell him I was a fool.

But he was gone.

And I was alone with my decision. That was something I wasn't prepared to deal with.

Chapter 31

Elora

I went straight back to my room. There wasn't any reason to stay in the common room alone. Melody had come down as promised, but Wyatt was gone. There was so much to discuss with her, and I wasn't sure where to start or how to even talk about this mess. I grabbed Wyatt's jersey and hid it under my pillow. The charm bracelet felt cold against my skin. I stared at the little beaver, then the number 55. Wyatt's number.

This was just so... too .... I couldn't even find the words for it. It made no sense. Wyatt wasn't Lawrence. Deep down, I knew that. I was pushing him away based on fear. That was just as obvious. I picked up my phone. The background was still a selfie of us together. I loved how happy he looked as I wrapped my arms around his neck. He'd never done anything to me to warrant this reaction.

Just as I was about to text him to come back, a soft knock shook my confidence. I set my phone down and opened the door.

"Hi," Carlos said, his eyes red and his normally perfect posture slumped. "Did you know?"

I stepped back and let him in. "I found out from Mom the night of the accident."

"Why didn't he tell me?" Carlos settled on the loveseat.

I sat on the edge of my bed and didn't say anything. There wasn't anything to say. This was between them.

"I love him," Carlos said, tears streaming down his face. "Why didn't he talk to me about moving to Jamaica before he decided? I don't understand."

"I'm sorry, Carlos." I wanted to hug him but kept my distance.

"Did you know about Marco?" Carlos didn't wipe his tears as he met my gaze. "Did he tell you about him?"

"Who's Marco?" Apollo hadn't mentioned anything about another man. Neither had Mom, so she couldn't have known. Mom's a notorious gossip. Apollo and I never could tell her anything without her telling somebody else, whether she really knew them or not.

Carlos snorted and slumped farther into the loveseat. "He was a sous chef on the ship, but he left three months ago." He stared at the floor for a beat, then looked up at me. "He went home to Jamaica. Near Negril. I overheard Apollo on the phone with him. That's the real reason he's leaving me, Elora. Your brother's in love with another man and doesn't even have the balls to tell anyone. He's using this resort as an excuse. The same resort Marco's working at."

My mouth fell open. What was wrong with people? Why couldn't they just be honest with each other? Rage scorched my chest, and my nails cut into my palms.

"I'm sorry. I shouldn't have told you that." Carlos leaned forward and put his elbows on his knees. "I just... You're family to me, Elora. The little sister I never had and all. You've been kind to me." He pushed off his knees and stood. "I'm leaving tonight. Apollo can find his way to the airport

Saturday on his own. I can't stay here any longer. I wanted to say goodbye."

I stood and wrapped my arms around him. "Just because you're not with Apollo doesn't mean you can't call me."

"I know. And I will. Maybe not for a while." He squeezed me tight, then let go. "I need some time to sort this out. Distance."

He sounded like me. It was like a bag of bricks sinking me farther into the well I found myself. "I understand."

"Are you going to be okay? I hate leaving you like this, but..."

"I'm fine. I mean, I will be. I'm... sorting things out, too." I fingered my bracelet. It did exactly what Wyatt wanted, reminded me of him.

"That's beautiful. Where did you get it?" Carlos lifted the hockey charm.

"Wyatt," I whispered.

"Wyatt's not that asshole who tried to hurt you. You know that," Carlos said. He always knew what I was thinking. It was creepy. "And he loves you."

"I ... know." The hesitation in my voice wasn't missed by Carlos, but he let it go.

He hugged me again. "Take care, little sis. I'll call you or email you in a few weeks or so."

I smiled, even though my heart was breaking for a different reason.

Wyatt

I did something I never did during the season. After practice, I sat on our couch and drank until I passed out. T.J. and Damon both joined me. It was stupid, childish, and I regretted it the next morning, but I couldn't get Elora's expression out of my head.

She didn't trust me.

It was clear that even my touch made her skittish. Lawrence really fucked her up, and there wasn't a damned thing I could do about it.

Lawrence was the asshole who did this to her. Another regret was not beating the living fuck out of him. I hadn't lied to Elora. Nobody on the team touched Lawrence. T.J. had come pretty fucking close considering his arrest and his suspension from the team. But he stood down. We did exactly what I told her. The entire campus knew he went after her. Lawrence dropped out, but he didn't leave unscathed. Apollo and Carlos found him first. I helped in that department. And I watched as Apollo pummeled the guy. Lawrence got off better than he should have.

I sat at the counter with a liter of water, four eggs sunny side up, four pieces of toast, and a pound of bacon. Only the bacon was shareable. Damon had his own greasy breakfast, and T.J. hadn't even rolled out of bed yet. It was too early after a night of beer, whiskey, and more beer.

That didn't stop the doorbell from ringing. I was going to kill whoever it was. By default, of being the closest, I had to answer it.

Melody stood on the other side with a jersey in her hand. It shattered me instantly. Elora was done, even if she didn't want to tell me. She'd sent Mel over with my jersey.

"Take it back to her," I said as I started to close the door.

Mel's eyes widened, and she stuck her foot out to block the door. "This isn't yours, Wyatt." She lifted on her tiptoes and glanced over my shoulder. "Can you ... give it to Damon for me?"

I snorted. "Hell no. Woman up and give it to him yourself." I pulled the door the rest of the way open. Damon muttered something under his breath that sounded like 'fuck.' I walked to my food. It wasn't easy, but I managed to pick up everything and carry it back to my room.

It wasn't long before I heard muffled arguing. I forced the food down my throat. The best hangover cure was a lot of greasy breakfast and water. The arguing faded, then the sobbing started.

I knew it wasn't Damon. He wasn't a crier. I'd seen him take an eighty mile an hour puck to the balls and not even whimper. Just as I wiped the last of the egg yolk up with my final piece of toast, the front door slammed hard enough to rattle my trophies on the top of my dresser.

I walked into the kitchen, expecting to see Damon's red face. Mel sat at the counter instead. Her shoulders shook. Not a good sign. I started to back out of the room when her head snapped up. Blotches of white and red covered her skin. Mel was an ugly crier. Great.

"Are you okay?" I asked, despite wanting to run to the hills. Or my bedroom. Or anywhere that wasn't here.

She shook her head. "He's hurting, and it's my fault."

"You want to talk about it?" Again, I didn't want to get involved, but Mel was Ellie's best friend. It wasn't disloyal to Damon. It felt like it, though. I should have his back first.

"Can I ask you a question?"

I hated that question, but I nodded for her to go on.

"Do you love Elora? I mean really love her, not the kind of love where you think you love someone." Her eyes glistened with more tears.

I leaned back against the wall behind me. "Yeah, why?"

Mel glanced toward the front door. "I care about him. I thought I loved him, but .... I'm not pregnant, you know. That's what made me realize that this wasn't... real love. Not for me."

Shit. Damon was ready to do whatever it took for her. He would've married her, dropped out of school, worked two jobs. The idea of being a father terrified him, but he was willing to do anything she needed.

"I couldn't keep ... I do care about him, Wyatt." Mel shook her head and pushed herself to her feet.

"Damon deserves someone who will love him without any doubts. He'll find her one day."

I watched her walk to the door. It took all my power not to ask her about Elora. That would've been selfish on my part. As much as I needed to know if she was okay, Mel needed to not deal with Elora's issues as well as her own.

She stopped with her hand on the door. "I saw Lawrence yesterday on campus. His face looks like shit."

"That wasn't me." My blood ran cold. That son of a bitch had the balls to show up here? I was ready to hunt him down and destroy him. "I heard he dropped out."

Mel shrugged and opened the door. "I just thought you should know. Elora's terrified right now. Of everything. With Carlos gone, she's got one less protector around. Apollo's leaving too."

"She has me," I pointed out. "She will always have me."

Mel smiled sadly, then disappeared out the door. I didn't like that. Mel knew something I didn't. And when did Carlos leave? Damn it, I hated not knowing what was going on with her. I couldn't protect her if I couldn't get near her.

But maybe I didn't have to.

Chapter 32

Elora

I couldn't take hiding anymore, so I went back to class on Friday. My head ached, and I suffered through the pain for some sense of normalcy. It felt good to get outside. I smiled politely whenever someone asked how I was doing, but I pulled away from them. BA, before the accident, I would've seen their concern as sincere. How many other Lawrences were out there? Just waiting to pounce?

Instead of lunch, I headed toward the pool for a swim. There was a water aerobics class taking up much of the shallow end, but there was still room for me to stretch out a few laps. The minute I stepped into the water, the world felt right again. I still hadn't gotten used to the chlorine, and I floated better in sea water, but the movement of the water, the strokes, the caresses against my body felt like home. Even my head ached less while I swam.

The class ended, and I kept swimming. My mind opened up as if that dark cloud of doubt couldn't stand the water. Every moment with Lawrence played in my head like a movie reel.

The first thing he said to me was, "You're pretty tan. Where you from?" Harmless enough, right? But the touch, that was creepy. I hadn't thought of it at all. His finger slid down my arm, like a caress.

Then there were the jokes. He'd put his arm around me and told another classmate that he and I were two peas in a pod. His hand had landed over the top of my boob, and he'd stretched his fingers out before claiming he hadn't known where his hand was. Once he'd said my favorite Belize shirt fit me perfectly, and it would look great on his floor. I laughed it off because he smiled playfully when he said it. In retrospect, that was the last time I wore that shirt. Even my subconscious knew then what I finally figured out the hard way.

Of course, the song was the tipping point. I knew that song was for me. He'd been pushier about inviting me to open mic nights even though I encouraged him. Deep down, I knew he wasn't the person he portrayed himself to be.

Why didn't I see it then?

It took me two laps to figure that out. I hadn't seen it because I hadn't *wanted* to see it. Lawrence and I had our roots in the Caribbean in common. I loved growing up among the islands. He reminded me of home, and home was my safe place. I wanted my friendship with Lawrence to be a safe place.

I pulled my head out of the water, both figuratively and literally. My fingers dug into the concrete edge of the pool. There were signs. I just didn't see them. I didn't *want* to see them. That was my failure. I made that choice.

Pushing off into a backstroke, my thoughts drifted to Wyatt. The first time we'd met, he'd assumed I was a puck bunny. I had no idea what that meant at the time. A smile ticked on my face until I turned in the pool. Wyatt hadn't pretended to be someone he wasn't. He'd been sweet even before we started dating. He bought me hand warmers just because. He'd listen to my stories, and he'd treated me with real kindness.

I whacked my wrist against the edge of the pool, pulling up in the nick of time before I caused more head trauma.

Wyatt was everything he shared with me, and so much more. He never faked who he truly was.

I was using my own bad judgment about Lawrence and transferring it to Wyatt out of nothing more than a misguided fear. There wasn't anything to be scared of except possibilities. And I wasn't one to run from experience.

My wrist throbbed. I pushed my goggles up onto my forehead and inspected the swelling. The abrasion burned and turned the skin bright red. My fingers moved, so it wasn't broken. The swelling worried me.

I climbed out of the pool and hurried to the locker room. Getting dressed wasn't easy, and I opted to keep my wrist pressed against my chest with the sleeve of my sweater hanging loose. After stuffing my hair haphazardly into a Ridder U beanie, another gift from Wyatt, I grabbed my bag and hurried out the door.

And I almost ran into T.J.

"Slow down, Elora. You might hurt someone." He held me at arm's length, then noticed my loose sweater sleeve. "What happened? Are you okay?"

"I hit my wrist. It's no biggie. I just need to ice it." I stared up into his dark eyes. The first time I'd met him, I thought he was a colossal jerk. In hindsight, I thought he was the predator that Lawrence turned out to be. How wrongly had I judged him? Other than that first encounter, he'd been quiet around me. "Why are you here?"

"Just walking by." He nodded toward the dorms and glanced over my shoulder. "Come on. I'll walk you back."

I turned around and caught Damon's profile. When I looked at T.J., he had the gall to look slightly embarrassed. "What's going on?"

He looked around again before meeting my gaze. "Rumor has it Lawrence is back on campus. Wyatt... well all of us really, thought we should keep an eye on you."

"You're spying on me?" That pissed me off. "I can take care of myself."

"Says the girl who ran into Dean Stuart's car." He glanced down where I pressed my wrist into my stomach. "And who takes her anger out on the pool."

"It was an accident, thank you very much." Even though I was irritated with him, I was glad he was there. I didn't want to run into Lawrence alone.

"I'm sure." T.J. lifted an eyebrow.

And I wanted to slap him. "Why do you have to be such a jerk?"

"Why do you have to pretend to be so perfect?" He crossed his arms and glared down his nose at me.

"I'm so not perfect," I snapped and started to walk around him.

"No shit. If you were, you wouldn't have dumped a guy who worships the ground you walk on. You wouldn't shit on his friend who got suspended from the team because of a minor arrest."

That stopped me, and I turned back around. "What are you talking about?"

"You don't know that Wyatt would do anything for you? Great girlfriend." He sneered at me, and I've never wanted to hit someone until that moment.

"I meant who got suspended?"

He closed the distance and leaned into my personal space. "I did. Because you were hurt, and Wyatt freaked the fuck out. There was no way I was letting him drive to the hospital. I may be an asshole, but I have my friend's back."

"What did you do?" I felt all the blood draining from my face as I stared at T.J.

"Ran a few lights. Then I didn't pull over at the sound of the siren." He stepped back and grinned like a maniac. "I made sure he got there for you. And what did you do? You broke his fucking heart because you couldn't handle a little adversity in your life. Lawrence is an asshole. But Wyatt isn't Lawrence. He deserves better."

He couldn't have hurt me more if he'd hit me. "I know that," I said in a small voice.

"Then why are you doing this to him? He asked us to watch out for you because he fucking loves you enough to give you the space you demanded and to protect you from any other shit that could happen." T.J. shook his head. He opened his mouth to say more, but I tackle-hugged him with one arm. "What the hell?"

Tears rolled down my face as I squeezed him hard. "Thank you."

"For what?" His tone dropped to a softness I didn't know he had, and his arms wrapped around me.

"For being a good person, even though you're a jerk at times. For taking care of Wyatt. For watching out for me, even though you hate me. For being the only person to tell me the brutal truth."

"I don't hate you, Elora. I could never hate you." His chin rested on the top of my head. He snorted, then he let go and stepped back from me. "Wyatt's a good man. Treat him like it."

"I will." I turned and started toward the dorm. Without looking back, I knew T.J. was shadowing me. Part of me wanted him to walk by my side, but I was also glad he stayed back.

When I got to the dorm, I glanced around for him. T.J. wasn't anywhere to be seen.

But Lawrence rounded the corner, the look of murder in his cold brown eyes.

Wyatt

My phone buzzed, interrupting the music thumping through my earbuds. Not that an incoming text was going to stop me on the treadmill. Coach gave us the day off from the weight room. We had a light skate later in the afternoon. He liked light workouts the day before games.

It was the first home game Elora wouldn't be at. That thought was too much in the front of my mind. I was doing what she asked, giving her the space she needed. It was so much space I drove off campus to workout. Hugh's gym was the perfect refuge. I pounded through the last mile like my ass was on fire.

Hugh stopped beside the machine as I walked another quarter to cool off. I popped out one of my earbuds.

"Good run?" he asked, leaning on the handrail.

"Yeah. I'd rather run outside." I nodded toward the window. It was sunny, but the temp had dropped into the high forties during the day. Getting a cold wasn't on my agenda. The meteorologist said we'd get our first frost overnight. I loved the first frost. It meant winter was on its way and snow wouldn't be too far off. Of course, after I heard that, I thought of Elora and realized she'd probably never seen the grass covered in the frozen dew. Ten minutes later, I was on my way to Hugh's to work off my feelings.

I was so whipped.

"Heard you ran in to Veronica the other day. How'd that go?"

I stepped off the treadmill and reached for my towel on the floor. After taking a long drink from my water bottle, I looked him dead in the eye. "Enlightening. Why? What did she say?"

"She said you've forgiven her." Hugh shrugged but I could tell he didn't believe that bullshit. "She also said she thinks you'll forgive Lucas soon."

I snorted and walked to the free weights. "As usual, she's lying. That's not at all what I said." I put my towel and water bottle down, then selected twenty-pound dumbbells. Nothing too heavy to wear me down for a day, but enough to work out the aggression building inside me. "I told her I wasn't angry at her anymore."

"What about Lucas?" Hugh hated how that had played out. His nephew and my girlfriend both screwed me over. He blamed himself, but that was stupid. He didn't make Lucas stick his dick in Veronica.

I set the weights down after a set and faced him. "Lucas can rot in hell for all I care. Why? Why bring this up now?"

Hugh closed his eyes and looked over my shoulder. "Because he's here, Wyatt. And he's heading this way."

"Bullshit." I turned and stared at my former best friend, my former mentor. Lucas had lost muscle the last several months. His hockey body had turned into a dad bod. Even his hair had developed streaks of gray. He'd cut it short, almost shaved on the sides. I looked at Hugh. "He come here a lot now?"

Hugh shrugged. "More lately. You okay? Do you want me to head him off?"

"Do you want blood on the floor?" I wasn't kidding. If he got too close, I might punch him in the face. Then again, maybe I needed to deal with this. That's what that therapist said. Deal with the issues head on and all that bullshit.

"Not particularly. It's a pain in the ass to clean up." Hugh stood beside me. "I'll get rid of him for you."

"No." I looked at my friend. Hugh was a good man. He'd never treated me like anything other than an extended member of his family. I clasped his shoulder. "I'll deal with him. Just stay close. I don't want you to clean up blood, and I'm not going to lie, I want to beat the living fuck out of him."

Hugh nodded.

"Wyatt," Lucas said. He had the kind of voice made for TV, smooth and soothing.

For the first time since I walked in on him banging Veronica, I looked him dead in the eye. "What?"

"Veronica said you wanted to ... talk things out." He didn't look like he really gave a shit.

"She lies to you, too? Good to know." I reached down and grabbed my water bottle and towel.

"You didn't talk to her?" he asked, confusion wrinkling his face into fine lines.

"I talked to her." I flipped the towel over my shoulder. "And I told her I wasn't angry at her anymore. I'll never forgive her, but I'm not pissed at her. You, on the other hand, I will hate with the passion of a thousand suns. So get the fuck away from me."

Lucas rolled his eyes. What a prick.

I stayed calm, and I was proud of that. The anger boiled inside me. I wasn't going to let it win. "What? You think I should forgive someone I thought of as a brother for fucking me over?" Miss Bostic was right. I needed to confront this head on. "As much as Veronica hurt me, you hurt me worse. I looked up to you. I thought of you like family. Jesus, Lucas, you acted like Veronica was annoying you when she was sucking your dick. I cared about her, but I loved you like a brother. So go fuck yourself. Rot in hell and stay away from me."

"Would it help if I said I was sorry?" he asked, not at all flinching at my targeted words.

I shook my head. "If you're sorry, it's only because you got saddled with a wife and kid you didn't want. You don't give a shit about anybody but yourself. I hope you treat that kid better than you treated your friends." I turned to Hugh. "I'll see you later. Right now, this place reeks."

"Hold up," Lucas said, but I didn't stop.

"Let it go," Hugh said.

I didn't turn around. There wasn't anything more to say to him. I never wanted to see that man again in my life. The anger would never go away toward him, but it didn't have to take over my entire life.

I was never looking back on that shit again. When I got to my truck and climbed in, I realized something. Elora taught me that. She didn't look back, only forward. She needed to be reminded of that.

Maybe giving her the space she needed was a mistake.

I took my phone out of my bag. It was time to call in an expert.

Chapter 33

Elora

Fear gripped me. I didn't want to tear my gaze from Lawrence, but I needed to feel safe. T.J. had to be nearby. A quick glance showed he wasn't in sight. He must've thought I was okay since we were just outside my dorm. But I wasn't. I was alone. With a crazy man charging me.

I turned back toward Lawrence. His anger, his hatred, all showed in his expression. The man I'd met had disappeared into someone else entirely.

And I was done with it all.

I'd been pushing my own anger down for the last several days. I let that overpower the fear. It wasn't easy. It wasn't smart.

But I did it.

I raised my hand and yelled, "Stop. Don't come near me."

"Or what? You'll send your brother to beat me up? I already survived that." He slowed his pace, a lion stalking his prey. "Or you'll have your boyfriend tell everyone lies about me."

"They aren't lies," I snapped, keeping my voice loud enough anyone nearby would hear what was going on. I hoped, anyway. "Don't come any closer."

Lawrence laughed, but he stopped less than a foot from me. "You think you're so superior. You think—"

"I think you're a child who throws tantrums when he doesn't get what he wants." Fear laced up my spine, and I stepped back. Out of the corner of my eye, I saw someone in the common room. I wasn't alone this time.

"Whore," he said.

And I laughed. "I fell in love with someone who wasn't you, so that makes me a whore? You're an asshole. Leave me alone."

He laughed, too, and then he grabbed my arm.

This wasn't happening.

I wasn't going to let it.

"Fuck you," I said, kicking his leg. That wasn't going to be good enough. I screamed at the top of my lungs for help, and I kicked again. This time nailing him in the knee.

Lawrence collapsed, I kept screaming.

"You fucking bitch," Lawrence said as he pulled me back toward him.

"Let go of me!" I screamed. "Somebody help."

He grabbed my other foot, trapping them both down so I couldn't kick him again even though I tried. He got to his feet fast, standing on my toes and grinding them into the sidewalk. "Stop fucking screaming, Elora." His voice was far too calm and his eyes far too deadly. "Stop fighting this."

I stilled my body, preparing myself for what was next. Lawrence sneered and lowered his mouth toward mine. And I bit him. The shock of what I did loosened his grip, and I scratched his face. He fell to his knees.

"Elora!" someone shouted. I turned toward the voice, knowing it was safer than Lawrence. I looked toward the door to see Melody standing outside it, holding a golf club. Claire and Deidre stood behind her, along with four other women from our floor. Melody smashed the nine-iron into Lawrence's groin. "You son of a bitch, stay down."

"I called the police," Claire said as she took my arm and pulled me away. "Are you okay? Did he hurt you?"

I nodded, not sure which question I answered. Both were yes.

Lawrence started to push to his feet, but Melody shoved him back down with her foot. "I said stay down."

Claire gripped my wrist, and I winced. "Did he do this?"

"No. Yes." I shook my head. The panic seizing my chest started to let up. I didn't let it win. It wouldn't win any more than I was letting Lawrence win. "I did it at the pool. He just aggravated it."

"Only you would say that," Deidre said with a smile. Just like her to lighten the mood. She glared at Lawrence. "Anything else hurt?"

"Other than a few scrapes, I don't think so." Tremors started in my hands, then up my arms. I wasn't sure if it was anger or panic or something else entirely, but I started shaking uncontrollably. "He was going to, though. He was going to get his revenge."

"It's okay now," Deidre said, putting her arm around me.

"Yeah, we got you." Claire did the same. I let my friends hold me up. "We need to watch Melody. She might kill him."

The sirens sounded and lights flashed from the parking lot. Local police ran around the building. I recognized Officer Martin immediately. The other three had their guns trained on Melody. Officer Martin's gun pointed at Lawrence.

"Drop the weapon, ma'am," a male officer said in a steady voice.

"It's a golf club. And not until you cuff this asshole," Melody said. She glanced up and saw the guns. Her eyes widened, and the club fell from her hand. "Sorry."

"You heard the lady. Cuff him and read him his Miranda Rights. Miss Castellanos, are you okay?" Officer Martin asked as she lowered her weapon and walked toward me.

I shook my head. I wasn't okay, but I would be. The shaking eased and I met Officer Martin's intense gaze.

"Is this the guy?" she asked.

I nodded and turned to watch two of the other cops cuff Lawrence. "He's the one who chased me into the car. He ... he grabbed me and ... I kicked him." A horrible thought hit me. My heart skipped, then seized into a fresh wave of fear. "I won't get in trouble for that, will I? He attacked me."

Officer Martin smiled, and it was both kind and wicked. "Not if I can help it. I need to get your statement."

I nodded, and Officer Martin led me to her car so we could talk. Lawrence was put into the back of the other car, still cuffed. The male officer who had told Melody to drop the club took her statement. Claire and Deidre talked with a different cop, and the other women who'd come to help me shared what they saw. The stories were consistent, and there were plenty of them.

Officer Martin wanted me to see a doctor, but I refused. Once she was satisfied, she left with the others.

I didn't have her call anyone. Apollo would have freaked out. And there was only one person I wanted to talk to. One person I *needed* to talk to. I started walking the two blocks toward him.

Wyatt

I opened the door to see the smiling face of my sister. She looked mostly like our mother, with dirty blonde hair and bright hazel eyes that already knew your deepest, darkest secrets. I grinned and pulled her in for a big hug. Sirens sounded and lights flashed off nearby buildings. For a split second, I wondered what was going on.

"Safe neighborhood? Or do I need to tell Mom you're living the dangerous life?" She quirked her lips into a crooked smirk. Man, I had missed her. Then I realized what she had on. My Minnesota Wild jersey. Little thief.

"Calamity Jane, you won't tell Mom anything. And I expect you to leave my Wild jersey here when you leave." I stood back and let her inside, closing the door to the noises of whatever emergency plagued someone.

"Jesus, don't call me that." She slugged my arm playfully. "You know the rules, finders keepers."

I ignored that comment. "When I called, I didn't mean for you to just show up at my place. Why are you here?" I pointed to the chair and sat on the couch. "Not that I'm not glad to see you, but shouldn't you be back home?"

"Nope. I moved to St. Paul two weeks ago." She laughed at my shock. "Nobody told you? I thought for sure Mama would've made that announcement. I was going to surprise you tomorrow at the game."

"Seriously? Why?" I scooted to the edge of the cushion.

"I like nursing, but I want more. So I'm going back to school to be a doctor. Well, a pediatrician." Her grin widened, and she, honest-to-God, bounced on the cushion. "Albie didn't mind moving to the city, and A.J. is too young to know what's going on."

"That's great, Janie." My sister never ceased to amaze me. She'd been my biggest supporter for years, but I realized I hadn't really been hers. The four-year difference wasn't a big now as it once was. She'd graduated early a year ago and started working as an RN immediately.

"But I'm not here about me. What's going on? Your message was vague." She leaned back, resting her arms on her lap then switched it up by sitting in Lotus position.

"Still, you could've called or texted back. You didn't have to drive two hours. And when are you starting school? The next semester doesn't begin two more months."

Jane rolled her eyes. "I still have to work. Once I was accepted, Albie and I started looking for jobs immediately. We moved early because I was hired at a clinic, and he's got four interviews tomorrow. Now, are you going to tell me what's going on with you, or do I have to pin you down and tickle it out of you?"

"That hasn't worked since I was six."

"Do you want to test that theory?" She lifted her eyebrows.

"There's this woman—"

"I knew it," she said, almost leaping out of the chair. "You're finally over that bitch, Veronica."

"Jesus, I didn't realize you hated her that much." I lifted my hands to catch her if she did try to tackle me.

"She cheated on you, Wyatt. Of course, I hate her. Just like you'd hate Albie if he did anything to me." She scooted to the edge of her seat. "Now tell me about this one."

I smiled at the thought of Ellie meeting my sister. That would be a sight. Jane was a force of nature. I had no doubt they'd be fast friends. "You'd like her." I gave a vague rundown of how I met her and rushed through our quick relationship to what was happening now. "So do I keep giving her space?"

"That's tough, but I would say yeah. Give her a little more time." She reached over and tapped my leg. "You needed time over the summer to get Veronica out of your system. Mom and Dad were about ready to throttle you for screwing Allison over like you did."

"I made no promises to her." I crossed my arms and sat back. My foot started a nervous tap. "Allison knew what she was getting into."

"Allison's been in love with you since second grade. But that's not my point, and you know it." She jabbed her fingernail into my knee. "You needed time. So does she. If it's meant to be, it's meant to be. Let her come to you."

The doorbell rang, and Jane jumped up to get it. I followed her because this wasn't her house. Jane yanked the door open. Over her shoulder, Elora's smiling face fell.

"Ellie?" I wasn't expecting her to show up so soon. Actually, I was prepared to go to her and beg her to trust me. After talking to Jane, that was definitely a bad idea.

Anger flashed across her face. "That didn't take long."

"What?" I asked, but she spun on her heel and took off.

"Shit. You better go after her." Jane stepped out of the way, and I didn't wait. "Hurry up, little brother."

Ellie was halfway down the block, but I hoped like hell she didn't think my sister was anything other than my sister. One, that's gross, and two, that's gross. The family resemblance should've been obvious.

Chapter 34

Elora

I couldn't believe it. It had only been a few days. It had only been a few *hours*. He'd given me that bracelet because he thought I was going back to the yacht. I should've known he was saying goodbye then and there. He had his rebound from Veronica, and he was really ready to move on. Maybe I should just go home.

Fool. I was a fool.

"Elora, wait up," Wyatt shouted behind me.

I kept going.

"Damn it, Ellie. Why do you keep doing this to yourself?" He was right behind me, and I half expected him to grab my arm. But he didn't. "I'm not Lawrence, so stop looking for the worst in me. That's not who you are, and you know that."

Tears sprung from my eyes, and I kept walking.

"That was my sister." His voice had a desperation in it that made me stop. "Her name's Jane. Remember? I told you about her."

"She lives in South Dakota," I pointed out, still not facing him.

"Not anymore." Wyatt came around in front of me and held up his hands. I dropped my head, staring at his bare feet. They're sexy bare feet. I was so pathetic. "Before you call that out as bullshit, I just found out she moved to St. Paul. She planned on showing up at the game tomorrow to surprise me."

"Why's she here now then?" I asked, still not able to look at him in the eyes. A cold breeze lifted my hair, and I shivered.

"Because I needed a woman's advice about you. I texted her. Instead of calling me, she just showed up." He moved closer to me, but he wasn't touching me. His toes twitched, and he shifted his balance from one foot to the other. "After this morning, I thought ... I was pretty sure you were done with me. I wanted to chase you, beg you to see me for the man I am and not through the lens Lawrence clouded you with. But I wanted to respect your wishes, Elora. I didn't know what to do. So I went to the one person I knew who would tell me the truth."

"Your sister?" I lifted my head slowly to meet his gaze. "She's your sister?"

"After everything Veronica and Lucas did to me, do you think I'd move on that fast without knowing where we stood?" He lifted his hands to touch me but let them fall back to his sides. "I wouldn't do that."

Tears filled my eyes, and I grabbed him around the waist. "I'm sorry." I cried against his chest as he caressed my back.

"For what, Ellie?" he said gently. His fingers caressed along my spine, and I melted into him.

"For letting that jerk cloud my judgment." I leaned back and looked into his intense gaze. "I'm terrified that everything I've thought about people is wrong."

"Because of him? You can't let him ruin who you are." He kissed my forehead softly. "I love that you're so open, honest. I love that you see the world in nothing but sunshine."

The wind whipped through the air. Even Wyatt shuddered and that made me smile.

"I love that you see the best in people. Even when they show you their worst." He grinned. "Like the first night I met you. I was a dick. Instead of getting to know this gorgeous girl, I let my anger cloud my preconceptions. But you were so sweet, and you didn't get mad at me when you learned what a puck bunny was."

I laughed under my breath. "I had no clue."

"But you learned about hockey. Not for me, but because you wanted to know the game. Your curiosity amazes me. *You* amaze me." He looked around and shuddered again. "It's getting cold. Might frost tonight. Can we go inside and finish this conversation?"

I squeezed him against me, not worried about the chill in the air. There were more important things than a little cold air. "I have to tell you something."

His head twisted so fast I thought he might get whiplash.

"Lawrence ... he tried to hurt me. Earlier." I pursed my lips and let the whole story out. His body tensed as I relayed what happened, and I squeezed him tight with my good wrist. "He won't hurt me anymore, Wyatt. I won't let him."

"You fought him off? By yourself?" Anger flashed across his face. "Where was T.J.? Damon?"

I pushed against his shoulder. "You shouldn't have asked them to follow me. It wasn't fair."

"I should've been the one watching out for you." He sighed and pressed his forehead to mine. "I was giving you the space you needed, but I heard he was on campus. And I knew he wouldn't give up. I just wanted you safe."

"I know. And T.J. stayed behind me until I got to the dorm." I stepped out of his embrace. Wyatt's anger showed in his eyes, but I had to tell him one more thing. After everything he went through, he needed total honesty from me. "I asked T.J. why he hated me. He said he didn't. He said it was the opposite."

Wyatt half-smiled, and he almost laughed. "I've known since the first night we meet that he had a thing for you. Girls don't turn hockey royalty down often."

"It doesn't upset you?" I couldn't believe that he wasn't jealous or mad.

Wyatt shrugged and reached for my hands. "Yes and no. He risked everything to get me to the hospital after you.... I'm not happy about his crush on you, but I know you're not Veronica. And he's not ... he's not Lucas." He squeezed my hands, and I winced. That anger flashed again, but he just pulled me close to him. "I saw him today. At Hugh's gym. Coach gave us a light workout day, but I needed to burn off some energy. Lucas had the balls to approach me at the gym. After I told him to fuck off, I realized a couple of things."

"What's that?" I asked, slipping my freezing hands under the hem of his shirt. He shivered, but I didn't think it was from the cold.

"Lucas had hurt me more than Veronica did, and I needed to stop looking back." He leaned down and brushed a kiss against my cheek. "You taught me that, Ellie. Life isn't about living in the past. It's about learning from it and moving forward. That's how you've always lived. It's time I started doing the same."

I smiled and turned my head. Wyatt's lips found mine, and he kissed me like glass. Only I wasn't going to break again.

"Come on. I'm actually cold, and I want you to meet my sister." He wrapped his arm around my waist, tucking me under his shoulder.

"Wyatt, I'm still scared," I admitted. "He could come after me again."

His arm tightened around me, but he kept his voice easy and light. "He won't. We'll get a restraining order against him, and you'll never be alone unless it's in your room or my room."

"Do you have any aspirin?" I lifted my wrist to show him how swollen it was. "I should've been paying more attention to my strokes."

"What were you thinking about?" he asked softly.

"You."

He kissed my temple and kept me tight against his side.

"I was going to come see you after I changed. To talk. To stop projecting my fears about Lawrence onto you." I snuggled against him. "I'm sorry."

"Don't be sorry. Just be Elora." He stopped just short of the door. "Ready to meet my sister?"

"You've met Apollo."

"Oh, we have to get Jane and Apollo together. That will be interesting. Ready?" Wyatt kissed the top of my head again. I loved that he did that.

"With you, I'm ready for anything."

Epilogue

Wyatt

"Where's Ellie?" I asked my sister. We'd just gotten our asses handed to us by the other team, and I really need my girlfriend's smiling face to cheer me up. Losing by six goals was not fun. Everyone except for me and Damon was pissed at T.J. for his suspension from the team. We'd find out at his hearing with the athletic director if T.J. would be gone for good or reinstated, but that wasn't until later next week. He had his appearance in front of the judge first.

"Broody much? She's going to meet us at the party."

My face must have shown the panic, but Jane just tapped my shoulder like Mom would have.

"Don't worry. Claire and Deidre are with her. They're going back to the dorm to change into their costumes." Jane looked down at her clothes. "I'm not going. Albie's ready for me to be home, and I miss A.J. Spending last weekend here, and now tonight, that's a bit too much for even me. I'll meet you and Elora for breakfast in the morning before I head back to St. Paul." She held her finger up between my nose, making me go cross-eyed.

"But I expect pictures. Whatever it is Elora has planned for tonight, she thinks you're going to love it."

I smiled wide. "Probably will."

"I like her, Wyatt." Jane fell into step beside me as we walked toward her car. "She's sweet, but she's genuine. You know what you're getting from her."

"And she's kind, beautiful, smart, curious—"

"Yeah, yeah, yeah." Jane waved to cut me off. "She's perfect for you. She takes one day at a time." We stopped by her car, and I waited for the other shoe to drop. "Maybe you should rethink your future, little brother. You've got time, but ... Mom and Dad aren't going to retire for another ten to fifteen years, if they ever do. Rushing back to South Dakota after graduation might not be a good idea."

"I've got time." A year and a half before graduation, but that was plenty of time to make some decisions.

"Yeah, but it will fly by." She smiled sadly. "I wish I wouldn't have denied myself medical school. I thought nursing would be enough. I just don't want to see you fall down that same rabbit hole."

"What else am I going to do?" I asked even though I had started thinking the same thing.

"That's for you to figure out, not me." Jane patted my cheek gently, then added a harder slap. Just like she did when we were little. Some things never change, and that's not a bad thing. "Now be a good little boy and go to your party."

"You're a dork." I hugged Jane. "I'll see you in the morning."

I waited until her taillights were out of sight before walking to my truck. T.J. waited for me. His suspension and arrest didn't stop him from wanting to be at the arena, to support the team.

"Your sister's smoking," he said, tossing the toothpick he'd been chewing on over his shoulder.

"Think she'd leave Albie for an unemployed hockey player with no prospects?"

"Not even." I tossed my bag in the back and climbed in. "Going to the party?"

"Yeah, I figured I'd find some puck bunny to spend some time with."

I glanced at me out of the corner of my eye. "As what?"

"An unemployed hockey player with no prospects," he said with a smile. T.J. played off his guilt from leaving Elora alone to face Lawrence the week before, but I knew he felt guilty as fuck. He should, and I was going to let him. "Think I'll get laid?"

"Probably not." I started the engine.

T.J. and I didn't talk on the way to the apartment. There wasn't anything to say. We'd hashed out a lot over the last week. I didn't ask him about his feelings for Ellie. Honestly, I didn't think he was as serious as he thought he was, but T.J. kept his emotions in check. Ellie had been one of the few who shot him down, and that wasn't normal for him. His infatuation wasn't going to ever be anything more than what it always was. It wasn't my place to make him talk about it. Elora made it clear to him that they were just friends, and he seemed to take that okay. I knew I could trust him. If he didn't have my back, he wouldn't have taken all the heat from the cops for me.

Ten minutes after changing into suitable costumes, me in a pirate's eye patch and normal clothes and T.J. in a black t-shirt that said, 'this is my costume' and black jeans, we walked over to the frat house.

"Hey, Wyatt," Betsy Hardgrove said as soon as we stepped through the door. Betsy was a nice enough girl, but she wasn't interested in anything but a good time. Which made her perfect for T.J. Before I met Elora, I would've hated a girl like Betsy. But who was I to judge?

"Hey, you remember T.J., right? Our goalie?" I stepped out of the way, so Betsy got a good view of my friend.

"The one who got arrested?" She practically purred at him. Considering she wore a skintight cat costume, it was perfect.

I left them to do whatever they were going to do and went on the hunt for my girl. Melody stood near the hall, dressed as a sexy alien. A tall blonde guy with close cropped hair stood next to her, with his hand around her waist. Mel hadn't wasted time moving on. Damon was still wallowing and refused to come out for the late Halloween party. It was technically November, but Halloween had been on Wednesday. This wasn't the first Halloween party either. Just the biggest.

Melody nodded at me, then pointed toward the kitchen. I smiled and kept going. The kitchen was twice as crowded as the living room. Ellie wasn't going to be in here. I pushed my way out the sliding glass doors. It was cold outside, but given Elora's aversion to crowds, she'd be somewhere in the yard and near a bonfire.

It didn't take long to find her either. I spotted my name and number on her back as she huddled with Claire and Deidre near a firepit.

"Ellie?" I said loud enough to get her attention.

Her body stiffened. Then she stood and turned toward me with a huge grin on her face. I started laughing immediately. She had a pair of my old hockey gloves on with one of my broken sticks in her hand. On her head was a set of bunny ears, and someone had drawn whiskers on her cheeks. A fake bunny nose covered her own.

She strolled up to me with a grin. "You like it?"

"I love it." I bent down to kiss her quickly.

"Now am I a real puck bunny?" she asked as she spun in a circle. There was even a white bunny tail on her tan leggings.

"No, you're my puck bunny." I pulled her into my arms, and I kissed her hard and deep. A chorus of sexy noises along with 'get-a-rooms' filled the air, but I didn't care this time. Ellie was my girl, and I loved her. She'd changed my world in so many ways. All I wanted was to make sure she was happy.

"I love you," she said when I finally stopped kissing her.

"Love you, too, Ellie-Bunny," I said, dropping another kiss on her plastic bunny nose.

She smiled like the world revolved around me. Damn it, I never wanted her not to smile, and I was going to do everything in my power to make this woman happy. No matter what it took. She was my endgame.

~~Get Hooked on~~ Ridder U ~~Hockey~~

Don't miss Nolan and Grace's story in Hooked, the first short in the Ridder U Hockey series

Also by Lynn Stevens

Anthologies
Read Shootout, my second story in Ridder U
Hockey, in Let's Play
Read One Wish Only in Holiday Kisses

Just One... series
Just One Summer
Just One Song
Just One Chance
Westland University series
Full Count
Game On
Stealing Home
Girls of Summer series
Extra Innings
The Rebound
On Par

Standalone Novels and Novellas
Swipe Left for Love
Roomies
This Time Around
Rebel Hearts

About Lynn

Lynn Stevens flunked out of college writing her first novel. Yes, she still has it and no, you can't read it. Surprisingly, she graduated with honors at her third school. A former farm girl turned city slicker, Lynn lives in the Midwest where she drinks coffee she can't pronounce and sips tea when she's out of coffee. When she's out of both, just stay away.

www.lstevensbooks.com

Made in the USA
Columbia, SC
15 January 2022